The Fairyland Chronicles

Volume One

Dust Wars

by
David Levante

Published by
Quirks and Foibles

An imprint of The Print Register Ltd
Scotland KW9 6NL

www.printregister.com

ISBN 978-0-9956298-7-5

For Felix

2009-2014

Preface

There's really no easy way of saying this, so I'll just be blunt: it appears that I'm the King of the Fairies. OK, I can already hear you muttering variations on 'this is nonsense', 'garbage, 'you've been drinking again' or words to that effect. But no, for better or worse I really am, and this is my story.

First of all, let me introduce myself. My name is David Levante and I'm possibly the most average person in the world. I'm a lawyer's clerk, work 9-5, Monday to Friday with a whole hour for lunch and I mainly answer phones and file paperwork for my bosses, a firm of small town lawyers.

I'm married with two kids, a dog and a cat and when I get some time to myself, I read books, watch TV and when the notion takes me, take in a game of football. Generally, I spend the rest of my time with my family doing Dad things (taxi service, money lender, you know the score) and mostly enjoying them. In other words, my life is a straightforwardly happy one and was totally uninteresting until the damned Fairies got involved.

Now I want to make this clear, I am not writing this from a police cell, or worse, from a 'secure psychiatric unit'. I think that's the name, I always thought of such places as mental asylums but I know that I'm not in one. I've told no-one else about what I'm about to reveal to you but some of those close to me know the whole story and others, I'm sure, suspect that something's up.

Here we go then, welcome to Fairyland and all the madness that ensues therein. Let me acquaint you with Heads of the four Divens, who have to report to me as King, the sneaky humans known to all as Haferlincs who flit easily between our world and Fairyland, and also where some of the best portals to the other world can be found. You never know, you might find that if you visit these sites you too can nip in and out of Fairyland as you wish.

But more importantly, the reason that I've decided to go public with this is that I want you to know that there really is a magical world out there that's most definitely much closer to you right now than you think.

1.

At work, I spend my days in an open plan office with beige walls, a beige carpet and, no surprise, similarly boring furniture. The only splash of colour is the blue seats. My desk faces into the room, all the clerks around me are the same and there are about ten of us in the room. According to some Feng Shui expert, this gives us a better karma or something but all we know it's actually our bosses making sure we can't see the outside world, in case we want to escape.

I've the usual clutter associated with a lawyer's office at my workstation; lots of files on and around the desk, the obligatory computer and, of course, a picture of my wife, kids and pets. This reminds me when I'm writing up another contract or whatever that there is more to life than work.

However, to break this monotony, over time a number of extra-curricular activities have been developed by the staff. Most of these involve drinking (an easy way to forget the workplace) but one in particular, the Friday walking club, appealed to me. It gets me out at lunchtime, means that I don't have to spend hours in the local bars to socialise with my colleagues and also helps keep me fit.

You must understand, I'm heading towards the half century and no matter what I do, my waistline seems to expand on a yearly basis. I don't participate in the walk every week (rainy days don't really do it for me, you see) but most of the time, it all works out quite well.

It had been suggested some time previously that we, as an office staff, should include the local cemetery in one of our lunchtime walks. The cemetery had been added as a destination because in the middle of it was a 500 foot high hill that none of us had ever climbed, despite being locals. My kids, especially my son Milo, had also mentioned that we as a family should be climbing it (something about a project, he said) so I agreed to do the recce with the walking club. Anyway, it looked as if it wouldn't rain that day and the break was especially welcome that particular week as the workload I'd been dealing with was a bad combination of both onerous and very boring.

So, with all of this in mind, come Friday lunchtime, it was onwards to the walk.

"Would you please get a move on," shouted Shona from the bottom of the stairs – no elevators to be used when we were going walking. "We've only got an hour and you know the boss will go crazy if we're late back."

Shona is our office manager, the 'Seer' is what we call her, as, like the three wise monkeys she sees and hears all, but mostly says nothing. She's also pretty good at bossing us all around but right then she was standing at the door, dark hair pulled back into a pony tail and with a good stout pair of walking shoes on.

"Hold up," came the reply from Hayley, one of our recently arrived lawyers and by far the youngest of the walking club. Fresh from university, she had the uncanny knack of making people of all ages feel good about themselves and I've no doubt that she'll be a really good court lawyer someday. She jumps around with the boundless energy of the young and has managed to somehow get on designer training gear to complement her short blond hair. I suppose that if you have to look good, you just have to look good.

Making up the normal foursome was Jim, the man who looks after the building for us and the other tenants ('facilities management, David' he explained to me one day). He, as usual, appeared as if by magic from some cupboard or other as we all congregated at the bottom of the stairs. Jim always had a quiet aura of authority about him but was actually good fun when you got him by himself. He'd dressed for the day as he always did with a smart cap and sensible outdoor clothes, but nothing fancy.

As we strode off, I suppose if you looked at us we were a fairly unusual combination of walkers. There were no fluorescent jackets, backpacks or hiking boots (in fact Hayley had on some sort of designer tennis shoes to finish off 'the look'), just a bunch of office workers making headway in a determined fashion with the one hour rule bearing down on us all. At least the weather was staying good, it was nice and sunny with a little breeze but not too hot.

In the past, we had already walked the length of the town canal, down to the football stadium and through 'the islands' which were an integral feature of the river that flowed past our office. The cemetery suggestion was, I suppose, meaning that we were running out of options. I mean, a bunch of lawyers wandering around a graveyard doesn't really send out the right message when one of your specialities is writing last wills and testaments.

Never mind. As you can imagine, the chat on the way there was the usual nonsense, who did what at the weekend, who was seeing whom in the office and what juicy cases had come our way. If I look back on it though, I suppose the three of them had more spring in their step than normal. I remember that there was even a muttered 'at last' from Shona as we walked through the cemetery gates. Needless to say, I didn't think anything was amiss at all.

As I walked through the gates, I was reminded of the one and only other time that I'd ever been here. A few years ago, I had a bit of a mix up with my family about where they were to be picked up after visiting the grave of a newly deceased relative. I'd come here to Tomna Hill and Cemetery, not realising that it had been closed to new arrivals about 20 years back and that I should have been at a new cemetery a few miles away. It had been closed because by then it was completely boxed in by roads and the aforementioned canal.

It is, however, still maintained as an ancient burial ground where it is said that some graves date back thousands of years. The striking feature, though, is Tomna Hill in the middle. Forming a central point, it has steep slopes but a very flat top which is about the size and shape of a football pitch. The slopes are also covered in mature trees and lots of hidden gravestones making it a bit spooky, especially when the wind gets up. The rest of the graveyard is a flat area completely surrounding the hill and, as I said, chock full of dead people. On the way in, there's a gatekeeper's house which at that time had been for sale for months – no surprise there I suppose.

Striding through the entrance, Shona was hurrying us all up. "Come on folks, we have to reach the top."

"But I'd like to have a quick look at some of the graves if that's OK," I replied, "I've never really been properly in here before." I also fancied myself as a sort of amateur genealogist.

"No time, David," said Jim. "As normal, we're on a deadline," he said grinning and shaking his head.

"Yeah, and Shona's on a mission as usual." I came back with, raising a snort from Shona and a giggle from Hayley.

"What's the quickest way up?" said Hayley.

"Right there," said Jim as a set of granite steps that I hadn't noticed before appeared in front of us. "Race you all up," he shouted and promptly disappeared into the trees.

He was followed with remarkable speed by both Shona and Hayley leaving me, being as I said middle aged, unfit and slightly overweight (which I'd normally never admit to), at the bottom thinking 'no chance, I'm taking my time'. I took the first step and finally joined them all at the summit a long time later.

If you ever go there, the top of the hill is still the same today. It's got a big open circle in the middle and some spectacular gravestones and memorials at each end. I suppose that even in death, the rich of the town like to lord it over the poor. One or two of the memorials are like mini houses and must have cost some serious money.

As I reached the last step, I looked around and saw no-one other than the other three, who were all standing in a huddle in the middle of the circle. I wandered over to join them, trying to speak normally while getting over my breathlessness.

"Ha, ha," said Shona, "the fairies will get you if you keep panting like that."

"Right now the fairies or anyone else can do what they want if they can get me a seat," I replied.

By way of explanation, the hill is also supposedly one of many fairy hills across the country (and the world, I suppose). Local folklore says that depending on the circumstances you find yourself in when you're at the top of the hill, you might be taken by the fairies to some big party where you will enjoy yourself like never before. The only problem is that when you return to 'our' world, about 150 years will have passed. I presumed that this story had been around for much longer than the graveyard that now occupied most of the hill.

The other local fairy tradition, explained to me in detail by my kids, is the 'fairy ring' of mushrooms that appears each year in our front garden. Apparently if you jump into the ring you also join the little people at a party, only this time when you come back you don't remember anything.

At the time, I just thought that this was all a lot of hocus pocus and mumbo jumbo. To me, both traditions seemed to contradict each other meaning that the whole fairy thing was nonsense and really just an old wives tale to help frighten kids.

With all of this in mind I jokingly said. "And where's the party, cos to be honest, with the week I'm having a few beers would work wonders right now."

And that's when everything changed. Forever.

2.

As I stood in the middle of the circle beside my colleagues, I noticed some sinister looking black clouds forming overhead. By overhead, I mean right over my head, about 50 feet up and like a vertical tornado that wasn't moving. The wind had also built up just a little bit, causing some dust devils to swirl around the central circle area of the hilltop.

At the same time, Jim, Shona and Hayley all moved back quickly about 30 yards from me to three equidistant points around the circle, creating a triangle around the point at which I was standing. The thing was, I'm also pretty sure that they actually hovered backwards with their feet not touching the ground. Weird. They had also changed their appearance. Shona was now wearing a long black dress, her hair was down and she had acquired a seriously bling silver necklace with a really unusual symbol made up of a big scary bird hanging from it.

Meanwhile, Jim was now in ceremonial flowing white robes while at the same time holding a carved dark wood staff and clearly giving hand signal directions to someone I couldn't see. Hayley had also changed into what could best be described as a silvery grey jumpsuit and was carrying what looked like the Olympic torch, but had somewhat strangely managed to retain the trendy tennis shoes.

Standing in the middle of this, I'm not afraid to admit that after trying my best not to faint, then trying to run and being unable to move, I promptly wet myself.

"So this'll be Mr Levante," said a squeaky sort of voice from behind me.

In the movies, you'd expect a deep God-like tone to make sense of all of this. But no, it was high pitched and to be frank, a bit embarrassing. I managed to turn to try to see who was speaking but a ghostly darkness had fallen on the hill and I couldn't see anyone.

"Eh-ehm," came a sort of 'Excuse Me' cough from the same high pitched voice. It was then that I realised that it was coming from below me, hence me not being able to locate the source a moment ago.

Standing about 18 inches tall and dressed in green robes a bit like Jim's white ones, but with the addition of long yellowish hair and a vivid red baseball cap, this 'little person' was clearly speaking to me. As he came into focus I also noticed that he had really piercing purple eyes set into a face that looked like it was made of old leather.

"Who's asking," I said, trying a bit of bravado that I really didn't feel. "And by the way," I carried on while looking at the rest of them, "what exactly's going on?"

In truth, that's not really what I said. As I recovered some sort of composure there were significantly more swear words in the original version, but I'm sure you get the idea.

"My name is Sandels," said Mr Purple Eyes, "and I'm honoured to finally welcome you to Fairyland. We have waited a long time and I'm delighted that you're eventually able to join us. I'd like to thank our human contacts Shona Cool, Jim Staff and Hayley Starlighter for bringing you to us in our time of need. Please take a seat." He then actually bowed to me.

Now you'll forgive me for being a bit confused at this point. I didn't know Shona, Jim and Hayley as Cool, Staff or Starlighter nor had I any expectations when I agreed to the climb that I'd actually meet any Fairies, never mind one as unusual (to me) as Sandels. As well as the robes, he too had a big wooden staff, but with the same symbol as Shona's necklace on top of it. His robes were also held shut by what looked like an old skipping rope.

So, with substantially more swearing to all that I could see, I asked again, "what exactly's going on?" I did sit down, mind you, because a wooden throne-like seat had appeared behind me and it made more sense than just standing there in wet trousers.

"Let me explain," he said in the same voice. Honestly, it was like he was breathing in helium before every sentence. "For many years we knew that we may have to call on you in your special capacity to us at some time. Shona, Jim and Hayley are your guardians – it took us a long time to get them together in one place, then to get to know you in the human world and finally get you here to this spot without you guessing that something was up – if you had, the spell would have been broken and we'd have had to start again. Mr Levante, there's no easy way of saying this and it might come as some sort of surprise to you, but you're actually the King of the Fairies."

Cue a very long deafening silence from me. Right now, as I felt a headache coming on, I decided that keeping my mouth shut might be best in the circumstances.

"He's right, David," said Shona from behind me, "it's been hell trying to keep quiet about it and I know that the whole thing will be a bit of a shock but please stick with the program for a bit – Fairyland really needs you now and Sandels here has been nominated as your guide. I'm here as a sort of sorcerer – a nice one might I add – and Jim, as well as looking after our office is actually the guardian of Tomna Hill."

"And I've got the best job in the universe," chipped in Hayley. "As you'll have heard, in this world I'm Hayley Starlighter which actually explains what I do. In the human world, there's all the research into the universe and the stars it contains – what you don't know is that at night, I sometimes fly through space with my torch keeping all the stars that support life, like our sun, alight. For Fairyland, we also use it like the old sailors did as a means of communication – I put out and relight dead stars across the universe to create patterns that the Fairies can communicate with across galaxies. To normal humans, they just appear to twinkle. In fact, Shona might be called Cool, but it's me that the really cool one here," she giggled.

More silence from yours truly.

"Once again, we are honoured by your presence," said Sandels. "Might I have the pleasure of recording your first official words as our new King."

In keeping with how my answers had gone so far, the actual words have quite sensibly been deleted from history. The record now shows them to be something along the lines of: "Thank you kind Sir, notwithstanding the strange circumstances that I, a mere lawyer's clerk, find myself in, I am honoured to have had the highest position in Fairyland bestowed upon me. Let me lead you and the people of this land with courage, fortitude and wisdom. I remain and always will be the humble servant of the people."

It's truly amazing how quickly you fall into being a politician when the need arises.

At this point, though, I burst into tears. After wetting myself, swearing at my work colleagues and their little friend, something else had begun to dawn on me. No, not that I was going mad (although this was a distinct possibility) but if this was in any way true, I remembered the 150 year rule. This meant that I'd never be with my family again. My wife Bethany, son Milo, his little sister TJ, Paws the dog and Felix the cat would never see me again as they'd be long gone by the time I got back.

When I broke down, I was actually quite touched that there was immediate compassion from Sandels and the others. They couldn't understand why I was upset; after all I was now apparently King of the World as far as they were concerned. Through the sobs, I explained my new predicament. As you will probably understand, I wasn't taking the whole episode very well.

"No, no," said Shona, "that's a lot of nonsense. The 150 year thing is just a story that people use to stop their kids climbing the hill. In fact it's the opposite."

"Yup," added Hayley, "what really happens is that human earth time just slows down – it equates to about a tenth of a second for each year you're here in Fairyland. How do you think I can undertake the star lighting duties and train to be a lawyer at the same time?" She said this with a genuinely guileless look on her face, making me almost believe it.

"OK, take me back and prove it," I responded, "and anyway, come to think of it, how do I get back home?"

"Aahh Sir, it takes a bit of time to learn the process – until then, Shona, Jim and I will ensure that you make your way back through the portal when you've assisted us here," added Sandels, somewhat unhelpfully from where I sat.

Now, on the basis that I had come to the conclusion that I must actually be dreaming, I thought what the hell, let's go with the flow and just humour them. After all, they were all looking at me expectantly and when you do a mundane job like mine, it's not often you get to play King for a day. So, although I was still very much in a state of confusion, I decided to join in the fun.

3

"Sandels, please tell me a little about yourself and also, some more about what is going on – what do you mean about me being King and why are my colleagues looking so funny?"

"As you wish, Sir. According to prophesies that Jim, Shona and Hayley have been working towards, you are our King. At this stage, there is no need to go into any more details other than to say that now that you are here, it would assist us all greatly if you could maybe act like a King as we progress through the welcoming ceremony."

"And I'm King of what exactly?"

"Well, Sir, you are King of the OutFax territory, one of the territories that make up Fairyland. Kings only appear to us in special circumstances."

He said this in a way that didn't really invite more questioning so, being the polite sort, I moved on.

"And yourself?"

"I am now approaching 1,000 years old and am seen as an elder of the community. I work across all the Divens in the OutFax Fairyland territory. This is only possible because the Heads of all four Divens have bestowed the ability on me – there are only three other Fairies that have the same elevated position as me. It is because of my experience – I have also travelled to all corners of the OutFax territory – that I was chosen by the Heads of the Divens to greet you on your arrival. I have a wife of 940 years, two children, four grandchildren, seven great grandchildren, nine great, great grandchildren ….."

"Whoa, whoa, I get the picture on the family – how many 'greats' do we end up with," I said, thinking we'll be here all day, and also not understanding a word of what he'd said before that.

"Just one more, Sir… we all live quite long." He said this with one of these withering looks combined with a pout that long serving secretaries give to new bosses.

"Ok, apologies for that – but what's a Diven, who's a head and why is it called the OutFax?

"Well, Sir," you could see that he was clearly not happy about my line of questioning, "you'll find out more about our territory shortly but each Diven is probably best described as a distinct region or tribe within the territory. All the subjects of our territory belong to one of the Divens and each of the Divens has an elected Head. In normal times, the four Diven heads of the OutFax govern the territory like heads of government. They are assisted by elders like me."

"And my colleagues, who now seem to have had a name change, do they govern as well?"

"No, Sir." I could see that he was getting even more exasperated by the minute. "They are Haferlincs. In other words they are humans who like yourself, Sir, can move between Fairyland and the human world. This helps us keep a balanced society in both lands, given we both occupy the same planet."

I was truly lost. But, at the same time I was getting the distinct message that he definitely thought he was very important in all of this and wasn't used to having his authority questioned. I thought a more personal touch might help matters.

"And what about your name, how did that come about and do you have a surname, or is it just Mr Sandels?"

"No surname, Sir, and I was named for my footwear."

"So it's just Sandals – S-A-N-D-A-L-S?"

"No Sir, S-A-N-D-E-L-S."

Feeling that I was getting nowhere fast, I decided not to question this. After all he was still squeaking and to be honest, it was getting on my nerves. This proved to be a good move, because I would later discover that spelling wasn't one of Fairyland's stronger points. They drove around in karrs and sometimes hitched a ride on ayroplains for example. I was already confused enough about Divens and OutFaxs so, keeping matters moving to the best of my ability, I just looked at my very silent work colleagues and their new miniature friend and said:

"Ok folks, sorry, subjects, Fairies – what's next?"

My new found acceptance of the situation seemed to move us all on a bit and with a look in my direction that said 'Thank heavens, at last', my new purple eyed pal lightly tapped his stick to his baseball cap and I suppose what you'd call a ceremony began.

4.

To begin with, Jim stood forward and banged his staff on the ground. The stationary tornado above my head disappeared and a clear night sky took its place. I thought that this was a bit weird given it was lunchtime but never mind, I was just about past caring by this point. Then the trees on Tomna Hill all flattened into the ground and Shona took centre stage beside me, with Sandels taking up the wingman position on the other side. We now had an unusually clear view of the graveyard below, but not the town, as there was just darkness beyond the graves. Hayley flew off, star lighting I presume. She later said to me that when you and I saw shooting stars it was actually her bumping off the earth's atmosphere for fun and I can assure you, there were a few that day.

Jim then gave a second bang of his staff (it was pretty impressive this time, a deep bass drum noise) and all the grave stones sank into the ground, to be replaced by lots of what can best be described as, well, Fairies. Every one of them was about the same height as Sandels, and they were all looking at me. There were thousands of them, all crowding forward but in numbers stretching back as far as my eyes could see. All that was needed was a quick "All hail the King" and the fantasy would be complete.

"All hail the King," squeaked Sandels.

"All hail the King," came back a sports stadium sized roar from the assembled Fairies.

I went to speak, thinking that it was a really difficult time to be put on the spot, when Shona whispered "Sshh," in my ear. "As you'll have gathered, Sandels is in charge so you say nothing. I mean nothing. If you feel you have to do anything, just nod."

I therefore nodded – first to the crowd (my people!) then Shona, Jim and finally Sandels.

"People of OutFax," began Sandels, "Our King is here to save us." Big roar. "King Dave" (I'd have been happier with 'David' but just nodded) "will now invite the Heads of the Divens to an audience with him. This will be in private in the Tomna Hill precinct but each of the Heads will hold a gathering afterwards in their own Diven to inform you of the outcomes."

He looked at me and I nodded yet again. At this point, I realised that we had been slowly rotating. It was clear that there were indeed four distinct segments of 'people'. We did one final rotation with more regal nodding from me, some staff waving from Sandels and some muted clapping from each segment in turn.

This all seemed a bit short to me. After all, all these Fairies had come along to see the new king and Sandels had just dismissed them in short order. I also noticed that the crowd had started to quietly disperse with the mildly upset manner of kids in a school playground who had come to see a fight, only for it to be broken up right at the start by a teacher.

As King, none of this was acceptable to me and I wasn't having them walk away disappointed with their first encounter with King Dave. So, living the dream, I did the first thing that came into my head. I stood on the chair (sorry, Throne), put my fist in the air and screamed:

"FREEDOM!"

Well, all hell broke loose. Shona dug me in the ribs, Jim looked horrified and Hayley briefly came back to earth, waved her big torch at me and disappeared again. Sandels actually looked shocked, as opposed to his more normal wearisome pout. The people stopped, turned back and then really looked at me. Dammit.

I nodded.

They roared expectantly – all the segments together this time and much louder than before.

Dammit, really; dammit.

To try to dig myself out of the hole I'd clearly put all of us in, I then proclaimed in as serious a voice as possible:

"It is in truth not for glory, nor riches, nor honours that we are fighting but for freedom – for that alone, which no honest man gives up but with life itself." Where did that come from?

This brought on a huge roar which meant that I was clearly hitting the mark as King. Way to go David.

I then proceeded with a more formal speech that history now records about me being delighted and honoured to be their King, etc which seemed to both go down really well and round things off nicely.

This led to even more staff-waving from the little man and much nodding from me as we went through one more rotation as an encore, only this time it was completed with cheering and smiles all round from a much more buoyant assembled crowd, complete with me punching the air in each quadrant like a game winning football manager.

I nodded at Sandels, who indicated to me that the show was now definitely over, but at least the Fairies all went off chatting and smiling and at the same time appeared to be much happier than before.

"What was that all about," he said, "Shona told you to be quiet – there's protocol you know. Sir."

The 'Sir' was clearly an afterthought and said with an edge of menace. Great, to add to my problems I now had a high pitched, pissed off fairy on my hands. So, thinking to myself 'Always enjoy the moment David', and in a bid to take charge I said with what I thought was a suitably regal tone:

"I am your King, Sandels, and I'd appreciate a bit more respect. You haven't had the decency, as my supposed guide, to tell me why I'm here or what any of this nonsense is about and I'm just expected to nod at your command. No way, mate, or as

King, I'll be commanding Shona and the rest to get me home and you and your little friends can sort out whatever issues you have by yourself. Didn't you see their expressions when you dismissed them - they were clearly searching for leadership so whether I was right or not, I don't care, but I put a few smiles on faces and by the looks of things there needs to be a bit more of that around here."

Satisfied by my outburst, I returned to nodding again, trying, and failing I'm sure, to look Kingly.

He burst into tears. Shona also sniffled and Jim talked about failure before we started. I felt really bad as I'd clearly not made the best of starts in my new job as King. So to help fix things, for the next few minutes I did my best to gee everyone up and after a while there was some more normal chat, including some light hearted comments about my outburst, which seemed to calm everyone down. Sandels got the message though: You make me King Dave, I'll be KING DAVE. The lawyer's clerk was coming of age.

5

This, however, hadn't really moved matters forward. I still had no idea what was going on and to be honest, I was more confused than ever.

At this juncture, Jim stepped forward again and did a bit more staff-banging. The night sky disappeared, it became sunny again, the trees were restored and for a minute I thought that I was back to walking club. Then I saw that Sandels was still there – again, dammit. Then a little more banging happened and four doors came out of the ground about 10 feet away from us on each side, matching up to the segments that had made up the Fairy crowd. Tim, Shona and a returning Hayley all stood off to one side.

Recovering his composure, Sandels once again took charge.

"I will now announce the heads of the Divens, Sir. Please note, there is nothing to be read into the order of appearance. When they have all been announced, the formal audience will begin. At that time, Jim, Shona, Hayley and I will retreat to allow you to undertake the necessary court business with the Heads."

I just nodded, this being all I could sensibly think to do while not wanting to cause any further offence, but at the same time still being as clueless as ever.

"May I present the Head of the Diven of Thought – Struugs."

A door opened and another 18 inch high man wandered out, nodded at Sandels, walked over and did what I thought was the first normal thing that had happened all day: he offered to shake my hand. I accepted the offer and he then sat down on one of four chairs that had somehow appeared in a line in front of me. Struugs looked like a miniature college professor: Chinos, open necked oxford button down shirt, loafers and all finished off with an improbably coloured orange blazer. His hair was about as orange as his blazer and all over the place and it was clear that this was a fairy that didn't give a hoot about sartorial elegance, but at the same time he had a pretty serious look on his face.

"May I present the Head of the Diven of Hope – Snouques."

Now this was a real fairy. If you ask any kid to draw a fairy, they'd draw Snouques (this was pronounced 'snooks'- see what I mean about spelling). She was all ballerina like, dressed in wispy white with a full set of wings allowing her to fly easily, while at the same time brandishing the obligatory wand – this too was white and seemed to be made of some sort of carbon fibre. She was classically beautiful with black hair, a slightly dark complexion and large black pools for eyes. She topped all of this off with a truly bewitching smile that I thought could get many a man into real trouble. She flitted over, kissed me on the cheek and took her seat, slipping the wand into a side holster and winking at Struugs on the way. I was beginning to realise that this lot weren't really the respectful type of subjects a new king hopes for.

"May I present the Head of the Diven of Works – Ded-i."

Pronounced 'dead eye', he seemed pretty straightforward as he walked right out and over to me wearing jeans, a black T shirt, black baseball cap and an equally boring backpack. He stood in front of me, gave a half grin, made a 'thumbs up' sign, turned, did the same to his co–heads and took a seat with one leg draped over the arm of the chair. No deference from him then.

"May I finally present the Head of the Other Diven – Hooligan Pict."

And so appeared the tomboy of the bunch. "Call me Hoopik," she announced, "everyone else does". As you would by now expect, I just stuck to nodding. With short scruffy dirty blonde hair, a healthy outdoor tan and dressed in a sleeveless vest top with combat pants and ninja boots, Hoopik strolled over, nodded to the other three and then climbed up on my knee (remember, they were all only about a foot and a half tall) and proceeded to stare at me. This was pretty unnerving but got worse when she pulled at my ears and opened my mouth to look at my teeth, I think. For the first time in my life I began to sympathise with horses. One last tug on my nose, a quick smile and she jumped off, rearranged a mad looking belt with pouches that she wore around her waist and joined the rest, this time sitting on her chair cross legged.

Yup, absolutely no respect for the new King Dave at all.

"Sir, Heads, I must leave you now. May you have fruitful deliberations and bring peace to the OutFax territories."

"Thank you Sandels," I said, "you have been most helpful and a good friend to the nation," trying to say something appropriate.

Being me, I didn't know what to do next. This didn't last long, however, as they all started to shout at once.

I variously heard "Help us", "Thank God you're here", "So how do we stop the killing?", What's the plan", "Why did you take so long", "how can you save our dust" and other pleas for help. After the relative calm of the ceremony and then their introductions, they all seemed to have lost the plot.

"Good luck, Sir," said Sandels as he faded away.

You guessed it, with really no other option available, I just nodded.

Much later on I also learned that Shona and the rest of them also weren't very sure whether I'd be any use as king. They'd all discussed it out of earshot as they moved away from me and the Diven heads. According to what I heard afterwards the conversation went something along the lines of:

Shona to Sandels "How do you think it'll all work out?"

"I really don't know, but I hope for everyone's sake that something special happens."

Hayley, looking serious for a moment, added "it's a real issue, after all David didn't have any time to settle in or even have the risks explained to him."

"He must have had an inkling of some sort?" questioned Jim, "I mean, every one of us Haferlincs had some sort of feeling that there was more to life before we found the path to Fairyland."

"Well, if he did, he kept it all pretty quiet – then I suppose it's not really something you'd talk about, especially in a lawyer's office," said Hayley, mainly to herself.

"Too late now anyway," came the squeaky answer from Sandels, "I tried to persuade them to leave it off but apparently the worst violence in ages happened at Luskentyre Beach yesterday and after that, the four Heads told me to give you all the nod to go and bring in Levante. The fight for dust has moved up a gear in a way that I haven't seen in at least 800 years and the Canooque-F's front line is now only 50 miles from our main dust valley. It's too close for comfort and the Heads are convinced that King Dave has the key to beating them off. Having met him, I have to say that I'm personally not so sure, but as I said, it's too late now."

4000 miles away somewhere in Northern Canada, Arverlang, the Head of the Canooque-F Fairyland territory, was awakened by one of his minc-ling servants. The Canooque-F was one of the four other territories that made up Fairyland and Arverlang was their dictator leader. He hated the OutFax.

"It's happened like we thought it might and it looks like they've found something that's making them much happier."

"How do you know?" demanded Arverlang.

"Starlighter's been out on the prowl – we can't work out what the messages say but it's getting a reaction on all fronts. They're not quite partying but we get a sense of relief across the board."

Sitting up in bed and stroking his black and grey beard, Arverlang narrowed his yellow and black striped eyes and looked right through the minc-ling.

"Call my henchmen to the circle – we'll do a final push and sort this lot out once and for all. I want every one of the decapitated bodies of these useless Diven Heads posted at the four corners of the new United Territories of Fairyland."

The minc-lings ran off to get the message to the armies of the Canooque-F – it was time to finish off the OutFax forever.

#

6.

Meanwhile back at the hill.

"Oi, oi, ….OI," I shouted, "calm it down, will you. I can't believe that any of you could be the Heads of anything the way you're behaving. Now tell me….. What. Is. Going. On?" My outburst was as a result of them ignoring my nodding and after them all shouting in unison at me, getting into some massive squabble between themselves about things I hadn't a clue about. However, even to me it was obvious that they were clearly in some state of panic about something. I was also getting the idea that they thought I might have the solution. My headache was now really taking hold.

"It's a nightmare and we're losing," shouted Hoopik, "The Canooque-F's forces are knocking at our back and front doors and we're running out of options fast. The first Fairy killing in 500 years happened at the beach yesterday and it won't be long before the Fs work out how they did it. You've got to help us, King Dave, and we know you can – the Book of Groges said that you would be the saviour and right now, we need some saviouring. So, please get to it, big man, will you?"

I had no idea what she was on about. OK, she was clearly distressed and the shouting increased as she spoke but, honestly, they had to realise that I'd only came to this nonsense about an hour beforehand. I'd also discover as time went on, though, that Hoopik could get a bit hysterical. She affected this cool urban guerrilla look and worked the macho girl bit pretty well, but when the pressure was on, she broke like everyone else.

However, after my shouting at them the others had calmed down a bit but still looked equally concerned about the whole thing. Struugs was now on his cell phone, texting or something, and had been all the time Hoopik lost the plot and the other two, whilst no longer shouting did still look really upset about something.

Struugs put his phone down and said, "Well, King Dave, welcome to the mad house. What my hooligan friend was trying to say was the following:

"We, the OutFax territory, are one of five such territories across the known world. We have good working relations with three of them but have always had a bit of a problem with the fifth – the Canooque-F territory. The problem is Fairy Dust and the fact that they don't have very much of it. Now, they're based in what you know as Canada and periodically try to help themselves to our, and anyone else's, Dust. For the last 800 years there have been skirmishes but nothing serious until a guy called Arverlang became Head of Canooque-F. The Fs don't have Divens although they used to, until this Arverlang idiot came along and got rid of the competition, making it the first Fairy Dictatorship - and that dictator is him. His people live in fear but are also genuinely short of the Dust this time. We can't work out what he's done with it but it can't be good – if he was sensible, the Dust would last for years and new Dust could be produced in the normal way but hey, ho, he isn't and now he's hell bent on taking us on.

"As Hoopik said, the big problem was the death yesterday. It's incredibly difficult to kill a fairy."

I must have had a questioning look on my face.

"You see, in many respects, any battles that normally take place between the different territories of Fairyland are really for recreational purposes but the upping of the Fs quest for Dust combined with a Fairy death takes it to a whole new level. Also, the fairy that was killed came from Hoopik's Diven hence the slightly irrational tone to her argument so far."

"You'd be the same if it was one of yours – I'm the one who has to speak to the family," she shouted at him.

"Anyway, to continue, this death changes things, as the Fs saw it happen and will be trying to work out how they did it. If they do, we're stuffed. As Hoopik said, it's in the Book of Groges that the next King of Fairyland would have the answer – and that, King Dave, is you. So, to quote the Hooligan, 'please get to it, big man.'"

Jesus, this was rapidly turning into a nightmare and if I was asleep, I was now willing myself to wake up soon. Then, in amongst this craziness, all of a sudden Snouques was sitting on my lap trying the sympathy route. I tried my best to explain that there were some things that couldn't be fixed with a smile and big eyelashes but she just pouted. I was beginning to think that these weren't fairies, these were kids, and my immediate thought was that I sometimes have difficulty relating to my own, never mind this lot.

"There's got to be a practical solution Dave," said Ded-i. "After all, the book says so". No 'King' from him then.

Then they all sat still in their chairs and looked at me expectantly. Dammit, what was I meant to do now?

You've got to understand, I'm not the best under pressure. So far I'd already pee'd my underwear and burst out crying and I was now trying my very best not to have a total panic attack. After all, there's a reason I'm a lawyer's clerk and not an actual lawyer. But trying to act as if I fitted in and praying for Sandels to come back and help I asked:

"What's this about a book – are there some sort of instructions somewhere?"

"It's The Book of Groges, King Dave," answered Struugs. "I suppose it's the closest thing that we have to a spiritual guide but it also gives us answers when issues like this come up. The only thing is that very few of us have ever seen it and we don't know where it is, although Sandels was adamant that it would have the answers we needed. I understand that you're the man to find it and then by reading it, tell us how to sort this death thing out."

This was just getting worse and worse.

"Right, let's get some order to this," I said, trying to wrest back some sort of control. "Where's Sandels and the other three, are they still here?"

"Yeah, they're over in the far corner," said Ded-i. "You want me to get them?"

We were soon all back as one big group.

"Next thing, is there any chance that we can all go somewhere a bit more comfortable – this throne is killing my back and I don't like discussing matters of the realm outside, if you see what I mean."

In my head, I was actually saying 'David, you're going mad, you're joining in even more', but I couldn't see any other option at that time.

"We could retire below the hedge, Sir," said Sandels. Oh please, please help me, I thought. I was starting to accept him for what he was and even getting used to the squeaking as time went on, but sitting under a hedge wasn't really what I was hoping for.

"Yeah, good idea," said Struugs. "Let's go."

One of the bigger graves nearby had a big hedge around it and, being tiny, the five Fairies amongst us disappeared easily into it. I looked at my office colleagues for some help but all of a sudden, they too just shrunk and entered the hedge as well. As the new King, right then I have to say that I felt pretty useless. Then my new Fairy seductress friend came back out of the hedge, wings in the air, and touched down gently on my left shoulder, managing to stroke my neck in the process.

"I can make you fit, King Dave, we just need to use the magic wand," she whispered in my ear. It was clear even to me that this girl could be just trouble with wings but at that time, I was running out of options so I just shrugged my shoulders and said OK.

All of a sudden I was their size and lo and behold, in front of Snouques and me was a door in the hedge. What the hell, off we went.

The door took us into what would best be described as an old elevator where the rest were waiting. Sandels hit a button and we went down for a couple of seconds. There was a 'bing' noise and the door opened to a large, poorly lit room that was arranged as a lounge bar. I thought that there was no-one else around until I saw an old man tending a horseshoe shaped mahogany bar at the far end. Around the room were lots of empty booths with stools upturned on the tables.

"Who wants a real drink then?" I said in a bid to add some levity.

"Me," came back all eight voices around me. So now I was in a bar with a bunch of alcoholic Fairies and something called Haferlincs. My life was just getting better and better.

The drinks were ordered and shortly afterwards we were all sitting comfortably in a big corner booth. At the bar there had been no mention of payment and if questioned, I decided that I'd just say that Kings don't carry cash and then look at Sandels questioningly. Some light blues music was playing in the background, I was getting used to my new pals being the same size as me and I was beginning to relax for the first time that day. I also had my first taste of Fairy Broo ™ and it hit the spot. Just to explain, Fairy Broo ™ looks a bit like really light coloured champagne but is served with ice and also comes with two raspberries and some parsley in each tall glass serving. It also has a kick like a hungry mule.

"Let's get back to the war, Sir," interrupted Sandels, a man with a real talent for ruining the moment.

Taking the lead, I said, "OK then, I have some questions. I want clear answers and I don't need any bickering between any of you. I also need a few answers from Jim, Shona and Hayley with no interruptions from anyone else. Sandels, you have my permission to hit anyone with your big stick who doesn't obey. Jim, you leave yours on the floor."

"Yes, SIR." said Sandels. I actually thought I saw a grin crack his 1000 year old face. I had to shoot a warning glance to Ded-i and Hoopik though. On to question time.

"First, is all of this real?"

"Yes," said Shona, "I realise that it's a bit difficult to take in right now but it all is. And to answer what will almost certainly be your next question, no, you're not stuck here – Jim, Hayley and I will get you back out as soon as we can. To do that, though, we have to make some progress on the war issues that the people of the territory are facing."

"OK, I just want to say publicly and for the record that I still think I'm in some sort of personal nightmare but we'll go along with it in the meantime. Next, how big is this OutFax territory – in human world terms where does it stretch to?"

Ded-i this time. "From the North Sea to the Pacific Ocean and from Iceland to the top of Africa; in North America, the Southern border is Costa Rica and it used to be the US-Canada border to the north but the Canooque-F have now taken a chunk that includes Idaho, Kansas and Pennsylvania."

"Where does the Canooque-F exist?"

"The whole of the Arctic, Greenland, the bit of North America Ded-i said and some of Norway. They are mainly in Canada," answered Struugs.

"What's so special about Fairy Dust?"

"This," said Snouques. "Watch me". She took out her wand, clicked a little switch on it, waved it about and some dust came out of the end creating a Chinese take-out meal for eight.

"Wow." Not very regal I know, but about as polite as I could get. I was also starving and this was impressive stuff.

"Dust makes everything work in Fairyland," Snouques went

on, "and as every little kid on earth will tell you, the real power behind everything is Fairy Dust. Each community in the Divens, and across the world, has its own trained dust dispensers like me, but there are only certain places on earth that you can get it. You can make synthetic Dust – that's what Struugs was on about when he said the Fs could make their own - but right now it's still easier to dig it out of the ground if you can, hence the war. The Dust is magic – it works out what you want and delivers it. If you wish for too much, though, let's put it this way, it's not always a good outcome. As King, you'll automatically be a Dust dispenser and you'll be able to create some pretty special wishes with it. I can, of course, give you private lessons if you want." This was followed by another wink and a pout. She really never gave up, although the human male that I am was enjoying the 'dream fantasy' and was quite happy to go along with this.

"Where do you get the Dust from?"

"Geological fault lines." This time it was Jim, clearly with his 'facilities management' hat on. "We have two of the best in our territory, hence the fight. They're the Great Glen in Scotland and The San Andreas in California. In dust terms, they are, and no pun intended, gold dust."

"Next thing you'll be telling me the Loch Ness Monster is the Guardian of the Fairy Dust," I muttered pretty much as an aside.

"She is," said eight people in unison, all with happy expressions.

"I'm delighted to see that you're beginning to understand, Sir," said Sandels without a hint of irony. Oh God. Anyway, I put my straight face on and went back to the questions.

"What can I do – although right now, I'm sorry to say folks, I don't think I have any answers for you."

"Oh but you do," said Hayley. "It's within you, King Dave, and when we link you with the moon and the stars we'll find the truth."

I thought 'Really?' but this time I had, for the first time, the sense to not say it out loud.

"You need to read the Book of Groges pretty quickly as a first step," interjected Struugs. "Hopefully from that you'll see something that'll make sense."

"Seems like a plan to me," I replied, the Fairy Broo ™ clearly taking effect. "But one last question, am I just the King of the OutFax or am I King of the whole of Fairyland?"

"Just the OutFax, Sir, no need to get ahead of oneself at this stage." No guessing who was playing party pooper again.

And that was really it for the evening. We got stuck into the food and there was then what could best be described as a more general conversation amongst new friends and we even forgot about the war for a while as the Fairy Broo ™ was flowing freely. As time went on and they all seemed to calm down a bit, I sort of remember Hoopik and Ded-i doing a duet, Sandels performing a high pitched aria and I think Jim was playing a lute as the night faded away; really great stuff, this Broo drink, you know.

7

I'm waking up. Slowly, almost luxuriantly. Then I realise that I'm at home, in my own bed and I can tell from the way that the sun is shining through the window that it's morning. The dream (or nightmare, or whatever) is still fresh in my mind though – very, very clear indeed. But then I remember, it's Saturday; Bethany and the kids are away for the day so it's just me at home and I must have slept through them leaving. I can also clearly recall being at work yesterday, going for the walk to Tomna Hill and then coming back to the office, having a moan about how slow Friday afternoons can be and then coming home.

This was weird. It was the most vivid dream I've ever had and I remember all of it, every last detail. Thinking back, it was really quite enjoyable. I was King, the Fairies treated me the way I'd have expected, given my exalted position (well, most of them, but I suppose that's dreams for you) and for once, in a work sense, I seemed to have a real purpose in life.

Never mind, on with the day. I knew that there was laundry to be done, and some weeding in the front garden. This I remember from the 'You're the one having the house to yourself so you can make yourself useful' conversation the night before. Oh well, better get up and start with the list or there'll be trouble later I thought.

"Davie."

I sat up slightly in bed as I heard the voice.

"Davie."

A bit more insistent this time, definitely there alright. I pulled the covers up to my neck.

"Davie, would you get out from under the covers and look at me for God's sake."

Oh Shit. The voice was in the room and sounded like an old man who smokes at least 40 cigarettes a day and drinks too much – really deep and gravelly. This was not good, I'm going mad and never mind what had gone before, this was real. I hid completely under the bedcovers.

"Davie - NOW!"

I pulled the covers off my head just a little bit so that I could see the room. There was no-one there. In an irrational moment and remembering that Fairies were small, I looked over the side of the bed and there were no little people either. This must be what lunatics mean when they say 'the voices in my head told me to do it.'

"Over here Davie."

Still hiding behind the duvet but now peering over the top edge, I turned the other way towards the voice and with it, the chair that sits in the far corner of our bedroom. There were some clothes on the chair and our black and white tom cat was, as always, using them as a bed. It too was looking questioningly at the bed so it must be hearing the voice as well.

"Please don't hurt me," I whispered, sounding a bit like Sandels from my dream, while looking around the whole room and seeing no-one. "And please leave now. If you're real, there's some money in the jar beside the kettle in the kitchen. Please take it." I retreated under the covers again.

"I don't want your money, you moron, I live here. And would you at least look at me when I'm speaking."

Once again, I peeped over the duvet thinking the chair was now speaking to me. But no, the only change was that the cat was now sitting up and appeared to be shaking its head at me.

"Davie."

Oh shit (again). You guessed it, it's the cat. I'll have to see a doctor. Then I started to wonder about stress at work, or maybe early onset dementia. No, it's probably a tumour in my head, I was thinking, meaning I would die, I mean if it's making me see the cat speaking, then it's clearly inoperable. And I still had the laundry to do.

"It's OK Davie, calm down, it's me, Felixx, speaking to you. You're not going mad and if you must know, this is pretty difficult for me as well."

"HELP!" I screamed to no-one in particular.

"Give it up, would you - you idiot - and just accept the situation. You finally accepted it in the OutFax Territory yesterday so why not here. I mean, if you take on the throne of Fairyland from a group of foot high pests without question, you can at least listen to your cat – God knows, I've listened to you enough over the years – 'Puss, puss, puss', 'Chase the string', 'Mind the dog' – as if I can't see it already - 'Have a worming tablet'- yeeugh - 'Who's a lovely big boy then' and all the other crap you say to Paws and me."

Wait a minute, the cat's not only speaking, it's also giving me abuse now. And calling me 'Davie'.

Then he said, "You'd better go to the bathroom so the same problem you had yesterday doesn't come back, eh Davie?" He also nodded his head and winked.

He had a point so I meekly went to the bathroom, did the necessary and washed my face in very cold water. I came back to the bedroom to find that he'd moved to the bed. I stood by the door, just in case I had to make a run for it.

"Right, let's get to business. Everything that happened yesterday was real. We just made sure that when you came out of Fairyland to go back to the office you wouldn't remember what had happened until this morning. After all, there was a danger you'd be in jail by now if you had had a chance to think about it and speak to anyone – God knows what would have happened if you'd tried to explain to all the others in that cattle pen you call an office. And by the way, you thought the Fairy Broo ™ was good. Damn right, it had some really special dust that your new pal Snouques put in it to make you forget – heh heh."

I just continued to stare. I may have nodded.

"Anyhoo, I'm your new guide – a guide cat eh? First time ever, heh, heh. Here's the rules. You mustn't speak to Shona, Jim or Hayley about any of this in public unless all three of them get you alone and they bring it up first. Obviously, you can't tell anyone else either, Davie, or it'll be the men in white coats for you and we'll all be in a worse position than ever. If I'm not around, you can speak to Paws. She mainly speaks Spanish these days but knows enough English to get the message to me. So, unless you're in Fairyland, it's you and me, OK".

Silence.

"OK?"

"OK." A whispered croak from me.

"Now, get dressed, go downstairs, have some food and then we'll have a proper discussion – I'll catch you in the kitchen as I want Paws to get the gist of this as much as possible as well. In the meantime I'm off to lick where my whatsits used to be – please note, and I've been waiting a long, long time to tell you this, I've never really forgiven you for that operation but we'll have a separate chat about that at another time. By the way, just for the record, it's Felixx with two x's; you people can't spell to save yourselves."

With that, he jumped off the bed, checked himself out in the mirror and headed out of the room. I was torn between bursting into tears again or getting really annoyed with the cat for having a go at me. Being me, though, and true to my profession as a lawyers clerk, I took the safe option and did as he asked. I was already worried about the 'separate chat' threat so decided that, as it had at least delivered me from Fairyland to home, once again the best thing to do was to 'get with the program', only this time it was our cat taking the lead. It's got to be a brain tumour.

After dressing, I crept downstairs and into the kitchen. This was where our lovely black Labrador dog Paws lived. She was by this time an old lady who had moved pleasantly into old age and really liked the comfort of the radiator in the corner. She'd come to us as a puppy when the kids were little about 12 years ago and was very much part of the family. Now, however, in my new state of madness, I was frightened of her as well – and this was a dog that didn't have a bad bone in its body.

"Morning Paws," I said as normal as I went towards the kettle.

"Buenos días, Señor Dave," came the answer back from the corner behind me, in the sweetest voice I've ever heard.

I closed my eyes and turned round, not wanting to look. As I opened them, the damned cat was there again, between me and the dog, who was now wagging her tail and, I swear, smiling at me.

"It's the best you'll get these days," he said. "She's really gone over to the other side."

Not knowing what to say or do, I made a cup of coffee, got a bowl of cornflakes and sat at the kitchen table. The dog settled back down into its corner and nodded off.

All the time I ate, the cat sat guard on the table right in front of me, with his black and white fur bristling up menacingly every once in a while. It clearly thought I was about to make a run for it and to be honest, it wasn't far wrong. At one point it hurried me up, saying something about not liking speaking to me while I was eating, although apparently it hadn't stopped me with him in the past. Its attitude was starting to really annoy me.

I finished the cereal and refilled my coffee, sat back down and looked the cat in the eye. It just shook its head again and said:

"Right, gather round everyone."

'Everyone?' I thought. Present were the recently demented me, an abusive talking cat and a dog that speaks Spanish. Really?

Then the cupboard door under the kitchen sink opened and

out popped Struugs and Ded-i. In unison they said, "Morning King Dave, sleep well, did we?"

The cat shook its head, I nodded - slowly this time - and the dog snored quietly.

Oh God....

"OK, let me have it." I said wearily, rubbing my face and hoping that maybe someday, I really would make some sense of this.

8.

"Here's the rules". This was the cat once again asserting its authority. Not only was it having a go at me in my own house, it was turning into a control freak as well.

"This is my territory," he went on, "and I'll be in charge while we're here. You pair can explain to Davie here what's to happen next and if he looks like he's going to welch on us, which given his performance to date seems pretty likely to me, I'll sort him out. Over to you."

I thought about interrupting to try to gain some sort of control – after all, I was the King – but the way the cat narrowed its eyes as it said 'welch' made me think the better of it. I said nothing.

Struugs this time. "You do remember the problem with the Canooque-F, don't you, and the fact that someone was killed?"

I nodded.

"Good, in that case we're back to where we left it in the Fairy Lounge yesterday. Since then, it appears that the Fs have got wind that you're on the scene and it's made them ramp things up a bit. They're trying all sorts of nasty stuff to get another kill and as we explained, they don't know how it happened. In fact, nobody knows how it happened as, in general terms, a fairy can even be decapitated and brought back with some dust.

"What we do know is that the Book of Groges is quite clear that when something like this happens, a new leader will make him or herself visible to the heads of the Divens of the territory where the death happens. In our case, this is you. Along with this, from what we can read into it, you'll be able to not only work out why it happened, but put measures in place to stop it happening again. Remember, the last killing was about 500 years ago and the leader who appeared then – it was in the Sou-Pa Territory – just made everyone about two inches bigger which solved the issue until now."

As the cat was still staring at me, I thought I'd better look involved.

"Why me?" was all I could think of.

Ded-i jumped in this time, perching on the edge of the table next to me. "Who knows, Dave, it just happens. There have always been Haferlincs like the three at your office and Felixx and Paws but people like you seem to be sleepers of sorts who only come to us in times of strife. I'm really sorry I can't help you – my Diven's main role is to provide practical solutions to problems and this time I'm failing, so all I can say is sorry, I've no idea."

"I'm the same," said Struugs, who by this time was lounging around in the dog's bed, much to the obvious disgust of the cat.

"My Diven – of Thought – leads on philosophical issues and tries to think things through. Normally we come up with a solution and Ded-i's lot then make it work. I'm the same though, even my best thinkers are lost on this one so, like the D said, it's up to you I'm afraid."

"What about the other two Divens – what do they contribute?" I asked, trying to get back into the swing of things.

"Snouques's lot cheer everyone up and keep us all positive. It's needed sometimes as really, apart from times like now, we have a fairly benign existence and I suppose it can get a bit boring. They're also the primary dust dispensers for the OutFax." This was Struugs, who by now was on the dog's back pretending it was a horse. The dog slept through it all.

"We generally spend most of our time playing tricks on humans for entertainment – the more elaborate the better as far as we are concerned. It's actually true when people lose stuff, find it again and blame it on the 'little people' – that's our younger ones learning their trade. Some of our better ones, though, are the old 'end of the world is nigh' stuff where we leave clues for the gormless of the planet to pick up and persuade others to join them – it's amazing quite how gullible your lot can be. That's why this war is serious, not only is there a real survival issue for the OutFax, but things'll also get really boring in the human world 'cos we're not out having fun."

"Hoopik's Diven is different from the rest though – it's called 'Other' for a good reason. She tends to pick up all those Fairies that don't quite fit into the other three. However, she's really good at getting them together to make things happen and in practice, her lot flit between the rest of us and help out where needed. They're a pretty tight knit community though, hence the reason she's so upset at the death. In fact we're here alone because Hoopik is with the family and Snouques is out and about keeping the mood of the people up across the Diven."

I was almost starting to believe this and take it seriously when the cat jumped into the fray again.

"Enough of the history lesson, you lot," he growled. "We've got work to do. Right Davie, you'll need to work out from the Book of Groges what you're doing next."

"And where's this book?" I asked, apparently naively given the looks all round – even the dog opened an eye in my direction. And feeling a bit braver given I seemed to be the linchpin I added "By the way, please don't call me Davie – it's 'David' when we're at home or 'King Dave' in front of others, OK Felixx? Oh, and sorry, did I manage to say that with two xx's."

At this, the dog sat up, eyes wide open, Struugs fell off into the bed and Ded-i actually looked away. The cat, still right in front of me on the table, looked straight at me for what seemed like an eternity and said very, very slowly. "Well, well, it appears that you have some balls after all. Maybe everything isn't lost. Let's get the book." It jumped off the table, heading for our den, clearly expecting everyone else to follow it.

I almost said, 'Well I've got more balls than you,' but thought the better of it as it stopped and turned to look at me, all narrow

44

eyes again. It was clearly a mind reader as well.

Now, our home is only about 20 years old and has the usual assortment of rooms any modern detached house has. The kitchen (I guess the house builders would call it a 'dining kitchen/family room') is big enough for a table for us to dine at, a sofa, TV and space for Paws's bed, as well as all the kitchen stuff; granite tops, island cooker and a big fridge freezer. Off the kitchen one way was the utility/laundry room with a door to the back garden and on the other side, double doors lead to a combination of living and dining rooms.

Off the dining room is a little room stuck on to the back of the house that some would call a sun room and others maybe an office, but in our house it is 'the den'. The cat led the procession across the wooden floor of the dining room, showing off by taking a short cut under the table lightly tapping its claws on the oak planks. The den, where we were clearly now heading, was just big enough to have a couple of chairs, an old hi-fi, some book cases and a coffee table. In other words, nothing the kids would be interested in so in reality it was mum and dad's sanctuary. More importantly, it had a door that shut the rest of the world off when you went in and closed it behind you. This door was closed now and the cat was outside it, waiting.

'Huh, who's so smart now, eh?' I said, looking at the cat staring at the door handle a good two feet above it. (I did only say it in my head though, seeing no need to get confrontational.) Our feline mind reader turned to me with that 'special' look again and, given the progress of our relationship so far, I decided the best policy was just to open it. I did, however, hesitate just a minute to let the cat know whose house we were in, and who was King. In that moment, though, Ded-i jumped up and opened the door as it was clearly more important to all that we went into the room as opposed to me having a pissing contest with my pets.

We all packed into the den. "So," I said looking at the cat. "Why here? Tell me, is our den a bit like the tardis and we'll all be transported somewhere else now?"

"No you idiot, we're here to get the book," came the irritated reply. "You'll find it on the bottom shelf of the large bookcase, second from the left."

"Nonsense," I said, "that's just all the family history books that Bethany got at the charity shop – there's nothing about Groges or Fairies in there."

"Humour me," replied Felixx.

Once again the damn cat's right, the book's there and I now hate it even more.

I asked "How did that get there?", as I picked up what was a fairly unprepossessing eight by six inch book with no more than about 100 pages in it. "I've never seen it before." It was bound in blue cloth with old yellowing writing that did indeed say 'The Book of Groges' on the front cover. Under the title it said 'Yandermoo'.

"It's probably always been there," explained Struugs. "Like all things in Fairyland they're actually right under your nose if you're a human, it's just that you don't know how to look for them properly."

"Right Davie, we're going to leave you alone with the book to see what's next. We'll be waiting." And with that, the cat, dog and the two Diven heads left the room, even managing to quietly shut the door behind them. I didn't notice them go, however, because I'd opened the front cover and read what someone had written in pencil: "To young Levante, a gift for you, All the best, Yandermoo". I sincerely hoped that it wasn't a book of bad poetry.

I settled down in my favourite chair and put my coffee on the little table beside me. It'd gone a bit overcast outside now and I had to put on the reading light to see the faded print inside the book. I looked for a publication date but there was none; there was no mention of a publisher at all, in fact. Turning the first page, I came to a disclaimer. This was really strange. I mean, it wasn't written in old fashioned English or anything, in fact it was more like a warning that you'd get at the front of a TV instruction manual. There was a bit about not reading on if you didn't know how to undertake the instructions contained therein, hire an expert if you're not competent, making sure you had the proper tool kit before you proceeded and things like that. The other notable point was that the spelling was atrocious so this was clearly a Fairyland publication.

Given the obvious urgency of the situation, I flicked through the book to see if there were any quick answers to the immediate problem of how to stop Fairies being killed. Chapter nine was helpfully listed as 'Uneckspektid Deths' so I quickly proceeded to that section. The Chapter listed a number of circumstances that were apparently what the good people of Fairyland would consider unexpected deaths – 'death after eating a mouse' and 'death from staring too long at daffodils', for example – but there was also one on 'killed in battle, no resurrection''. This sounded like the one I needed and here's what it said (note: I've corrected the spelling).

In times of strife, normal fighting, which is seen mainly as good exercise and entertainment for our people, might take a turn towards the sinister. This may occur when the pentagonal balance of the territories of Fairyland is disturbed and one or more territories gain a power advantage over the others. This power shift can lead to circumstances in which what would be normal exercisional (I had to leave that one in) behaviour can actually kill, without the possibility of a dust resurrection. It is recognised that the cause of this is the creation of a triple vortex impact of force, with a subset of balanced projectile trajectories combined with concurrent impact orchestrations, into the lateral subjugation of the victim's postural and energy receptor acceptance. When such a death occurs, it is normal to expect the appearance of a new monarch within the territory of the deceased. The monarch will provide further guidance.

I was, and I'm sure you are, none the wiser. I hoped that I'd interpreted the bad spelling correctly but even then, I'd no idea what the 'cause' section meant. Even more worryingly, the book clearly indicated that not only would I know what it meant, but that I'd have the solution that would stop it happening again. The only thing I could think of at the time was that the bit about vortexes, orchestrations and subjugation sounded like the way big countries explain away unnecessary military action against smaller neighbours. This Yandermoo fella already had a lot to answer for.

I was brought back to reality (if that's what it actually was) by some scratching at the door. In the past, I'd have happily let the cat in to sit on the seat beside me. Until this morning, I always presumed that it wanted in to relax and get away from the stresses of the household and enjoy a few quiet moments with its owner. Now I knew it had just been spying on me all along.

Reluctantly, I grabbed the handle, pulled the door towards me and let the cat, dog and the rest of my new friends in. They must have been listening at the door because the scratching only came when I'd finally put the book down.

"Well?" came the question in unison (with what sounded like a quiet 'cuáles la respuesta' from the dog in amongst it).

"Well, indeed", I replied, waving the book about. "This is at best wholly unhelpful and at worst, unintelligible junk. Who's this Yandermoo by the way?"

Cue a collective intake of breath from the assembled crowd.

"Please keep it down," spluttered Struugs. "He might hear you."

"Yes, shut up will you," added Ded-i looking around nervously.

Through all of this, the cat just sat there, flicking its tail and waiting its chance.

"OK Davie, what's the score, how can we sort out this lot's problem so we can all get back to normal. And the rest of you, as I've explained, Yandermoo doesn't exist, it's just a made up name used by the folk who wrote this stuff centuries ago, so quit with the panics."

"Do you ever actually lighten up, Felixx," I said, feeling a headache coming on, "and anyway, like I explained, I can't see the answer from what the book says. I'm sorry."

I felt I'd let them all down. Badly.

Ded-i and Struugs looked lost, the cat was clearly more hacked off than ever and the dog took this as its cue to leave the room and pad slowly back to its bed, head and tail down.

"But it must be in there," said Struugs, more now in hope than certainty. "I mean, we've always been told that the Book has all the answers",

"Well, have a go yourselves," I said. "Here's the book." I offered it round the room.

"But we can't read it," came back Ded-i and Struugs. "The only readers are the Labichens of each Diven and they're all out at Luskentyre keeping a lid on things," explained Struugs.

I looked at the cat.

"Don't be ridiculous Davie, I'm a cat – I can't read books. And before you ask, Paws can't either – she used to but..."

"Yeah, yeah .... it's not in Spanish," I finish for him. "Just great. Where do we go now?"

"You could read it to us," said the cat, in its uniquely condescending manner. I just nodded and did as it had asked.

They had no idea either.

We returned to the kitchen. Or more properly, I went back to get more coffee and some headache tablets and the other three followed me. We were now back were we started with Ded-i and me sitting at the table, the cat back in command right in front of me and Struugs once again hanging out with the dog. I was still holding on to the Book. The headache was to me a clear sign that it was some serious medical malfunction that was making me hallucinate in my own house, with speaking cats, Fairies and dogs chatting a la Español. However, if I saw it through, I could hopefully make it back to bed in one piece.

As a suggestion to try to bring things to some sort of conclusion I said "OK, let's say the answer is in the Book but we just can't see it yet. If it is, we need to work out what the vortexes and all that stuff means and, much as it pains me, I'll try to read the rest of the Book to see if it's any help. It might be that we need to get the whole gang together again to try a group solution – after all, we seemed to be heading somewhere in the bar yesterday before the 'broo' took effect. What do you think?"

The cat yawned and rubbed its eyes, one at time. The other two looked at each other (the dog was asleep again) and nodded.

"OK," said Struugs. "We'll set up a meet."

"One thing," I said. "On the timing issue, is it not the case that thousands of years have passed in Fairyland if it's a tenth of a second for each human year?"

"You just aren't with us at all Davie, are you?" The cat shook its head again. "That's only when you're there. You see, the space time continuum bends a bit to accommodate us in Fairyland – ask Hayley, she's the expert – but the rest of the time it's the same so right now, we're only a day on." He said this as if he was speaking to an imbecile. So giving up completely, I just got up and headed back to bed.

"Whatever," I said as I trudged up the stairs, book in hand.

From the kitchen: "And what about the laundry, eh Davie - heh, heh?"

I won't repeat my answer here.

As I lay down, I prayed to God, Allah, the Sun God, even Yandermoo and everyone else for forgiveness in the forlorn hope that I'd wake up and it would be all back to normal. I fell asleep instantly.

I woke when the family came home which was close to lunchtime. Arrival shouting and other general noise penetrated my rest and I shook my head to clear the sleep from it.

"Is your father still in bed?" I heard from downstairs. This was not good. Footsteps followed on the stairs and the door opened with a bang.

"Enjoying yourself, are you?" My wife was clearly not happy with the situation; as she saw it, she'd been lumbered with the kids' stuff while I just lay in my pit. My excuse of having a sore head, the remains of which were still there, didn't work either.

After a short rant in amongst which was a begrudging offer of lunch with her and the kids, she left the room with another bang of the door and I tried to take stock of what was happening. Up to the present day, my life had been pretty benign. In the space of the last 24 hours, however, the whole thing had gone clean off the rails and I now had no idea what was happening. I mean, on the face of it, I was going mad. How else could any of it be explained? I didn't want to tell anyone, though, as I really did fear the consequences. After all, if you told someone what I'd been through, there was every chance you'd be shipped to the doctor and end up on some pretty heavy medication. The problem was also that the whole damn thing felt so real, but I guess that's what happens when your body and brain decide to go off on one. I sat up in bed and looked around. I noticed that the cat was asleep on the chair again.

"Felixx?"(note the two xx's). Nothing. "Felixx" – bit more insistent this time. Nothing again. So I got up, crept over and looked very closely at it but at the same time keeping my distance , just in case.

"Felixx"- this time in a sort of frantic whisper. It opened its eyes, yawned and then meowed, just like a normal cat. It then settled down back to sleep. I didn't know whether this was a good or bad result so I went back to bed for a re-think.

As I got into bed, I found the answer sitting beside my alarm clock. The Book was there, right where I'd left it when I'd baled on the team earlier on. I picked it up and yes it was the same book, yes the pencil inscription was still there and yes, the spelling was still very, very bad. I sat in bed for a long time trying to work out what to do. I looked again at the book and, given the grammatical issues, I realised that it would take an eternity to read leaving me genuinely stuck as to what to do next.

"Lunch is ready, if you can be bothered getting up," came the call from downstairs. Maybe some family time would help so I hid the book in the bedside cabinet drawer, under some old papers and other junk that had gathered there over the years. Time to take some stock, I thought, but first of all, time for some food.

As I was heading for lunch, unbeknown to me, the four Heads were meeting up in the Fairy Lounge.

"How did it go with King Dave" asked Hoopik as she arrived from the lift – the other three and Sandels were all there already. "I hope he's got some pretty good answers as I don't ever want to go through that again."

She was clearly distressed as Struugs moved over to let her into the same corner booth as the last time.

"No such luck," said Ded-i and he came from the bar with five Fairie Broo NA's this time, "he's the least likely King I'd ever have thought we'd get."

"And I suppose you've met lots," came a retort from Snouques, "I quite like him – he seems really genuine, if a bit lost, and if he's got even part of a legal mind we should get there."

"Getting there is not enough, Snouques." This was Struugs, looking up from his phone again, "we need some answers now and King Dave didn't have them. Even with Felixx threatening him - and he did a pretty good job - it's clear that King Dave's as lost as the rest of us. Having said that, he read us the relevant part from the Book and I don't think anyone would be any the wiser."

"Yeah, he did," said Ded-i, sipping his Broo, "and he did offer to read the rest of the book to see if it helps. I suggest we get him back in here tomorrow after he's read it and see where we go from there."

"Will it be me who calls him?" This was Sandels, who looked as miserable as ever.

"Yes – we'll all be back to Luskentyre this afternoon to lead the troops. It's all hands to the pumps right now," agreed Struugs, downing his drink and heading to the door. "I've got some serious thinking to do so I'll catch you all tomorrow here early on, OK?"

Four other glasses were raised in acknowledgement.

#

Arverlang sat fuming in the dark cave that he called home – no-one appeared to know what was going on. The minc-ling crept in and announced his presence.

"What now", he shouted, a 'welcome' that included a thump on the table in front of him.

"They've got a new King and he's got a copy of the Book" said the minc-ling from behind the nearest chair.

"So get me The Book as well you idiot" roared Arverlang.

"But we can't read it, Sir, you banished all our Labichens to other territories for reading 'unsuitable' material." This time he was backing towards the door.

"Then capture one of their Labichens as well and bring him here with The Book you clown. And don't come back until you have."

#

9.

The rest of Saturday passed peacefully with the family. The atmosphere caused by my unexpected lie-in thawed as the day went on and in mid-afternoon, Milo and I headed off to watch the local football team. Later that evening we all went out for pizza and I started to believe that things were, indeed, returning to normal. The only nagging problem was that the Book was still there, hiding in my bedside cabinet.

Sunday dawned as most do in our house and it won't surprise you that I like to follow Lionel Ritchie's advice in the old song, 'Easy like a Sunday morning'. The kids had been out and about early on and the Sunday papers had arrived back with them. TJ was waxing lyrical about some party that she was attending later that day and Bethany was working away on the usual Levante family Sunday roast dinner – genuinely, anyone would look forward to this. By late morning, I'd settled down with the papers and a cup of coffee in the den as everyone else did their own Sunday things. In other words, it was much like lots of other weekend mornings in households across the world.

Three coffees later and I had to nip to the toilet. I went to the little bathroom by the front door (the closest to the den) and locked the door behind me. I turned to face the toilet and ……… oh, no, here we go again. Sandels was standing on the toilet lid, one hand on his hips, the other holding his staff. You know, by this time I was so punch drunk from all of this nonsense, I didn't even make a noise. All I said was:

"You'd better move my squeaky friend or I'll pee on you." I waited.

Looking as unhappy as ever, he climbed off the toilet pan and let me carry on unhindered. At least today, I hadn't wet my pants. I took this as a good omen and a sign of progress.

"I find your reference to 'squeaky' a tad insulting, Sir," came the familiar whine from somewhere near the floor behind me.

"Well, as King, I find the fact that you want an audience with me in the bathroom equally insulting, if not just a little bit creepy," I retorted. Finishing and washing my hands, I put the lid down, turned round and was now sitting down on it so I could speak to him quietly without the family hearing. How do I explain this to them, after all they were all still in the house.

"We need to reconvene, Sir, to see what you learned from your reading of the Book of Groges and as your guide, I thought it best to catch you in the main portal in your house. This is in an attempt to save you walking through your home with me to make your way back to Fairyland without anyone noticing. Believe me, Sir, we could also have done this out at your back hedge where Felixx and Paws normally exit to the OutFax but I thought, in my wisdom, that here would be best." He said this with such authority and sense (if you suspend belief once more) that again, he made me feel just that little bit inadequate. Just perfect.

"So what now," I whispered.

"Come with me," he said, "come with me."

With this, as I stood up, he waved his big stick and I shrunk once more (involuntarily I might add) to his size. Adjusting to my new height, the toilet pan looking huge for example, I followed him as he went through the little plumbing inspection hatch that was fitted to the wall behind the pan which had handily turned into a door as we shrank. Here we go again, I've got no control over anything and I'm supposed to be King.

I thought; I'm going to have to have words with him. Probably later though.

I kid you not, through the door and right behind our hallway bathroom was a miniature version of a New York subway station, complete with a train at the platform. All I could think of was why did we have an underground station where outlet pipe should be? Never mind, way to go Davie. He indicated that we should get on the waiting train, which I did. We were the only passengers.

He banged his staff on the floor, the doors closed with a pssssh noise and we hovered off. We stopped a few seconds later at what I thought must be the next station and guess what, Felixx got on. At least he'd shrunk in proportion and wasn't bigger than me – I really don't think I could have coped with that. "The Levante House Hedge portal stop," said Sandels, trying to be helpful.

I nodded at the cat who did the same back as he jumped up on the seat beside me. I honestly couldn't think of any other response to the whole episode and remembering Shona's advice from the top of the hill just kept quiet. Sandels sort of settled down for the ride and the cat just sat there, staring into the distance. I looked at my travelling companions: a miserable, thousand year old grumpy git and a cat with issues that has made it very clear that it thinks that I'm not coming up to the mark. Just magic.

Another few seconds later and we were stopping again. Sandels and Felixx got up and waited for the door to open and I followed their lead as by then I had no other viable option that I could think of. This station was a bit more modern and significantly brighter than the Levante house effort and was helpfully signposted as 'OutFax, Tomna Hill'. More doors and elevators (this time going up) and within minutes, I was back in the Fairy Lounge with the cat and Sandels either side of me. So much for a relaxing Sunday morning.

"King Dave!" shouted Hoopik as she jumped off the seats in our corner (did I really call it that?), ran over and hugged me. This mob still didn't have a clue how to behave in front of royalty at all.

"What did the Book say?" came the question as I eased myself from her iron grasp and saw the rest of the gang (Hayley was there but Shona and Jim weren't) also looking expectantly in my direction.

"Ah-ha, right, the Book," I said, sitting down with the crowd. "Nothing really," was all I could muster.

"What do you mean 'nothing'," said Struugs from the corner, "you've had a whole day to read it."

I went to answer but the cat beat me to it.

"There's the problem, eh Davie, you didn't read the book at all, did you?" I told you it was spying on me.

This led to silence, a really disappointed silence if that's possible. Once again, I'd managed to let my new subjects down.

"Look," I said, trying to regain some composure, while at the same time trying my best to give the cat the evils "I had a quick flick through and it's so badly written it might as well have been in a foreign language. Even if I'd tried, I'd still be on the first chapter right now. Why don't we work with the bit that matters – vortexes etc – and see where we get to. I mean, collectively I think we're quite a bright bunch so let's see how we get on with that."

Thank the lord, this was followed by a few nods so I carried on.

"I need more info on this battle at Luskentyre – I had a look on Google maps yesterday and saw that it's a beach on the Western Isles of Scotland – so let's start by telling me what's going on."

They all talked at once and I couldn't hear a thing. I raised my hand and, amazingly, they all shut up.

"Right. I want to know who's in charge, how long's this war over dust been going on and what happened at the time of the killing – Ded-i, you start, the rest of you, silence until I say so. Sandels, you can use the stick again if you have to."

"I think you'll find it's called a 'staff', Sir." Honestly, he just never gives up so this time I just shook my head instead of nodding.

Settling down into his seat, Ded-i started, "It's been going on in fits and starts for about 100 years now. Until recently, there's been not much progress but then a couple of years ago, Arverlang made the move into the US and gained some ground like we said. We think he was going for an overland offensive to get to California but we managed to stall it in the Midwest. Off the back of this, he came in from the Atlantic and attacked us in the Western Isles off Scotland – we can only presume that the Fs are doing this to see if a seaborne attack works – if so, they can nip round the bottom of the islands and come for the dust in the Great Glen.

"If it works off Scotland," he carried on, "he could also use the same tactics to come down the Pacific coast of the USA to get to the San Andreas mines in California. However, through all of this we'd pretty much held them up until the death last week. This change in things has unfortunately given them a real boost – they've even transferred assets from the Midwest to Scotland to try to replicate the killing. We also understand that he knows about you – the Fs are aware of The Book – but we also know that he can't read The Book as he got rid of all his Labichens in a purge about 80 years ago. This means he's stuck with trying to copy what they did a few days ago."

I noticed as an aside that the cat had slunk off and was having a quiet drink with the barman. Typical.

Struugs came in at this point, "this gives us a little bit of an advantage – he'll think that you'll know how his lot killed Hoopik's warrior (he was called Naluke, by the way) and he'll be waiting to see what defences we put in place – knowing Arverlang, he'd then try to figure out what you're trying to protect. The problem is that we now know that you don't know what the reason was, but I think we can bluff him until we work it out. Any 'defences' we put in place would just throw him off the scent anyway."

"Maybe," I reply, "but it's not much of a plan is it? Where are your best thinkers, Struugs, can we at least get to work with them to see what they make of it?"

"They're in the war room," this time it was Snouques and her eyes actually sparkled when she said 'war room'. Again, this didn't make any sense to me.

"What war room?" a kind of obvious response from me. "I mean, if there's some sort of command centre, shouldn't we be there and not in the pub?"

Blank looks all round.

"OK, where is it – is it out at this beach you're all on about or in Kansas or ..... where is it?"

"No, it's just downstairs," said the cat from the bar, "and before you get upset with your new found 'people' Davie, just remember, they're Fairies, not humans and don't think like you and me." So the cat thought it was more like me than them. Astounding.

"Right, let's go – and that's a direct command – Sandels, lead the way." The cat stayed put.

10

After a few more seconds in the lift (going back down, but further than the Fairyland Subway) and the doors opened to a wide set of stairs. With Hoopik taking the lead, she led us up and into the middle of the most impressive command and control centre I'd ever seen. Just imagine the biggest combination of all the villains' nerve centres from every James Bond film combined with NASA's space station set up and you'll get the picture. Multiple 100 inch flat screen monitors beaming in live action feeds from the beach were banked four high all around us. Also, bear in mind that when you're a foot and a half tall, a 100 inch screen is a bit like being at the cinema. They were complemented by 3D surround sound and to get us even more in the mood for a fight, there was some more low level nightclub style lighting.

Wow.

However, just to remind me that, as the cat put it, things are not quite the same in Fairyland, to complete the decor there was a single lane swimming pool with sharks in it built into the floor around the edge of the room. The odd splash of water onto the carpet also indicated that the said sharks appeared to be racing each other round the outside of the floor area in lanes.

Wow again.

Also at floor level and all around us were about 70 'operators' for want of a better word. They sat in gaming seats, had headsets on and consoles in front of them and in many ways, it looked like the biggest computer game in the world was underway. In the centre of all this, in the obligatory 'big chair' – black leather, huge armrests with joystick controls etc - was what I presumed to be the war room commander. He saw us, issued some instructions into a microphone, unplugged himself and jumped down. As you'd now expect, he was the uniform 18 inches high.

"Sir, may I present Soopar-Komandur Del Fort." I was reading 'Soopar-Komandur' from the badge on his one piece black army style jumpsuit as Sandels introduced him. He might command but like the rest, his tailor clearly wasn't very 'soopar' at language. Bizarrely, he was also wearing a black bandana round his head and had his slightly thinning silver hair cut to military shortness. I was wondering who supplied the uniforms when he said:

"King Dave, a pleasure – welcome to the War Room."

Fighting an urge to ask to sit in the big seat, I just said, "Pleasure's all mine, Mr Fort, and maybe you could explain how all of this works."

"Come with me," he said this as he turned around and led us up to what could best be described as a viewing gallery, up at the back of the room and looking down on the operators, his big seat and the sharks.

"As you can see, we have a system that allows us to be virtually present at any battle site. The feeds come from helmet and other personal cams, as well as fixed position feeds set up by the battlefield commander. Our current battlefield commander is Jonnie 'the sheep' Rustler – a man experienced in making sure all the correct assets and support are in the right place at the right time.

My team of Noogmas – that's these guys," he said as he swept his arm across the area occupied by the operators, "act in unison with the battlefield Fairies to best work out war game strategy and then execution. As I'm sure the Heads have told you, in normal times, such battles are really just recreational as no-one can really get hurt. The killing has changed all that as I'm sure you are aware. It's my job to ensure that each Noogma and battlefield fairy has the right training and then gets the right job to do – it's a team thing. "

"So it's just like a huge war/computer game in normal times?"

I interjected.

"In many ways that's correct but it's a bit more involved – people do get injured but the on field dust dispensers help fix them up. They're out of action for up to a week, though, so even in more peaceful times, it's not for the faint hearted." He stopped, took out some sort of tablet and fired off a few emails or texts or something before looking back at me.

"You see," he continued, "in Fairyland there's big money and notoriety in becoming a top battlefield fairy. There's a bit of a music scene in Fairyland but it doesn't produce 'pop stars' the way humans do and it's really tied to the battlefield action. We don't really have a great history in literature – some issues with presentation have been mentioned in the past – so the great warriors are really our heroes. In fact, as well as your own regal presence, I'm truly honoured to have one of the greatest of all with us today."

With this he stood to one side and actually bowed to Sandels. Seriously? A great warrior – well, who'd have thought. The old man did crack a smile, though, so maybe there was something in this.

Struugs this time, "You see King Dave, this is why we chose Sandels to be your guide. I can see from your face that you are finding it 'unlikely' that he could be a great Fairy warrior but believe me, he was one of the most famous there ever was. So that you get it, imagine Elvis, Pele and Justin Bieber all combined with John Wayne and you'll get the picture."

"Bloody hell, Sandels." Not very appropriate for a King but there you go. "You kept this quiet."

"I know, Sir, but anything I may have done in the past is very much in the past – it's today's problems that are much more pressing."

Fair play to the old fella, I was actually starting to respect him a bit more. I'm also getting pretty impressed at my own dream making capabilities. Or the pressure points in my head. Hey ho.

"One of the other problems we have is that the Fs are also now parading the fairy who killed Naluke as the greatest there ever was," chipped in Snouques, "and from my perspective of trying to keep everyone cheered up, this is an added complication 'cos some of our battlefield Fairies now think that this guy has got some superpowers and as such, they're quite frankly scared witless."

"Yes," added Del, "there's the beginnings of a morale issue, King Dave. I've even seen it in here with some of the Noogmas and they're not actually fighting hand to hand. If we don't head it off at the pass pretty soon, we'll start to lose fighters and that'll be fatal."

They all looked at me. Once again, this wasn't good. Not good at all.

I decided that it was time to take charge. Now, you'll understand from the story I've told you so far, this isn't really my strength. I've happily wandered along through life and when the family came along, it made things pretty complete for me. Now, though, for whatever reason — be it insanity, an illness, a dream or God help me, a genuine call to help the poor Fairies of the OutFax territory, I'd found myself installed in a position of authority. Given all of this, at that very moment I decided to take that all important step up to the mark. Incidentally, I particularly wanted to show Sandels that I could do this and more importantly, also show the cat who was really the boss. Therefore, decision made, I put my hand up. They all quietened down.

"Del, what's the battle status right now — and can I have the attention of the Noogmas for a minute?"

"It's actually pretty quiet. I'll pass overall control over to 'The Sheep' for five minutes — will that be enough?"

"More than enough – perfect. Everyone, gather round."

The Noogmas all disconnected themselves from the battle and turned to face us. Del stood off to one side with Hayley, the four Heads took up positions on the other side and Sandels lined up beside me. Deciding that if this was indeed a dream and I was after all the King, I should say something appropriate, I started.

"Everyone, I am your King. I have come to you, as you will know, because a killing occurred and the Book of Groges predicted that on such an occasion, a new King would present himself to you. I am new to Fairyland and especially the OutFax territory but I am being guided by the most famous fairy warrior of them all, Sandels." I paused as he nodded this time. "Furthermore, I have the assistance of the four Heads and have now established a direct line of command for fighting purposes through to your commander, SK Del Fort. My immediate court is completed by the Haferlincs Hayley, here today, Jim and Shona, and of course Felixx and Paws who are currently undertaking other duties. I want you to know that as of now, I will take every measure in my power to beat back the Canooque-F, protect our Dust reserves for future generations and at the same time, as the Book has said, I will find the reason for the killing and implement measures to ensure that it doesn't happen again."

At this point, even the sharks stopped swimming and stuck their heads out of the water for a listen.

"Noogmas, you will be incredibly important in this mission. I may ask you to do double shifts or undertake some extra tasks – I hope that you and your families realise that this is necessary to secure very the future of the OutFax territory and maybe the whole of Fairyland as well. However, to fully lead our people, I am establishing a mobile control centre which will include full links to you, the battlefields and will also have the necessary facilities to research the cause of the killing. Everyone, I want you to join me in fighting off this threat to our democratic and unhindered existence. If you do, I give you my word that I will stand beside each and every one of you until we defeat the forces of darkness that are being thrust upon us and restore the OutFax to the free and happy territory that we know it can be."

I stopped and nodded.

There was bedlam. The Noogmas burst into applause, the Heads did a dance, Del and Hayley shook hands and hugged and then a distant roar of approval came through the sound system. I hadn't realised that this was being broadcast through to the battlefield Fairies as well and it seemed to have gone down pretty well there as well. The noise abated to more general background chatter and the sharks went back to racing.

"To work everyone, to work." This was Sandels, squeaking loudly and bringing the whole lot under control again. Del resumed his position in the big chair, the Noogmas went back to their consoles and it was just us again, on the gallery. I realised that I was now getting hungry – after all, I was missing the Levante family roast dinner.

"Look," I said, "are there any more formal quarters that I can operate from, or is it just the war room or the Fairy Lounge, and also, is there any food?"

"Well, there is the Royal Mansion, but it hasn't been opened in hundreds of years," said Struugs, "it's down another two levels if you want to have a look."

"And I'll get the food – what would you like?" this was Snouques pulling out her wand.

"Let's go then – and get us a feast fit to ready us for the fight." You can see that I was starting to get used to being the boss. I'd also reluctantly decided that if I was ever to return to a normal life, I would just accept the situation as it was and act accordingly – you know, when in Rome etc. etc. seemed to be the best policy.

So, King Dave was now fully in charge and ready to rock and roll – take me to the Mansion.

We made our way downstairs with a few more royal nods and waves to the assembled Noogmas before heading down on the lift again. When the car pinged and the doors opened, I noticed that the cat had managed to arrive at the Mansion stop before us.

"Though you might end up here," he said, "sorry about not going to the war room, but I can't abide these sharks." He then turned and walked towards a very regal set of huge oak double doors, complete with golden handles.

Hoopik whispered in my ear, "there's more to the sharks and him than he's letting on but I'll tell you about it later." The cat glanced back suspiciously but we ignored it because Sandels had opened the doors to reveal what I'd call a super modern penthouse flat. How bizarre – it even had floor to ceiling windows with panoramic views over the town and was fitted out as if it had been built by a high-end housing developer only yesterday. It was all neutral carpets, wood floors and modern cream and light oak coloured furniture and had that 'new house' smell to boot.

"Like I said, Davie," this was the cat, who by now had jumped on to an island bar in the middle of the main reception room that we were now in, "I thought you'd eventually end up here when you finally accepted the reality of the situation so Sandels and I arranged for a bit of a refit."

"But what about the windows – why does no-one notice them from the outside?"

"Remember, they're pretty small, Dave, and are actually hidden in the trees and gravestones on the hillside," explained Ded-i, " but also, like we said yesterday the whole Human/Fairyland interaction has always been that we're right under your noses at all times but for some reason, you just can't see us."

Remembering that I'd decided to 'just accept', I said, "OK, so where's the food then," looking around for Snouques.

She did us proud, it was indeed a feast. I sat down afterwards in a super comfy sofa and looked over the townscape in front of me, seeing our office in the distance by the river. So near, yet so far was all I could think. I was starting getting my bearings and thought that if I did have to hang around a while, at least the digs were pretty good. I even thanked Felixx for his efforts and I suppose by way of some sort of reconciliation, he purred a bit and rubbed up against my leg, before jumping up and over me to go away and do cat things.

The Royal Mansion (I was thinking of it as more of an apartment though) was set out as follows. Essentially it was a series of rooms in a big long line built along the hillside, all with picture window views to the outside. The main room that we'd entered into had the bar (this lot took their drinking seriously I was to discover) and as part of this, the barman had been co-opted from upstairs to take charge of food and beverage issues. To either side of the bar were a massive dining area to the right (it would sit at least 20 and was where we'd just eaten) and a sunken sitting room/lounge that would accommodate similar numbers to the left. This was where I was now resting. Further up to the left was a more formal study type area with a couple of desks and computers and on the other side, through from the dining area, was a kitchen and attendant utility & laundry facilities.

Corridors led off from each back corner of the main room to a series of bedrooms away to the left and various offices and for want of a better word, break out rooms, to the right past the kitchens. There was also a gym with an endless pool, more bathrooms than you'll ever need and a cinema that Ded-i told me could become a multi-screen facsimile of the war room. As you'd expect in a Royal Mansion, there were also various other members of staff who were either very frightened of me or were taking the 'be seen and not heard' mantra to a whole new level. We communicated with them via the barman whom I now knew simply as P.S.

With the help of Struugs and Ded-i, we designated the first two rooms past the kitchen as 'research' and 'procurement'. They put their best staff in each respectively and set them to work on what had caused the killing and hopefully after that, how we could address it. Snouques set up in the study area with Hayley; they were effectively the PR and communications team. Sandels and I set up a head office function at the dining table as I wanted to be in the middle of things and there was plenty of room to lay stuff out on it. P.S. was a bit put out by this but brightened when we allowed him to make one of the breakout rooms a separate eating area. Snouques made it even better by waving her wand and creating a mini food mall in the said room with different stands ranging from Thai/Chinese fusion to something called 'Vanda's Veggie Va-Voom' and a fast food outlet called MexTexToo. Yup, this was a fantasy of the first order.

This left Hoopik. I'd never really gotten my head around the meaning of 'Other' in Diven terms. She went around with an ever changing band of merry warriors following her who looked to all intents and purposes like extras from a Robin Hood movie. They flitted in and out of things but I couldn't really put my finger on what they did. She was right now sitting at the bar staring out the window, so I called her over as everyone else was busy settling in.

"Well Ms Pict, how are you?"

"Ok, I suppose King Dave, given the past few days," she answered as she sat down in an armchair over to the left of me. She didn't sound OK at all.

"Tell me, how can I help make things a bit better in your

Diven – I mean, I get that it's been pretty traumatic and I've come to realise that your Fairies are a pretty self-sufficient bunch, but I can also see that even those that make up your immediate entourage aren't at their best."

"I don't know. To be honest I'm a bit lost and that's a bad state of affairs for the Head of a Diven. Everyone in the Diven looks up to me, especially in a time of crisis like now, and I'm really afraid that I'm letting them down. If we could only find out why Naluke was killed, it would let us focus on something rather than all the wallowing in pity that's going on at the moment."

"Look Hoopik, this grieving process is entirely natural. I know that killings don't ever really happen in Fairyland but believe me, where I come from, it occurs all the time for all sorts of reasons. It's OK to feel lost and over time, you'll come to an acceptance if not complete closure – please just go along with me on that, will you." She nodded but obviously wasn't really buying it.

"I also know I've only just met you but I'd guess you're an action centred lady at heart," I went on, "so I'd like you and your Diven's help with a couple of things that would take the others away from their tasks in hand – d'ya think you could you see your way to helping me with this."

I didn't know if this would work but I'd an inkling that she'd rather be up and about doing things rather than sitting at a bar staring out the window thinking miserable thoughts about failure.

"OK." Still reticent but there was a questioning look in her eyes that gave me hope. A word on her eyes; she had the deepest blue eyes that had little stars in them that danced when there was a hint of mischief, meaning that they were truly unusual in every sense of the word. I think I saw a glimpse of a tiny little sparkle just then.

"How about I get Sandels over and check this out with him," I said. I remembered that she'd had a go at him about his age when we first met but I suspected that there was a deeper relationship there. It turns out that I was right.

"Yeah, the old man gets what we do so, let's see what you've got." She actually jumped up and retrieved old Sandels from the dining table herself.

"Ok you pair, what's the story," I said as they sat together opposite me this time, suspecting that they were maybe a bit closer than I thought.

"Aah, Sir, I've known Hooligan Pict for a very long time" – no surprise there then – "and in fact, in my warrior days, I was a mainstay of the 'Other' Diven; this was before Hoopik was in charge though. You see, Sir, the best warriors in the territory have always come from the 'Others' as the members of this Diven have traditionally been those that are what I suppose you'd call 'lost' and looking for some direction. As I discovered, there's no better way of giving direction than allowing one to fight for what they believe in. Hoopik's main issue right now, and forgive me for saying this my Hooligan friend, is that the killing means that the best warriors have been beaten and it's really hurting, isn't it."

A silent nod and a single blue tear on her cheek confirmed this.

"Right you two," I said semi-conspiratorially, "l want you to be the glue that makes this whole team work. Sandels, I need your expertise as a warrior to work out how to best fight the enemy off in the meantime. Hoopik, I need you and your team to provide us with the best you have in fighting terms but also to help this 'Sheep' fella and others locate anything we need to win this battle."

There were two nods followed by a quick gathering of Hoopik's team around us. They must have been listening in from wherever they were hiding.

"First off, you get on OK with Ded-i don't you," Hoopik nodded, "so I need you to ask him what would be best for a mobile command centre and then you need to find it – I don't want his lot getting too involved as they're combining forces with Struugs to see if they can solve the killing. Can you do this?"

This was answered by a 'Yes' from Hoopik and nods from her followers.

"Sandels, I need a quick lesson in Fairyland battle tactics while Hoopik gets us on the road – can you help me with this?"

This brought a 'Yes, Sir' from him.

We all stood up. "So let's get to it and kick some ass, people". Hoopik and her team variously shook hands or hugged me and then disappeared along the corridor to the right. I later learned that they'd commandeered a room that became known as Hooligan Command. As a favour, Snouques went along to help out and waved her wand, making it into a jungle themed HQ. This was complete with tents, nets, many, many weapons, a hundred degree heat and a monkey swinging through trees. It appeared that the Other Diven was back in business.

This left Sandels and me sitting there. He never changed – same robes, skipping rope and cap, same squeaky voice that I'd now got used to and that unique piercing glare from those purple eyes - when he managed to get the hair out of his face. He said "let's go to the cinema."

I won't bore you with the details, but with Del Fort and Jonnie 'The Sheep' Rustler's help, he used the multi-screen set up to run through a hundred years of battles and skirmishes. By the end of it, I had a basic grasp of the tactics from both sides and had mastered some of the more specific moves, but in many ways I was still thinking of it as one big multi-user computer game, with the obvious difference that this one now had a real fatality in it.

Listen to me; I was starting to accept that this was now real -

and I was starting to enjoy it.

The day was drawing to a close – in Fairyland at least. I'd gone around and had a quick word with everyone and individual plans were taking shape. When I'd stuck my head into Hooligan Command I was told by the monkey that Hoopik and her crew had gone off to 'acquire some assets' so I decided not to enquire any further. The cat, Sandels and I enjoyed an end of day drink with P.S. at the bar – this time it was something called EffBea lite – a golden coloured beer-like substance that thankfully wasn't nearly as powerful as the other broo stuff.

I was, as usual, a bit worried about my family but the cat reminded me about the time difference and the fact that as far as they were concerned, I was still in the bathroom and had only been there for a microsecond. He also said that Paws would alert us to any issues that arose on the domestic front. Hayley and Snouques had devised some messages for the good people of OutFax and the Starlighter said she'd shortly be off to deliver them (I was told by Snouques that there was a bit more to this but she'd explain it another time) and the other two Heads were so tied up in analysis, I left them to it.

So I went off to bed – a palatial bedroom as you would expect, with its own big window, a massive circular bed and a separate living room and bathroom off it. Lying alone on the big bed, I realised that I missed going to sleep next to Bethany and also yearned a little bit to hear the Waltonesque 'goodnights' that sometimes echoed around our house.

The cat snuck into the room a little later and jumped up beside me. It purred a bit and although we'd had our moments, it was my only link to home so I didn't have the heart to shove it off the bed. The last thing I saw before I nodded off, though, was Hayley zooming away through the night sky, heading off to tell my fairy subjects that King Dave was now in charge and help was at hand. I slept like a log.

#

As I slept, Arverlang sat in his cave and fumed, fumed again and then fumed some more. The minc-lings were now drawing straws as to who would tell him each bit of bad news.

No Labichens caught, no idea how they'd managed a kill. Idiots, all of them, he raged at anyone who would listen.

If there was no progress soon, the advantage would be lost and he knew this only too well. Give it another day or so and if there was still nothing, he'd go and do it himself, he decided.

Arverlang didn't sleep at all.

#

11

The next day dawned with the rising sun shining straight into the royal bedroom. My day actually arrived as a large head and ears appeared in front of me saying "Davie, Davie" in the now familiar low growl. So I'm not back home then.

As I sat up, Felixx moved over and said, "we really need to get to work today, Davie – it was a good start yesterday, even though I find that difficult to believe, and you've got to keep the momentum up. The good news is that your new best friend Hoopik seems to have found the solution to the mobile command centre overnight."

I yawned (not very regally it has to be said) and only covered my mouth when the cat gave me one of its looks. "Any chance of some breakfast before we get going?"

As I said this, the doors opened and a parade of P.S.'s staff came in. A large tray of food (full cooked breakfast, piping hot) and a massive container of fresh coffee were delivered on to the bed. Sometimes it's not so bad being the King after all. The cat even got a saucer of milk, but I did hear it moaning that the temperature wasn't right so all in all, it appeared that it was situation normal in the OutFax. The staff sensibly left us to it.

As I luxuriated on the bed finishing off my fifth mug of coffee and munching through a last croissant, I again briefly considered my sanity. It was clear that I was accepting the situation more and more and to be honest, at this juncture, as long as my family was fine and didn't find out about it, I suppose I was starting to consider as normal my move into the Fairyland version of reality.

Once again the cat brought me back. "Up we get, Davie."

"Look, would you stop ordering me around. Not only am I King, whether you like it or not, but it might come as a surprise to you that I'm actually a fully functioning adult and can behave like one, so I'd appreciate it if you'd just back off a bit."

It immediately took the huff and walked out through the door that the staff had left ajar. No surprise there then.

Sandels was next. He appeared as the cat left and took up the mantle of annoying 'helper'. "We had some new clothes made up for you overnight," he said, "it's full battle gear for when you're in the MobiCom-C."

This was a cue for the staff to return to the bedroom and present my new threads by laying them out on the bed. There was a pair of the standard issue ninja boots accompanied by a more regal version of the black jumpsuit that Del Fort had been wearing; as an example, this one had some gold decorations on it. There was also the obligatory name badge for the convenience of those that I would meet but didn't know who I was; 'King Dayv'. Well, at least they spelled 'King' correctly.

"It's wonderful Sandels, please thank the team very much." Best not to sound like an upset English teacher at this time, I thought. He beamed and squeaked all at once.

They all left me to go through my morning ablutions and get dressed. I dutifully did this, took one last stretch in front of the window as the sun rose over the town and headed out through the bedroom door. I went along the corridor, across the living room and went purposefully towards the dining room table for my first full day as a war commander.

It has to be said, there was already a lot of activity in the royal residence but more importantly, there was a positive buzz. The cat and Sandels appeared beside me and both actually said as much. We sat down at the dining room table and with the pair of them just looking at me, I decided to once again try to take charge.

"Sandels, gather the heads to the table in ten will you." He went off to do so. "And Felixx, a five minute update would be great, especially about this mobile command centre."

"I'll leave that one to Hoopik when she gets here but I think you'll like it," he said, "On other matters, there's been a bit of a lull at Luskentyre which worries both Del and me, and it's as if there's a bit of regrouping going on in the Canooque-F side of things. Also, when Hayley was out and about last night she picked up some rumours that Arverlang is on the move. If this is the case, it's pretty serious as he doesn't normally move far from his cave."

"Why's that – surely as leader he's out and about a lot."

"No way – he's totally paranoid and has got much worse recently. As you'll have gathered, we get quite a bit of intel from his side – that's because as you can probably imagine from what we've told you, he's not the most popular of leaders and lots of his people hate him. But remember, he runs a totalitarian state predicated on fear hence he's stayed in power so long. In fact, if it hadn't been for the killing giving his troops a boost, we thought that a coup was near. If that had happened, the irony is that you probably wouldn't be here and we'd be heading to another few centuries of peace with the battles going back to the old way – more entertainment really."

"A bit like WWE then." I commented on the side.

"What's that," said the cat, "do we need to take note of this WWE and disseminate it to the troops."

"Eh, ...no, best just leave it as it is just now."

At this moment, Sandels appeared with the four heads, all of whom seemed pretty upbeat, apart from Struugs. He'd also found Del Fort and as they arrived, a screen came down from the ceiling, as did a control panel from the table, allowing us a video link to Jonnie Rustler.

"Please be seated in your allocated positions and be ready to participate in King Dave's inaugural war commander meeting," announced Sandels from the other end of the table from me. "King Dave."

At this point glass screens came out of the floor, effectively cutting out the rest of the room. Sandels hit a button on the control panel and the screens went opaque. "You can't be too careful" was all he said.

Time to be Regal again.

"Everyone, thank you for coming. As you're all aware, a couple of days ago, I had no idea about any of this but I'd like to thank you all for your help in getting me up to speed and the efficiency and friendliness you've all shown while doing this. In summary, we've got to try to find out how Hoopik's fighter was killed, put a solution in place to stop it happening again and at the same time try to sort out this Arverlang guy once and for all. I'll now take suggestions of what to do next – Struugs, you first."

"We're struggling King Dave," he started, "we've looked at all the scenarios – as you will understand, the nature of the battles is such that the killing was caught on multiple cameras. We've analysed the moment from lots of angles and it's really not clear what Naluke did differently – in fact, when you look at others around him, they were all doing the same and some of them were hit by the same sort of arrow that appears to have killed him. In truth, I need more time and I really need Jonnie and Del to come into my team to work with all of us to try to figure it out"

This was followed by slow nods from Del, Jonnie and Ded-i.

"Ok. Ded-i, anything you'd like to add?"

"I've been at it with Struugs all night and agree with him – there's nothing obvious. Through a labichen, we've again looked at the passage from the Book of Groges as well and it's not helping either. My team is also of the opinion that if we get Jonnie, Del and maybe a couple of their guys in as well we could, for want of a better word, brainstorm it again."

The cat was staring right at me.

"Felixx?"

"Seems reasonable but for one thing," he growled, in between rubbing his ears with his paw, "who the hell is going to look after the battle if the experts are all here. It's fine right now with a lull in the fighting but when the Canooque-F realise that The Sheep and Del aren't in command on the ground, they'll really go at it and to be honest, I don't think we have anyone that can step up given how serious the situation is."

"I'm with Felixx, Sir," added Sandels, "it's too much of a risk taking these guys out of the fight."

"Aww, come on guys, surely there are others that can do this stuff," was my not so royal response.

"There may be a way." This was from Hoopik who had so far sat quietly throughout. "The guys mentioned this to Snouques and me through the night when we got back in. As we said yesterday, one of the best warriors of all time is sitting right here."

Sandels sat up at that point with a look of fear in his eyes as clearly this didn't sit well with him at all.

"Don't worry old man, we're not suggesting you get all kitted up again – Snouques and I think you could take over from Del for a couple of days; after all, you ran through every battle scenario with King Dave last night and you really do know what you're talking about."

"With permission, Sir," squeaked Sandels (I nodded), "It's not the fighting or strategy, it's the technology that makes it a non-starter – I've no idea how it all comes together."

"But we do," came in Snouques with a grin, "and we've got a plan."

She looked at me so I nodded again, just as the cat was shaking its head once more – miserable git....

"So, what's this great plan?" I asked - with a few other expectant faces also looking at Hoopik.

"OK," she said, getting out of her seat and heading to the top of the table. Continuing to stand, she started.

"We've acquired a mobile command centre – the Mobicom-C – and we'll get it out to the beach as soon as possible. I'll take charge out there with a couple of the better fighters working with me – The Sheep has already told me who'd be best on the deputising front. I also think it's important that I do this as it was one of mine that was killed, leading from the front and all that. Sandels will sit in Del's big seat and advise but Snouques will work with him to ensure that he can interface with the technology as it stands today. This leaves one thing – King Dave. As you know, Dave, the entire OutFax territory thinks that you're here to work this through 'cos you've read the Book of Groges and can sort the whole thing out. Now, we know that you can't ...

(this brought a really inappropriate withering look from the cat that quite frankly, royally hacked me off)

"....but it might be an idea to come with us to the beach to lead the troops."

My face must have said it all. I mean, bows and arrows and whatever else they use to fight might not do much to the good fairies of the OutFax but I'm not so sure how a lawyer's clerk would fare in these circumstances.

"I know, KD," she said, obviously seeing my reaction, "but it would really help with morale and we'll keep you well back. Anyway, there's an unwritten rule that you wouldn't be targeted anyway, so it should all be fine."

Now, at this point I was really thinking that things were getting out of hand. First this new 'KD' handle and then more time away from my Sunday lunch with a trip to the Western Isles of Scotland. It was Sandels that sorted it out though.

"King Dave," he squeaked, "this is your chance to really grasp the metal. I saw what you did on the hill when you decided to really become king and it was clear that all those in attendance really liked what they heard. If you do this, you could become the most famous King of all".

Now, call me a sucker for a sale, he managed to get me interested. Never mind the 'metal' comment, which in my pedantic way of doing things I'd normally correct, but he'd got to me good and proper. Also, even though I felt a bit like Alice as she was drawn further and further behind the mirror, I was also coming even more round to the view of 'what the hell, I appear to be here anyway' and once again thought, let's go with the flow.

"OK folks, let's do it," was the royal command.

We spent the rest of the time running through some more admin tasks but the decision was made. Sandels would be the man in charge, Snouques would assist and Hoopik would run the show out at Luskentyre. The rest would get to work trying to understand what had happened. The cat then nodded in some sort of approval, there was hand shaking all round, the walls disappeared and we were back in the dining room as was.

As things wrapped up and everyone went off to start the planning, I excused myself for a moment to go to the toilet where, as I sat on the only throne I think I had, I closed my eyes to mentally make a to do list.

The next thing I heard was my wife shouting 'lunch everyone'.

12

At this point, you'll understand that I was again close to tears. I just sat rigidly on the pan back in our house, nowhere near any Fairies and at the same time trying to work out what was happening. To all intents and purposes, all that had come to pass was that I'd gone from standing up to sitting down in our hallway bathroom with a minor blank spot in between. I could only be truly losing it.

As I sat, I tried to rationalise things. It couldn't be real because to my clearly deluded mind, if I actually was King, surely by now I could decide when and where I would go and more especially, I could decide when to go home. This wasn't the case, so it must be some sort of illness. I decided to look it up on the web that afternoon and resolved to get through lunch with the family. I'd try it on with the cat, though, just in case.

I made my way through to the kitchen where the family all sat waiting for me. "Last as always, Dad." This came from TJ as she tucked into today's roast dish.

"I'm just feeling a bit off," was all I could muster as I quietly sat and ate my food.

The cat was snoozing in the corner of the kitchen and Paws was in her bed, lying upside down, legs in the air and snoring as well. This was all pretty normal. After lunch, the kids headed off out and I said that I'd do the dishes. You'll have worked out that I really just wanted some time alone with the animals.

As Bethany headed out to give her folks her normal Sunday afternoon visit to see how they were, I shut the door so at least they couldn't run out on me. I gathered up the dishes, put them in the dishwasher and went to the cat. It didn't move an inch. I spoke to it quietly. Nothing. I then poked it in the gut, which made it open its eyes. Again, no movement at all. I went right down to its face and stared. Again, nothing; no recognition, no quick wink or anything and not even a sarcastic comment.

"Felix," I said in a loud whisper. Nothing.

"Felix – with two X's". Nothing.

Then the miserable little git just yawned and went back to sleep.

Giving up, I tidied up what was left and headed through to the den with my laptop. I really had to do some research to see what was causing what I was experiencing. I tried searching for hallucinations (a lot about illegal drugs came to the fore) and brain tumours (not nice or especially helpful) and out of body experiences (more about illegal drugs). Then I noticed that the last link listed on page one of Google said davidlevante.com . This came as a bit of a surprise to me as I'd looked before and never found another David Levante, never mind one with his own website. Also, I hadn't searched for my name this time.

As you'd expect, I clicked on the link and the web page said something along the lines of:

Seeing little people?, animals that talk?, Click here.

By the way, it's all changed now but at that time, all I did was click on the link. I was then faced with Felixx looking straight at me from a YouTube style video. On playing it he said, not very politely, to never poke him again and would I just please accept what was happening. He said there was a good reason for the times they couldn't speak to me and for the sudden trips to and from Fairyland but I'd understand in the future, but right now I should just shut up and put up.

Not overly happy, I went straight back to the kitchen to have it out with him and guess what, he'd gone. Paws did witter something quietly in Spanish which gave me some solace but at the same time almost brought back the tears.

My new state of confusion was interrupted by a shout from outside. Bethany was back and was calling me, saying something about Jim and a new campervan. With no real thought I wandered out to the front of the house and indeed, there was Jim from the office with a newish but not brand new campervan vehicle, although he called it an R.V.

"Just thought I'd pop by to show you my new toy" he said, beaming like a kid at Christmas "I was chatting over future holiday plans with my wife and we worked out that this was just the ticket as it allows us to travel wherever we want"

There was then the obligatory tour of the van. When we looked into it in more detail it became apparent that it was really quite big with a full shower and bathroom and four berths, including an end bedroom all by itself.

"Are these things not really expensive," I asked as we stepped back out to our driveway, and at the same time hoping I wasn't insulting him.

"Yes they are, but I had an inheritance from an old aunt that paid for most of it," he explained, "and we thought it was a really good use of the cash."

"Fair enough," was all I could think to say.

As this was going on, the cat had wandered out from somewhere and was heading into the new RV. I went to shoo him away but he managed to sneak past me and jump into Jim's new vehicle.

Bethany announced that she'd head off back into the house make some coffee for all and Jim went back into the RV to lock it up, or so I thought. As I stood outside the van waiting for him, I heard a familiar low growl from inside.

"Davie, in here now. And make it snappy, we haven't got long."

Here we go again. Was there no rest from this at all?

I somewhat reluctantly went back up the two steps into the side door of the RV. There was the cat on the table, tapping its paw in annoyance with Jim just sitting back on the seat beside him smiling.

"What now," I exhaled, "and you could have spoken to me in the kitchen when I was doing the dishes."

"I couldn't you moron, Milo had come back in and was through the door but you didn't realise, did you. Imagine if I'd taken you on, we'd both be in the doodoo."

Once again, the cat had managed to make me feel about three inches tall.

"Anyway, enough of that - we've got little enough time to get things sorted. Hoopik, out you come."

And so she did, from the built in wardrobe next to the seating area.

"Hi King Dave, how do you like the Mobicom-C, it's pretty cool isn't it," she said grinning her head off.

"Ok, I'm lost" was all I could muster "How does this get to where the battle is and why is it full size, would it not be better being in proportion as you might say?"

"Oh Davie, Davie," came back the cat, "you'll never learn – just accept that it'll be there. D'you know, all we wanted was to show you your battlefield digs and give you some time with your family before we all head to Luskentyre. Now, I'll warn you, enjoy this evening as in Fairyland time, it may be a while before you're back here. Just before you get ready to go to work in the morning, I'll head into the hall bathroom with you and we'll all get going from the there. In the meantime, Jim'll head off with Hoopik now and they'll make the necessary adjustments to the RV for what we want. Right, let's go and get the coffee that Beth's making."

So we're Beth and Davie to the cat then. Cheers, Felix.

As I was leaving the RV, Hoopik jumped up off the seat to give me one of her special hugs and at the same time whispered a quick "Thank you KD, really, Thank you" in my ear, before disappearing back into the wardrobe. I have to say this cheered me up a bit.

The cat then led the way back into the house and as Jim and I made it to the kitchen where mugs of coffee awaited all on the table, it gave a big meow for Bethany's benefit. She immediately scolded me for not feeding it and true to form it followed her away to get some food. Not before winking at me, though. I just drank some coffee.

Bethany came back and we then had a pretty normal adult chat. This was mostly about holidays and where Jim and his wife would be going during the measly breaks that our bosses reluctantly allowed us to take each year. Jim then headed off home with the RV and the rest of the day just turned into a Sunday evening like every other with some more nice food, some TV and then bed. Surprisingly, I slept like the dead.

When I woke I felt genuinely refreshed but more worryingly was also coming to accept the whole Fairyland thing as normal. Bethany was already up and about getting the kids ready for school so I had a quick check around the bedroom for the cat and Fairies but none were there. I also had a rummage in the bedside cabinet and came up with the Book as this time I thought I'd take it with me if I was, as the cat said, going to be away a while. As I went downstairs for breakfast, in the hallway I slipped it into my jacket pocket for later.

After breakfast with the family, I tried not to make tearful goodbyes as I left the table to go to the bathroom but I suspect to this day that the rest of the family was wondering what was wrong with me that morning. As promised, the cat appeared from nowhere and nipped into the closet just before me. I locked the door and was immediately 18 inches tall. The cat had shrunk as well. Here we go again.

13.

We said nothing as we boarded the waiting underground train. It didn't stop at the hedge this time but did stop at another station where Jim and Hoopik got in to join us. Their arrival put me in a better mood and we actually had some 'going to work' style gossip and chat as we made it over to Tomna hill. Within no time at all, I was back in the war room with Sandels squeaking a hello and the sharks bobbing a welcome from the water. As usual, the cat had disappeared.

"Welcome to the beginning of the rest of your life," said Hoopik who had taken up residence in the big chair.

"Firstly," I said, "Get off that now." If I was to be King of the battles, then I really wanted to sit on it and see what it was like from Del's perspective.

She did and I jumped on.

Wow.

I discovered then that when you were on the seat, all the screens and noise and battle tactics boards merged into a 3D version of the battlefield. It was just as if I was really there. I now understood how the whole thing combined the warriors on the ground with the Noogmas and whoever was in command back here. Hoopik appeared beside me in this virtual world.

"Pretty cool, eh," she said, "when we get out there, there'll be an equivalent seat in the MobiCom-C so that you and Sandels can see the same thing. The only change we've made is the extra seats we've added for Snouques here and me out at Luskentyre – normally it would be one each for Del and The Sheep. I saw in your eyes that you wanted to get on the seat when you came in the first time but we thought it might all have been a bit much to take in so we ushered you away."

'Holy mother' was all I could think. Here was a virtual world inside Fairyland which to me was another world anyway.

Madness. Before I jumped off the seat, though, I saw the sharks, only in this 'reality' they were in the water patrolling the real sea off the beach. One of them did the customary nod as they carried on with their duties. Even though it was just after breakfast, I began to think that I needed a drink.

Back from the fun of the chair, we gathered everyone together in the War Room. Present were Sandels, Del Fort, Jonnie Rustler, Felixx, Hoopik, Ded-i, Struugs and Snouques. Jim was elsewhere sorting out the RV and Hayley was doing a Galactic sortie for more information. Shona was at work, I presume. I handed over to the Pict.

"OK everyone," she said, "the latest intel is that Arverlang has moved from his cave to their equivalent of the War Room – rather unusually it's based under a kid's play park in Mill Street in Perth, Ontario so he's come pretty far south to get involved. Hayley has also picked up significant warrior movements coming across the Atlantic so it looks like the Canooque-F are indeed looking to up the ante at Luskentyre. The sharks are patrolling the seas and are speaking to deep sea whales and others so should know when they arrive – it's expected that they'll set up camp with their existing forces that are there already on the nearby island of Taransay, while we'll be on the mainland as always. It's too early to say how many we're dealing with but we're also bringing in reserves, although we are keeping a regular force in both Kansas and California."

"Why don't they just sail up the Caledonian Canal and into the Great Glen if it's the dust they are after," I asked.

"That's not how it works, Davie – we've already explained that they have to try it out at Luskentyre first," said Felixx with the sort of finality that made me think I'd be better saying nothing.

I nodded.

"Anyway," continued Hoopik, "we think things should be ready to go the day after tomorrow so we'll head off to the RV this afternoon. For safety we'll be travelling separately – King Dave, Snouques will take you out and I'll meet you there after Jim has picked you up. We'll rendezvous at a parking area that overlooks the beach at Luskentyre – it's just to the west of Seilebost. After that we'll work out where to set up nearer the beach for the actual battles – we'll probably end up close to the old graveyard at Luskentyre itself as there's an enclosed bit that we might be able to use and I think you were on a hill near to there, Jonnie?"

A confirmation nod came from The Sheep.

"Sandels, Del and Jonnie have worked through some new moves for the battles – we hope that these will work against the Fs. Also, they specifically exclude the tactics that were used by Naluke's platoon when he was killed so even though we don't know what killed him, we'll try to ensure that we don't undertake any movements that could be fatal."

At this point Del joined in, "we've got some new formations and some new music as well," he said "none of these have been used or seen before so should come as a bit of a surprise to the Fs."

Music? – best say nothing David, the cat's looking funny again.

I nodded.

Sandels took it upon himself to bring matters to a conclusion. There was real reverence when he spoke with even the Noogmas, who until this point had been minding their own business, also turned to us up in the viewing gallery to listen.

"I'm delighted, Sir," he began and I nodded again, "that not only have you allowed the Diven heads to take the initiative but you've also allowed an old warrior like me another chance to become involved – I have to say, I thought that 21st Century technology had put paid to any more battle involvement from me. Having worked through the night – in fact, it was a few days here as Hayley played with time to give all of us a bit of time to reflect as well as letting you get a good night's sleep, I think that we're as ready as we'll ever be to take on the Canooque-F".

He continued, "In my long time in Fairyland I've never seen anything so predatory and we really need to stop Arverlang in his tracks. Not only will he kill again if he gets the chance, he'll exhaust the entire Fairyland supply of dust in doing so. This would be a disaster for all. I've also watched you grow in stature, King Dave, and I know that you even being here has helped boost morale throughout the OutFax Territory. Your speeches from both Tomna Hill and here in the War Room have broken the record for download numbers onto Fairytaks and everyone I see is speaking about you. I wish you and Hooligan Pict the very best out at Luskentyre and we'll be doing our utmost to support you back here. All hail the King."

There was a big roar of approval in the room and once more, the same came from the beach. I realised then that a lot of this was ceremony and build up and even though he'd squeaked his way through it, it was clear that Sandels commanded huge respect in the OutFax. It was left to me to reply; this was clear from all the expectant faces that surrounded me.

"Thank you Sandels, you are a true hero of the OutFax," a big cheer followed from what appeared to be all over the territory. So it was going to be like that then.

"I realise that it has been a truly difficult time for all and that this is the reason that I've come to you. I want to thank my court as gathered here for the outstanding work that has been done in such a short time to allow us to take on the enemy that is the Canooque-F. Normally I wouldn't use words that strong but in this case, to take such obvious pleasure in the death of our brave warrior Naluke makes them an enemy of not just me, but an enemy of all the reasonable citizens of the OutFax and the rest of Fairyland."

Big cheer again.

"I want to assure you, my people, that I will do what I can to see off this threat. I intend making sure that Arverlang will never again be able to act in this way and that our dust reserves will be safe for all time. I want to make one special mention. Hooligan Pict and her Diven have borne the brunt of this. I want to pay homage to the dignity with which all of her people have taken on board this terrible blow. She has also volunteered to lead the charge against Arverlang's army at Luskentyre - as King I truly appreciate this and as such will make my own way to the beach to personally oversee and lead our armies from all four Divens. Mr Arverlang, if you're listening, bring it on my friend, bring it on, you can't hide in a cave forever."

There was bedlam. This included cheering, dancing, some singing, the sharks doing synchronised swimming and a distant cheer that as far as I could make out, seemed to come from across the whole of Fairyland. Meanwhile I was shaking like a leaf and was now panicking that in my over enthusiasm for the moment, I'd overstepped the mark, especially with the explicit threat to Arverlang. Sandels brought me back as we headed towards the Royal Mansion once more.

"Well done, Sir," he squeaked, "Just the job." He even patted me on the back.

"Trying to go for a new download record, eh Davie," was all the cat could muster as it passed us by, going only knows where. Ah well.

14.

Hoopik was waiting at the big doors with her band of close followers. She asked that I come to their jungle HQ for a sort of debrief. I agreed and said to Sandels that I'd meet everyone else for lunch on the food mall but this was more because I actually wanted to try out some of Vanda's veggie food with a bit of MexTexToo.

I entered the jungle room behind Hoopik with the rest following. The monkey, which had now been joined in the trees by a snake, bowed as I came into the room. I just shook my head as we sat down around a campfire that was burning nicely in a clearing in the jungle.

"How's everyone holding up," I asked

"Actually, not too bad," said Hoopik, "but we just wanted to get you by yourself before we go into battle."

This worried me.

"Firstly, we'd like to give you a real personal and heartfelt thank you," she went on, "I'm bringing in the rest of the 'others' right now though."

With that a virtual screen appeared in the trees. It's difficult to describe but it was like a hole in the jungle appeared with a big window to the world. Within this window, there were thousands and thousands of people; Fairies, that is. It was only then that I realised the size of the OutFax nation, before that it hadn't really occurred to me and I hadn't been in contact with that many of 'my people'.

As a result, the old David doubts immediately started to appear, something that Hoopik must have seen. She silently and quickly held my hand in a manner that no-one else would see. She gave it a quick squeeze and nodded to one of her lieutenants.

They pressed a few buttons on what appeared to be a remote control and one of the many faces in the crowd came to the fore.

It was a lovely looking lady who seemed to me to be quite sad. I'd no idea what was going on so just squeezed Hoopik's hand back.

The lady on the screens said, "King Dave, I'm honoured to be able to address you on behalf of the Other Diven. I'm Naluke's mother and I would just like to say thank you to you personally for giving us all hope. Your intervention has been really welcomed and I now know that my son didn't die in vain. If his death means that you can now stop this stupid war once and for all, it is a fitting memorial to my brave boy. Bless you King Dave and all that take the fight to the Fs."

Once again I was lost as to what to say. However, after another squeeze, I answered.

"I'm too am honoured to be able to lead the reply to this awful event. I'll make sure that Naluke's death will be remembered as the catalyst for a time of peace. Thank you for your kind words and I truly respect you courage at this difficult time."

Hoopik concluded, "Thank you King Dave. As you know, we're called the 'others' for a reason as we don't always fit. We all suspect that you too feel a little bit this way so we secretly think that this, along with the fact that it was Naluke's death that brought you here, means that you're really our King and we're lending you to the rest of the OutFax as well."

She squeezed again and I smiled happily this time. She finished with another "All hail the King."

This time it was just clapping. This was more fitting I thought and yes, I suppose I too was an 'other' in this strange world and through this, I guess it made me slightly more at peace with myself. Then the monkey jumped down and ruffled my hair, everyone laughed and the screen disappeared. The animals of Fairyland had a lot to learn.

I spent the rest of the morning meeting more of Hoopik's people, going through some battle tactics and keeping out of the way of the snake which appeared to have Felixx's eyes. In my general state of 'lawyer's clerk' paranoia, I was beginning to think he was everywhere.

We lunched with everyone else in the food mall. I had some of Vanda's food along with some MexTexToo and it was, as you'd expect, superb. After lunch, Snouques took me in hand because Hoopik had headed off saying something about gathering the troops and a garbage truck (or 'bin lorry' explained Ded-i somewhat unhelpfully), again leaving me well and truly in the dark. I also had a meeting with Struugs, Ded-i, Del and Jonnie who outlined their plans over the next week.

Essentially, they had arranged for some Labichens to come in and go through the Book of Groges (I'd made a copy for them) to further analyse what it might mean. They'd also got some Fairyland IT guys in to try to match up the recordings of the death battle with the Book and see where this got them. Struugs said they'd keep me in the loop and I promised to read to the book as well if I got a chance. I really wasn't looking forward to it at all and more worryingly, the four day transformation from clerk to King meant that I was now happier going into battle than reading a book. This was a change indeed.

"We'll give it our best King Dave," said Struugs as I went to leave with Snouques, "and Ded-i's determined to come up with a practical solution for you to implement. You may also have noticed that he kinda likes Hoopik which is giving him extra impetus but I don't think the Pict has twigged that she's got an admirer yet..." He smiled in a conspiratorial fashion and left me to it. Ever the gossips, these Fairies, I was finding out.

"You're all mine now King Dave," whispered Snouques in my ear as she led me down the corridor to the main bar in the centre of the residence, and she was also rubbing my back as we went. Not knowing what she meant, we settled in at the counter as she organised some of her people to gather what we'd need out at the beach. P.S. poured me an EffBea lite and Snouques took some sort of cocktail that had little fairy wings in it instead of the usual umbrella. She batted her eyelids at me and fluttered her wings as she took a sip of her drink.

At this point, I'd like to explain that I've never been really great with women. When I was growing up, all my mates always seemed to have the 'chatting up' gift, leaving me to sort of hang around and hope that some equally shy woman might want to speak to me. As you'll imagine, this wasn't the best plan as, when you think about it, they too were probably terrified of speaking out. I realise that it's different nowadays with social media breaking down lots of barriers but back in the day, King Dave was just Davie No Mates at the bar.

I met a few girls at parties, mainly because both they and I had drunk too much but I actually met Bethany when we were students and she was working as a barmaid for some extra cash. When you spend your nights sitting at the bar watching everyone else having fun, the only people left to speak to were the bar staff and even then, it was her that started it. We actually got together through a shared love of country rock music which again, twenty odd years ago, was pretty unusual and lovers of the genre were few and far between. The rest, as they say, is history, but if I'm honest, she's the one who wears the trousers in our house and it was even her doing that we live in such a nice area and with such a great home. You'll get the picture; lawyer's clerk, not lawyer etc.

Back in Fairyland, I was therefore deeply uncomfortable. Even me, with my non-working 'love' antenna, could see that Snouques was one of these women who loved to chat up (and tease) men for fun. I knew a couple of my pals back home who could take her on at her own game, but I was genuinely lost. The dilemma I had was that I was supposed to be King and be at ease in all situations. I tried to think what to do without embarrassing both of us which was not a good position to be in at all. Here we go....

"Look Snouques, I'm a married man you know."

Silence. P.S. walked away.

Snouques continued to bat her eyes, flutter her wings and sip her drink. I downed my EffBea lite in one. Snouques one, King Dave nil. Same old story.

I then thought that honesty might be the best policy. "Look Snouques, I've been married forever and have no idea how to socialise with ladies who behave like you do. I'm a bit lost you know."

She stopped sipping and said, very coyly I might add, "Ladies who behave like me?" An eyebrow was raised as well.

This was going from bad to worse. P.S. came by at that point and refilled my drink.

"Right you two, quit it." It seemed that Felixx had now joined us.

P.S. gave him an EffBea Lite and replaced my second one which I'd also downed in one.

"Snouques," continued Felixx, "Davie here is hopeless with women. God only knows how he got together with Bethany but I assume that she did all the work. However, he's also a straight up guy so we don't need any of your nonsense, OK."

"I don't know what you mean," she said by way of reply.

"Yes, you do," said the cat, which by now was right in her face, "all this lovey-dovey chatting up crap that you do to every new man that appears in the place. Quit it or I'll be having a word with Yandermoo."

This, remarkably, got a reaction. "OK," she said in an almost normal voice, "but I really like King Dave and I thought that he might be the one."

"Oh, you are an idiot aren't you? He's not a Fairy, he's your new King and he's married to someone else. I mean, I think he is indeed a 'special one' in many ways but he's definitely not the one for you. Why's it always the same Snouques?"

"I don't know, I always try my best and I never meet anyone."

"You always try too hard, more like it," said the cat, not willing to give up while he was ahead. "Now, behave normally - act like the pair of you are brother and sister or something. You too Davie, stop pussy footing around and act like the King you're supposed to be – think of her like a little sister who can help."

"Ok, enough," I intervened, "Felixx, thank you – I think. Now if you'll leave Snouques and me alone, I think we can take it from here."

He sniffed and walked off.

"Well, Miss Diven of Hope, can we 'hope' for a better working relationship in future. All your fussing makes me a bit nervous so if we can just talk normally, I'd be very grateful."

"Ok," she said, looking a bit depressed.

"Right," I said, choosing to ignore any moods that might be starting, "how do I get to the beach and how long does it take?"

"That I can answer," she replied a bit more brightly, and with her team arriving back carrying some boxes she went on, "but why don't we just get going. I always like going to a beach," she finished with, after rummaging through a box and putting on a pair of sunglasses. I suppose I'll never fully understand women, fairy ones or otherwise.

At this point, Felixx returned and said, "OK Davie, time to go – we've decided that it's best for Snouques to just stay here and help get Sandels ready so it's up to me to get you out to the beach. First, though, if you go to your bedroom you'll find that all your packing has been done for you – just have a quick check on it and then we'll be off. I'll be back here at the bar."

As a result of this, Snouques didn't look too happy at her beach trip being cancelled but after throwing her sunglasses back where they came from, she obviously decided that it wasn't worth an argument with the cat.

So I too did as I was told and headed off to the royal apartments. There I found a small case with some clothes in it and a backpack with some more 'stuff'. I guess this is the best you could call it as I didn't know what some of it was. In the spirit of things, though, I just went to pick it up and move off when a couple of Hoopik's team appeared and took them for me. Just how it should be for the King, I thought. We walked back through to the main living area.

"Couldn't be bothered even carrying couple of bags, eh Davie," said you know who from the bar, bringing me back to reality as usual.

We all headed off to the lift outside the big doors. Felixx explained that we'd be taking a train to the beach – a new tunnel had been dug to the Western Isles last year when it became clear that Arverlang wasn't to be moved. When we arrived up at the platform, we all hopped on the waiting train looking just a like a group of folk (but with a cat that speaks) heading off on holiday. I did wonder about asking for some 'Royal Protection', I mean presidents and kings normally have some sort of security guards with them at all times, but given the mood on the train, I thought it best to just keep quiet.

15

The journey was remarkably quick considering the distances involved. In no time at all, the train was pulling up at a half built station called 'Ak-ram'. It transpired that this was right underneath a General Store in Tarbert on the Isle of Harris which meant we were now on the islands that had Luskentyre beach on them. In Western Isles terms, Tarbert was the closest 'big town' to the action. Felixx explained, "It was Ded-i that chose the spot - he really likes the shop because it has so many things in it that he can use to solve problems and fix things."

We had a quick look in on the way past and indeed, the shop was a true representation of a general store in a small town. It had what appeared to be one of everything, including lots of things that you didn't realise you needed until you saw them in the shop. The other strange thing was that no-one noticed us. I mean, OK, we were only a foot and half tall but here we were, out in the human world with folks all around and nobody was seeing us at all.

"What's with this," I asked Felixx, "why can't they see us?"

"It's really strange isn't it," he concurred, "but that's just the way it is – no-one knows why we're invisible to most folk. Just live with it, Davie 'cos that's what we do. Anyway, here's Jim."

Now, this was when things became really confusing. Jim arrived in the Mobicom-C as planned, but it was full size, as was he. As he pulled up outside the shop, we all jumped into the RV via a little door that was meant to be for putting gas bottles into the vehicle to power the cooker and the heating.

Inside things were even more crazy. It was a bit like the tardis with the whole interior space being much larger than was possible from the outside and at the same time it was nothing like what I'd seen back at my house. Inside the RV, we had a smaller version of the war room with other rooms off it (it transpired these were basically the rooms of a house) and a stair that led to the vehicle cab where Jim was. I went up to see him.

"OK," I said with a suitably confused look on my face, "how does this work – how does the whole time issue work now and how come you're full sized and I'm not?"

"Don't worry, David," he came back with. "This is where it's all really puzzling to an outsider. In essence, when the RV is seen by a human and it's on Fairyland business, normally they only get a fleeting glance of it so while it really is in their world, they hardly see it. Have you ever been sure you've seen something - then it transpires that it isn't there when you look again?" I nodded, "Then here's the answer. For reasons beyond even me, it was easier to take it here in human time and then pick you up – just take it as read or you'll go insane trying to figure it out. Sometimes, though, the RV will just appear to humans as normal which is why I'm full sized when I'm up here driving. Like I say, best to not question it all too much."

"Just like I don't," said another voice from above the cockpit (there was apparently a bed up there).

I looked up and saw Jim's wife peeking over the side. Not her as well?

"Yes David, I'm a Haferlinc too so I'm along for the ride. You'll remember I'm a chef as well so I think you'll find that I'm the cook for the duration."

I nodded – it was all I could do. Here I was, 18 inches tall, speaking to giant versions of my work colleague and his wife. I was just starting to wonder if the cause of all of this was maybe the fact that last week I'd taken some flu medication and whisky together a few days before we'd gone on the fateful walk. I was brought right back to Fairyland, however, when Felixx called me back to the Mobicom-C war room.

"Davie, once again, just go with the flow, will you. I know it's difficult, me being a talking cat and all the rest of it, but please, for the sake of the OutFax, just get back to being the King – to be fair, you were getting the hang of it just before we left."

Well, well, praise from the cat – the dream was heading back on track.

"So...what's next?" was all I could muster. Great.

"Hi David." This came from behind me. It was Hayley. "I get that you're finding it all a bit strange" she went on, "but don't worry. Also, in terms of how the space/time continuum is affected by the flitting in and out of the human world, it's not a concern as I'll fix it. In other words, when you finally make it back home, it'll only seem that you've been in the bathroom for a few minutes max. More importantly, I've got some good news."

So everyone present - this being Felixx, the two minders who travelled with us (I had by now decided that they actually were my royal protection), Jim and his wife (although they looked like they were at the end of a huge long tunnel) and me - all looked at her expectantly.

"I've been out and about as usual and picked up quite a bit. I've had it confirmed that the Canooque-F still can't read anything written or my star signals. Also, the other three Fairyland nations are all keenly awaiting the results of this battle as they think that if Arverlang wins, they'll be next. As a result, they're taking steps to give tacit approval to help us if things get difficult. We can also communicate with them via the stars – isn't that cool?"

She sat down, all silvery with her fancy tennis shoes up on a seat, and beamed with a real sense of satisfaction. The rest of them were clearly delighted as well and it was very obvious that they were waiting for me to join in the praise. The only problem was that it just seemed pretty straightforward to me – why wouldn't they all want to help?

"Uh...OK, that's great," I said, nodding as usual.

"Aww, come on Davie, give the girl her due - this is spectacular."

"Sorry, but how exactly – and please be assured that I'm not trying to insult you," I said, looking at a clearly upset Hayley.

"The nations never get together Davie," explained Felixx, "this is ground breaking. You see, Fairieland has never been really united. Every territory just gets on with their own lives and from time to time battles the others in the aforementioned fashion. Like we said, Fairieland is a pretty peace loving place, exists mainly to create mischief for humans and also mine Fairy Dust, which in turn helps make both the Fairyland and Human worlds better places. Up to now, nothing has happened like this whole Arverlang thing so there's never been a need to work together. If Hayley is reading this right, then notwithstanding if we find out how Naluke was killed, we now know that we've got the backing of the other three in the war against the Canooque-F. Like I said, truly ground-breaking."

"Wow – OK then. Truly, well done Hayley. However, if this is the case, I'm thinking it best that we don't tell a soul.

As you would expect, there was a general sense of disappointment. David the killjoy strikes again.

I went on. "Look, if we tell all our people, then Arverlang will find out in minutes. Also, the heat might seem to be off us and I don't want that to happen as everyone might just think that we'll just gang together with the other territories and beat Arverlang. If he's got any sense, he'll immediately back down in the face of such overwhelming numbers but it'll only mean two things – one is that he'll bide his time and come back for another bite in the future and the other is that we probably won't find out why Naluke was killed as by then it'll seem less important. I made a promise to his mother that the first Fairyland death in 500 years wouldn't be in vane so I'm inclined to go with carrying on with Plan A whether we like it or not." I then hoped that none of this had been broadcast across the territory. I also sensed that I'd maybe gone a bit too far.

This brought silence. Complete silence.

"Who else knows?" I asked.

"Only Shona," said Hayley, "I told her on my way here but I doubt she'll have seen anyone else to tell."

"Someone, get her on the phone or however it's done here. And make it a secure line."

There was more silence.

"NOW." I said, this time looking at Felixx.

I don't want to bore you with the details but he wasn't happy, and neither were the rest. They couldn't see my point of view at all, but I persevered and in the end, I pulled rank. I also got Shona to join us and got her agreement to keep quiet. I could see that even the Haferlincs were querying my decision but I was King and that was that.

The reason had done it was actually twofold. I had to assert my authority at some point, especially over the cat, and I thought that this was a fairly benign way of taking the first steps in that direction. Also, in this case, I did actually think I was right. I'd see over time if I was, but I was discovering that's the thing about being a leader, you have to sometimes make some decisions that aren't clear to others. Oh, well, back to the battle plan.

There was silence as we moved off the meet with Hoopik. The atmosphere thawed a bit though as we made our way through the wonderful scenery of the Western Isles and finally, arriving at Luskentyre, we had some lunch at the parking spot overlooking the beach. It was weird being half human and half fairy. For example, if I sat up front with Jim and his wife, all I saw was a stunning white sandy beach, bathed in sunshine with deep blue water lapping at its edges. Move back into the command room, and the view was entirely different as there were then thousands of fairy warriors camped out on and near the beach. I'd imagine it was like any other army waiting for battle with ranks of people getting prepared, obvious support areas and lookouts posted everywhere, waiting for the Canooque-F to attack or us to take the initiative. The sharks made an appearance once in a while but overall, it was pretty calm.

The only strange thing was in both 'views' there was a couple walking their dog. They couldn't control it at all in the human view as it seemed to have a mind of its own and wouldn't listen to any commands from its owners. Flip to the 'other side' and this all became clear in the Fairyland view where it was fairly obvious that the dog was itself a Haferlinc and was actually chatting to the relaxing warriors as it was being pulled back and fore by its owner.

They had also parked their car beside us so when they gave up on the walk, dragging their pet back to their car, Felixx went out to have a word as the dog went for a pee. He reported back that the mood on the beach was quite upbeat and there was a huge expectation building about the arrival of 'King Dayv'.

The dog also apparently sensed that the RV wasn't all it appeared to be and, believe it or not, asked for a selfie with me. Felixx said that I hadn't actually arrived yet and that they were just the forward party. He later explained to me that this was his default position with anyone he didn't know, "just in case, Davie, just in case," was all he would say.

After lunch, and with me now having seen the enormity of what the battle forces were like in 'real' life, we headed south to the Uists. The Uists were the more southerly islands that formed the long thin line that made up the Western Isles. Jim explained that when battles were taking place on the Islands, each of the Diven heads came in by their own portal due the dangers of travelling when serious fighting was taking place, hence us meeting them at places away from Luskentyre.

In fact, as he gave me more background it became clear that they were never all together unless it was at Tomna Hill or if I asked them to meet up. Jim said that this was why the hill was so special to the people of the OutFax and why it had, for example, him as a guardian and at the same time was the location of the Royal Mansion.

Heading towards the island of South Uist, he said to Felixx to come up and keep a look out for Hoopik. From this, there was more chat about garbage collections and recycling that I, as you'll have guessed, just nodded at due to not having a clue about what they were saying. Hayley had also left after lunch, saying she'd help locate Hoopik's portal. It was when the cat picked up some binoculars, I gave up and had to ask.

"Ok, I'm totally lost," I said, "if it's a portal, why don't we just drive there and get her?"

"It's not that simple, Davie," said the cat, still scanning the horizon, "she's on the local garbage truck. Normally she'd jump off and message us but given the heightened state of security, she's staying on the lorry until we find her. Luckily, this is one of the days it comes north from the Isle of Barra to collect bottles for recycling, so it saves us a trip to the far south of the Islands."

"Why on earth is she on a recycling truck?" I asked.

"You can ask her when you see her but I think it's because it moves around and also because Scippur, a dog that works with the crew, is one of her main Haferlinc lieutenants. Scippur's now like part of the truck's staff and travels on the lorry everywhere, hence I think it's easier just to appear in the truck with him. Needless to say, Scippur's the only one who can see her but he's also super protective so heaven help anyone he doesn't know if they try to get into the cab."

That's me told then – probably best that I'd stuck to nodding.

A shout came from the RPD in the back (that's Royal Protection Detail – I'd asked them if I could call them that and they were delighted). They now insisted in being called RPD One and RPD three. As they were so happy, I made no comment and just agreed.

"We've caught sight of Hayley about 1000 feet up waving the torch about a mile down the road near the junction for Lochboisdale – that'll be where Hoopik is."

The cat swung the glasses round and gave a paws up as confirmation. "ETA 10 minutes everyone" said Jim.

The recycling truck was parked up at the local Co-op supermarket and it appeared that only Scippur was in the cab. As before, no-one else could see us so the good people of South Uist were also going about their daily business, totally unaware that Royalty was amongst them. Probably just as well as they too would be likely to join me in the asylum if they knew what was going on.

Scippur jumped out of the open cab window, did a quick recce and came across to speak to Felixx. Believe me, to you it would be the weirdest thing seeing a cat and dog chatting as if they were old friends catching up, but given the circumstances, I thought it was fairly normal.

The said Scippur was brought over for a Royal introduction. "Feasgar math, ciamar a thathu, Dayvrigh," he said, which meant nothing to me.

"He likes to speak only in the Scottish Gaelic language," explained Felixx, "he says it's in case there are any spies – he said 'good afternoon, how are you King Dayv', or something like that"

Honestly. I've a dog back home that only speaks Spanish and here's another that's addressing me in the local lingo.

"Scippur, as your King, I appreciate your caution, but if you can understand me, please feel free to speak English."

"OK King Dayv, but don't blame me if anyone hears us," he said, with the most furtive look you can imagine a little white dog ever giving. Just great, I thought, a paranoid Gaelic speaking terrier is Hoopik's main lieutenant.

The RPD then appeared and gave us an all clear – it was good to see that these guys were starting to get into the swing of things.

I just smiled to Scippur, nodded as was my want, and asked, "Where's Hoopik?"

"Over here," she said, jumping from the cab. Her band of regular followers also appeared from the back of the truck where all the bottles were. I swear that one of them was drinking dregs from a whisky bottle but I chose not to say anything. Hayley also hovered down to join us at that point.

"Everyone into the RV," ordered the cat, back to its usual role, "and Scippur, once again, thank you for your help." This led to high five paws from both and no comment from me.

"Scippur, it was a pleasure meeting you," was all I could think to say, "you've been of great assistance to Hoopik and the rest of the OutFax and I have no doubt I'll meet you again."

"Mar sin leibh," was the answer as he headed back to the lorry cab, just as the crew were coming back.

The drive back north was uneventful and proved useful in gathering the necessary intelligence on who was where and what the battle group status was. We managed to link the two command centres together and by some version of virtual reality, Sandels, Snouques, Hoopik and I were able to sit as a group hovering just above the beach, giving us an astounding 360 degree view of what was happening. We also caught the sunset which was a blaze of red and orange hews that was so beautiful, it almost brought a tear to my eyes. I now fully understood the meaning of the phrase 'big skies'.

We arrived back at Luskentyre just as dusk was falling and parked up near the old church as planned. Jim's wife made us all dinner and with the RPD offering to take shifts on guard, we all went off to sleep in our individual rooms around the command centre. Just as I was nodding off, I heard a distant sea bird calling good night and once again was comforted by the sight of shooting stars outside my window.

#

Back in Ontario, Arverlang was as unhappy as ever. There was still no news of being able to capture a labichen and it seemed to him that the general mood was that the OutFax were on the up.

"You need to sort this mess out," he shouted to no-one in particular. "Get the Henchmen out to the beach and get to winning this battle, will you. We're winning, you idiots, and we need to keep the upper hand."

A minc-ling stuck its head out from behind the nearest door and said a meek "Yes, sir" before heading off to carry out the latest instructions.

Still fuming, Arverlang too went off to sleep but with a promise to himself to fix this once and for all.

#

16.

The next day arrived at a bright and sunny Luskentyre. Honestly, when the weather is like this, I think that this beach (and it has to be said, some of the others that we passed on the trip to get Hoopik) have got to be some of the most scenic on the planet. They're also pretty much deserted, making it great as a 'get away from it all' location and also, it seems, one of the best locations for Fairyland battles to take place.

The plan was for me to be formally introduced to the troops. Apparently, the arrival of the RV had caused the rumour mill to get going and by all accounts, anticipation was high as breakfast was being served to both us in the command room and the troops out on the beach. Felixx outlined the plan:

"We'll get you ready while the RPD and Hoopik's band clear the way for you to go on to the beach in your Royal capacity. I'd imagine that we'll be done by lunchtime after which, the sharks are telling us that the Canooque-F may start some initial skirmishes. Imagine a practice session and you'll be pretty near to the mark."

"What exactly do you want me to do?" I asked.

"Follow us, shake a few hands, meet some of the troops and give one of your 'download special' speeches is about all that's required."

"What about meeting Naluke's battalion? – shouldn't I see them?"

"I hadn't thought of that," said Felixx, "what do you think, Hoopik?"

"I like it King Dave," said, "we can sort it for you to have some time with them."

"What about over lunch?" I came back with.

"No need," said the cat, "we can eat back here."

"Sorry Felixx" I said, "No way my friend – I'll be eating lunch with the troops. If they're good enough to fight for the OutFax, the least I can do is sit and have some food with them."

As usual, this didn't sit well with him but Hoopik did the diplomacy thing and he eventually relented, albeit reluctantly. I also asked how Ded-i and Struugs were getting on with Del and The Sheep but I took from the funny looks and noncommittal comments that things hadn't moved forward much on that front either. Call me a coward, but a big bit of me wasn't looking forward to leading Fairies or anyone else into battle where another fatality could occur. To me, the sooner the team back home worked out the cause of Naluke's death, the better it would be for everyone.

Notwithstanding this, I headed off to my room to get my Royal togs on. I thought that the black jump suit was best in the circumstances (complete with the King Dayv badge and gold thread decorations) and I even found a matching black baseball cap in my bags. Shortly thereafter, Field (or more correctly 'Beach') Commander King Dave was up and ready to meet the troops.

The all clear was given once more by the RPD, and leaving Jim and his wife behind to mind the RV, we set off across the grass to the beach. Hoopik had planned it all in detail and the Noogmas were controlling the crowds, leaving a passageway clear through the gathered troops that led to a large field tent where it transpired ground command was located. I did some hand shaking and chatting on the way through as you would expect and after about an hour, we arrived at the tent where The Sheep had left two of his team in charge. They made a big fuss about greeting us and then led Hoopik, her little band, the RPD, the cat and me on to a stage that had been built at one end. Sandels appeared on a big screen behind the stage as the assembled troops filed into the tent and we took seats that had been placed to the side of the stage.

"Warriors of the OutFax," squeaked Sandels, "Please welcome King Dave." I stood, and not knowing what else to do, saluted the crowd. There was a huge roar of appreciation after which I sat back down when I felt Felixx tugging at me.

"We all know why King Dave has come to us and, to enable us to move on to more peaceful times, he has already built a task force to properly interpret the Book of Groges and work out why our fellow warrior Naluke was killed in battle. However, as we also know, the killing has given Arverlang a huge boost which has led to massed forces gathering on Taransay, meaning that we may have to defend ourselves again before a final solution is found. As our new leader, King Dave has decided to lead from the front and has therefore, as you have seen, joined you on the beach today. I give you King Dave."

Taking the cue and as the inevitable applause died down, I moved to the front of the stage having been handed a microphone by RPD three.

"Fellow warriors," Big Cheer (but I could already sense the cat rolling its eyes behind me....), "normally I'd say, let's get out there and destroy the Canooque-F. However, I recognise that these are not normal times and 'destroy' could mean more deaths and please forgive me for saying this but I genuinely don't want anyone else to die."

This led to some murmuring – maybe not so good, David, not so good.

"Let me explain. I fully back our troops to win any battle and will help in any way. But I also understand that it is not the Fairyland way to decimate your enemy and kill your fellow Fairies. But be warned, Arverlang is like that and we want him gone. This doesn't mean killing or destroying his warriors as I'm convinced that many of them are as unhappy about the turn of events as we are – after all, they might be next to receive the same fate as Naluke. I'm sure that this message will make its way to Arverlang's troops – we want a fair fight but we also want to stop the killing. So if you're listening, people of the Canooque-F, we have no argument with you as fellow warriors, our fight is with your lunatic leader and his henchmen who seem intent on destroying the Fairyland we all know and love. Remember, we are here to make the Human and Fairyland worlds a better place, not fight to the death. But, if we are forced to fight dirty, my friends, we will. So, as I'm sure he'll hear this again, be sensible, Mr Arverlang or be afraid, be very afraid - we're coming to get you and we are still the best army in the world."

This had the desired effect. The usual roars and cheering took place and first Hoopik, then finally Sandels, said a few more gee up words before we moved back into the throng to meet more of my people.

"Come this way, King Dave, and meet the musical directors," said Hoopik as we came off the stage.

"OK," was all I could think to say. After all, what did music have to do with wars between territories?

This was where I was to learn a bit more about the structure and ceremony that went with each battle. Music was played through huge outdoor gig sized speaker systems at specific times in the battle sequences. Needless to say, the type and genre of music had evolved throughout the centuries, as had the technology, but the message was that this was a very important aspect of Fairyland culture, hence my meeting the Luskentyre directors. It transpired that the Fs also had a similar set up and it all worked in a way that each side could only hear their own music. We made our way over to a platform outside the tent that at first glance appeared to have much technology on it as the war room and any of the biggest music festivals you've ever seen. Up we went, Sandels first.

"I'm delighted to introduce you to the twin DJs known as DarcRoola, Sir."

I shook hands with two men that I was later to discover made up one of the top musical acts in all of Fairyland at that time. Normally, I'd have thought that DarcRoola and their ilk would have had gigs at concerts and nightclubs, but it appeared that in Fairyland, their main purpose was to perform at Battles, like the one at Luskentyre. Dressed in white 'morph' suits, with very dark glasses and accompanying dark hooded cloaks, the DJs were also clearly delighted that they would also be spinning the discs or whatever for the King.

"Welcome to the groove, King Dave and I'm sure you'll be appreciating the sounds you hear out on the beach" said one of the two.

"Yes, thank you," was about the best I could muster. I mean, back home Milo and TJ listen to 'music' by people with names that sounded the same to me as DarcRoola's and I have to say that most of the time it just sounded like a lot of noise to me. I was acutely aware now that I had a track record in Fairyland of putting my foot well and truly in it, so less was probably best when it came to commenting on the music.

"We've mashed up a few new tracks in your honour, King Dave," he went on, "we'll open the next battle with 'All hail KD' and we'll be closing with 'Luskentyre Lullaby, bye'. We've drawn down some serious bass on these, man, and we hope you'll give them the royal blessing."

He then let me hear shortened clips of both tracks and I was pleasantly surprised to find that I actually quite liked them.

"Yes, please consider them blessed, DJs, and thank you once again for honouring me in this way." David the politician was back again.

Everyone looked suitably happy and I did a cursory inspection of the stacks of equipment before thanking both Mr Roolas and their posse (they called them that, not me) before moving on with the tour.

"Thank you for seeing them," said Hoopik, "they've got a real knack of being able to play the right sounds to support the warriors at each stage of the battle. They're also one of ours and knew Naluke pretty well so are taking things a bit personally."

"What happens with the tracks they write – is it just one off performances?" I asked, as we made our way across the field to a big white tent, set off to the side.

"Every major battle has new music written for it by both sides and it is normally used in any documentary or TV coverage - it will also be available as downloadable tracks. There's normally about 10 new tunes for each battle."

"I must admit, I like the idea of 'All hail KD'," I said with a wistful smile, "but what are the others?"

"This time round, the tracks are 'All hail KD', 'Commencement Part 1', 'Mad Mad', 'Tarbert', 'The other party', Recommencement – AKA Commencement Part 2', 'Arrowflight', Harrisian Heaven', 'Naluke my brother' and finally 'Luskentyre Lullaby, bye'."

She said this with a real passion so I just nodded and carried on following Sandels.

The next stop was at the aforementioned big white tent. This, believe it or not, was the makeup department. I was duly ushered inside, by this time just accepting anything they said to me.

"This time, Sir, I would like to introduce you to Yonnamakk, our head of makeup."

"Delighted to meet you," I said to a very pleasant dark haired Fairy who had appeared in front of us. "Tell me about the makeup elements of battles."

I asked this because I was genuinely mystified. I mean there's music and now makeup – it was looking more like a night at the theatre than preparations for the war.

"Certainly, King Dave, and thank you for coming along to meet my team." With that, and with an outstretched arm, she indicated rows and rows of seats that had Fairy Warriors on them having their faces made up. Bizarrely, it looked like a huge beauty salon that had been taken over by an occupying army. She continued:

"Each warrior has an individual look that is painted on to his or her face before battle commences. These patterns have either been specially commissioned or more likely, handed down through the generations of each warrior family. Some are really intricate and it is believed that proper application of the design will assist the warrior greatly in the fights ahead. The top warriors' designs are also available on t-shirts and the like for their followers to buy."

There you go, who'd have thought. I nodded again, first to Yonnamakk and then to her team of makeup artists.

Then the cat appeared beside me.

"Time to move on, Davie, you've seen the war paint and the musos – I think that's enough for now."

So, with a final farewell to the makeup staff, we then retired for lunch. It appeared that the main tent that we'd started in doubled as a mess hall so I led the Royal party to the nearest queue, joined the troops in line for some grub and after grabbing our food, was led to Naluke's battalion's table to eat with his colleagues. It appeared that my earlier message and the more general tour I'd taken afterwards had been pretty well received and as lunchtime turned into the afternoon, we headed back to the RV, complete with more shaking of hands and chatting on the way back.

Just before Hoopik and I went back on the seats to join Sandels and Snouques , there was more faint praise from the cat.

"I don't know how you do it Davie, but just when you look like you've totally lost the dressing room you seem to manage to get it back every time. Good luck with the battles." He then promptly went to sleep, almost like any normal cat in the afternoon.

17

Let me try to explain how the big seats thing worked with those on the ground. Along with the music and makeup elements, the battles were set out like old fashioned medieval film sets. There were battalions setting up in what looked like big long lines on the beach, each facing towards the opposition. This was the same for both sides and there could be a number of different fronts facing off at the same time. When those at the front line lost a skirmish or needed replaced, the next lot moved up. The weapons of choice were bows and arrows, swords and knives. They had apparently tried guns but the bullets just went straight through the Fairies and larger shells when fired from artillery just threw the participants up in the air with no other harm. They'd also tried planes and drones but it transpired that there was a previously unknown invisible shield above each battle that rendered them useless.

So, from a command perspective, it was really a case of co-ordinating hand to hand combat. Within this, and alluding to my earlier WWE comment, sometimes the overall battle would stop to allow two top warriors from each side to take part in what was in essence a very violent one to one fight. This could be a wrestling match, or alternatively a sword fight, or any number of different combinations but no matter which it was, the 'bout' as it was called would continue through to incapacity. To get to this stage, there was a really complicated scoring system that involved numbers of arrows fired and hit, numbers of cuts, including lost limbs as a bonus would you believe, and the related speed of recovery via the dust dispensers. There were set moves, a bit like chess, that had proven successful in the past but there was always the chance to develop wildcard tactics on the hoof. This was apparently Sandels' strength although in his day, it was done from a huge high chair in the middle of the battle with instructions dished out via a megaphone.

Computing technology had transformed centuries of tactics and although the principles were the same, the battles now sometimes moved at extraordinary speed and on multiple fronts, hence the Noogmas and their field equivalents, whose job it was to keep track and feed the commanders the intel necessary to win each manoeuvre. There was also a lot of ceremony, though, with set procedures at the beginning and end of battles. These were set to music and played out in a sort of 'wind them up' way in the beginning and a 'chill out' way at the end. The overall winner was the side who had gained the most points and also the side that won the most individual bouts.

In terms of timing, there were different classes of battle; some were timed by mutual consent (those were televised if you can believe it) but others started and finished when what appeared to me to be a random set of circumstances. As an example of past fights, some involved birds flying past, the appearance of a fox or badger, sometimes combined with the right position of the moon relative to the sun and the stars. The rules have been written elsewhere but with the inevitable spelling issues that you'll understand come as part of it, I'll just wish you good luck trying to interpret them.

So it was within this madness that I took my place alongside the other three. My job (so I'd been told) was to dish out the really important instructions. I was told that these would be fed to me by Sandels and the others when required. For once, and having seen the reruns, I had no wish to try out any other ideas of my own as you honestly did need to have done this for a while to get to grips with it. I, therefore, was just there in a leadership capacity to keep everyone going until Struugs and co had sorted out the Naluke mess.

Sandels and Hoopik were the real commanders and while Hoopik had up to date on the ground experience along with a truly awesome grip on the technology, Sandels was being fed the pictures of what was going on in a way that looked like it had done when he was on a high chair. As we were about to discover, for an old man he could still really develop possible forward moves and execute them via Hoopik with remarkable alacrity. Snouques's job was to co-ordinate the dust dispensers on the ground (they were like the Red Cross in our world), make sure that Sandels was OK with the technology and to collate good news snippets for forwarding to the troops.

The Noogmas carried out the instructions as devised by Hoopik and Sandels by sending them through to the troops and at the same time lifted battlefield stats from individual intelligence feeds from the beach, analysed them and fed them back to screens that Hoopik, Sandels and Snouques could see. In this particular battle, as well as being fed what to say, I had also been given the job of taking info feeds from outside sources and passing them on to Snouques for analysis. Overall, each battle was a combination of wit, waiting the others out, recuperation when individual bouts were taking place and at times, sheer speed of action.

It was sensational.

You must understand, sitting in the 'big seat' was both phenomenal fun and highly addictive. The highs were better than any other 'adventure' experience I'd ever had (although, as you'll have worked out I've not really led the most exciting of lives) and the lows were devastating but you always wanted to go back for more. And I was the leader for a day; way to go David. Let me just say for the record, even if this whole journey is a form of madness, a dream or just a dreadful illness, very little in my life to that point had come close to the feeling I got when I was in the commander's seat.

We were just setting up and the warriors forming into the battle formations when Hayley and Shona appeared on my virtual info screen.

"King Dave, David," said Shona, "You'll never believe this. We've been hearing both on the ground and from Hayley's galactic sources that the Canooque-F forces on Taransay did manage to link into your mess room speech. It appears that apart from a few nutcase henchmen of Arverlang's who are there and like the idea of killing, the bulk of the troops are sick of the way things are and, as you pointed out, are for the want of a better word shit scared that they're next to die. Overall, you've managed to gain huge respect from the other side as well."

At this point, I kid you not, Felixx faded on to the screen, shook his head, and faded back out, leaving Hayley and Shona back with me.

She went on, "as a result, they'd like to offer a one hour TV special ceremonial battle to begin with - this could take place this afternoon with the regular battle tomorrow. This is the Fairyland way of showing respect to a new battlefield leader and I'd strongly suggest you accept. We can patch you through to their on the ground commander – she's called Ess. Let me know."

"Give me a minute, will you," I said, remembering that it was my job to really only do what I was told today.

I drew the attention of the other three and asked for an offline conference and as King, it was granted immediately. I told them what was happening and they agreed that it was a good idea. Given Sandels' legendary status in the warrior world, I suggested that he speak to Ess and sort it out, with my blessing of course.

The upshot was that the plan went ahead with an hour's grace to set up the TV links and to prepare both sides. Ess explained to Sandels that she'd managed to persuade the more violent of her warriors that this tactic would soften us up for the real battle tomorrow and they'd bought it. I later learned from

Hayley that Ess had been about to launch the much talked about coup against Arverlang just when Naluke was killed, changing everything, and deep down she still didn't like what Arverlang was doing to the people of the Canooque-F .

Over the next hour, boat loads of Canooque-F warriors started to come across the water from their base on the nearby island of Taransay. In the general spirit of co-operation, the sharks formed an aquatic guard of honour as the boats beached one after another. By the time the battle was ready to commence, there were about 4,000 warriors on the beach which were more or less equally split between the two sides. I handed off to Sandels and Hoopik who took charge from that point onwards. In our virtual world and about the equivalent of 100 yards away, Ess appeared with two others in similar battle seats and there was a brief nod of acknowledgement from both sides as we both floated above the battlefield. A message flashed on my screen telling me to make a brief introduction to the proceedings for both protocol and TV purposes. As you would expect by now it also had a footnote reminding me to hand matters back to Sandels in short order. I stood up in my new virtual world and what I took to be a Fairy TV producer appeared below me and counted me in by hand signals. I was definitely getting used to this.

"People of Fairyland, and specifically today, people of the OutFax and Canooque-F territories, I am honoured that the great warriors of both armies have agreed to this introductory battle in recognition of my first day in command of our warriors. I shall now pass over to Warrior Ess for the Canooque-F (cue Big Cheer from them) and our very own Emeritus Warrior, Sandels, for the OutFax (cue Big Cheer from us)"

I sat back down.

And so to the battle. It started with a Maori warrior style Haka type of face off by each side, all done in perfect synchronisation to heavy bass driven dance music. Both sides seemed to know the moves, as did those on the sidelines watching. It finished with a mass of arrows flying in both directions after which Hoopik and Ess counted in the first rows of each side to fight hand to hand. From that point onwards, I lost any perspective on what was going on. Scores appeared on a large scoreboard beside us and were projected into the sky on the beach. There were movements on different flanks at times and there were some casualties but, once again, it was the speed of movement that got me. I just took to watching the battle and nodding when anyone looked in my direction.

Then a red light flashed on my screen with a message that said "est five mins – one to one –wrestle. You to announce. Names TBC." I had a guess at what this was but looked over at the others for help. Snouques leant over and said that given the scores on both sides we were close to a bout and it was protocol for me to call it and then announce who would fight for us – Ess would do the same for the Fs. Snouques said she'd count me in via my screen so that I stopped the action at the right time, at which time I had to ring a bell that had appeared beside me and say (loudly) "I call for a bout". This didn't strike me as particularly regal but there you go, what did I know?

The said numbers counted down from 10 on my screen, first in purple then in red as three, two and then one came up.

"Now," said Snouques

I rang the bell.

The action stopped and another short burst of dance music took place during which the name of our wrestling warrior appeared on my screen. It was also becoming a form of autocue as, after the music stopped, I stood and read from the screen.

"As overall commander of the OutFax warriors, I call a wrestling bout. (pause for cheers - which duly came). I will call upon Ji-Musc, warrior grade one, to represent the OutFax at this time."

The screen said to sit down and nod, which I duly did. There were more cheers and music played as the said Ji-Musc came out of a dugout that I hadn't seen before and made his way to a ring that was about twice the size of a boxing ring and had appeared in the middle of the thousands on the beach. When I asked later, I discovered that the warriors who took part in the bouts were kept on the side lines warming up, a bit like in baseball. They only fought in the bouts, which I only understood the reason for when I saw the fight take place and a bit like UFC, it was fought until one of the participants was incapacitated.

Then Ess came on. "As overall commander of the Canooque-F warriors, I accept the wrestling bout. (more cheers). I will call upon In-2 You-It, warrior grade one, to represent the Canooque-F at this time."

There was more cheering on both sides as two warriors, accompanied by the obligatory dance music, were escorted by their support teams to the ring. Within 30 minutes, we were ready to go and it was clear from the atmosphere that anticipation levels were sky high.

After some preliminaries from a referee, who quite sensibly left the ring in short order, the two warriors just hammered into one another. There were no rounds but each side had ten time outs that they could call and to say it was brutal was an understatement. Snouques reminded me, though, that neither could be killed so while it looked horrific for a human, they'd be back fighting in no time. In practical terms this meant about a month as a minimum. The Fairies loved it; there was partisan singing, some allied fights in the audience, drink thrown all over the place and about 20 minutes later, In-2 You-It was declared the winner with our guy stretchered off for some dust treatment.

There was then a break of about 10 minutes (this I learned later was for TV commercials, some things being the same wherever you are) after which I was again cued up and counted in to gracefully accept the win of the Canooque-F and then start the whole thing over again.

The second half, if you can call it that, was as far as I could see a re-run of the first, with Ess calling a sword fight bout at the appropriate score level, me accepting as I should and us winning this time round. I thought it was a draw but apparently sword fights outclass wrestling in some circumstances so we won. Before I could get too excited, though, Felixx appeared and reminded me that it was effectively an exhibition match to welcome me to proceedings, so what did I expect.

And that was it for the day. There was some clearing up done and there was more music played, although this time it was the chill out variety. There was even a team of cleaners who came on to the beach and picked up the detritus of battle. The Fs stayed at their side of the beach and I guess you could say it was a bit like old fashioned battles where both sides just camped out on an open piece of land, awaiting the order to charge. As another glorious sunset appeared, we closed down the command room for the night and sat down to dinner in the RV. I did stick my head up into the cab to see the sunset and sure enough, on the human side of the spectrum, the beach was deserted as you'd expect. Once again, I questioned my sanity but given that was really hoping that I'd make it back to my house some day, I just popped back down into the RV to sit with the rest of the gang.

The atmosphere was quite relaxed and Felixx was holding court with Jim as they enjoyed some Fairy Broo ™ while they recounted battles of old. We had a quick video conference with Ded-i, Struugs, Del and The Sheep back at base but the only progress they'd made was that they thought that Naluke's death wasn't an accident. By this they meant that their initial analysis showed that such events normally happened after a specific sequence of actions took place - apparently this nugget was buried somewhere in The Book - so the next step was to try to analyse the steps leading up to the death. The only problem was that The Book wasn't so clear as to the timeline – in other words, the sequence could have conceivably started months or even years before. By this time, and given how busy the day had been, I was getting a headache so excused myself from the group and headed for bed. On my way across to the Royal Chamber (the RPD called my bedroom this and I didn't have the heart to argue) Hoopik stopped me for a quick chat.

"King Dave, just a quick one to thank you for what you did today. It means a lot to all of us, but my Diven are just chuffed as to how things went."

"To be fair, Ms Pict, I don't think I did much other than do what I was told. I'm knackered though – even watching the battle takes it out of you so I hate to think how tired everyone else is."

"No, King Dave," she came back with, "You went with the flow, came out to the beach and have taken the role of High Commander at a battle. Very few people will take on that responsibility and I'm hearing that your PR is growing across the whole of Fairyland, not just the OutFax. What this means is that if we have to go down the route of asking the other three territories for backing, it should be much easier given the leadership role you've assumed. It might also give Arverlang something to think about"

Well, like anyone else, I'm once again aware that I'm a sucker for praise and I did have a smile on my face. I was also very aware, though, that I shouldn't get ahead of myself (a mixed vision of Felixx and the snake popped into my head) so I just said thank you and that I'd continue to try to do my best. With that, she gave me a hug and I headed off to bed. One and Three took up positions outside the door and I think I was asleep before my head hit the pillow.

In Canada, Arverlang was, as usual, not in the best of moods. He'd watched the battle on TV and while he was annoyed that they'd lost, he was even more upset that it had taken part in the first place. He couldn't understand why this David, or Dayv, or King Dave had managed to get so much respect in such a short time.

He was also incandescent every time Ess was mentioned as, notwithstanding that it was normal protocol to have a welcoming introductory battle, he was of the opinion that it was treason by her to have given David such respect – he'd let it go ahead because he thought it was actually some sort of Trojan Horse ruse to get close to the OutFax and then ambush them. When this didn't happen, he lost the plot so badly that the minc-lings all took off for the afternoon.

As a result, he had resolved, though, to take charge himself at the beach and had arranged for the necessary transport. The Canooque-F had also built a tunnel to Taransay which meant that within an hour, he was on the ground, holding counsel with his battlefield henchmen in the middle of the night.

"I'm in charge now," he said "and that fool Ess is in prison – I'll decide what to do with her later. I'll be taking on the High Commander role tomorrow but it's imperative that the OutFax and that moronic idiot David don't find out I'm here yet– OK?."

There was murmured assent from the group of 20 around him.

"Tomorrow, when you're out in the field, you can also make it clear to our so called warriors that any losses will mean them joining Ess – that should sharpen their act up a bit – OK?"

More murmured assent.

"At the same time, have any of you clowns worked out how we killed Naluke? No? Well it's just not good enough, you fools, do I make myself clear."

"Yes, Mr President" came back 20 voices.

"Right, get to it and we better win tomorrow if you all know what's good for you. You, yes you on the right, get me a drink. The rest of you – disappear"

At that point, his minc-lings prepared his bed, he got his drink and he was left to plot the downfall of his new nemesis of five whole days, a lawyer's clerk called King Dayv. Who'd have thought.

\#

18.

It was another dry sunny day that dawned for the big battle. I was quietly confident that with Ess pulling the strings in the Canooque-F seat, we should win and hopefully put Arverlang on to the back burner for a while, allowing us time to work out the reason for the killing. I was up and dressed again in the royal black jump suit, to which a medal ribbon had been added overnight. When I asked, RPD Three said that it was in recognition of my win as a High Commander the day before. I thought that it was a bit contrived but just showed my appreciation and left it at that.

I had a quick chuckle to myself, though, as I imagined telling my fellow clerks in our room of workstations back at work that I was actually a King of a Nation and had won battlefield honours by taking charge of our territory's warrior army and winning. I then thought of the doctors who would spend years analysing my unseemly behaviour. I was brought back to the present by the cat.

"OK, Davie, big day and all that but if you just do as you did yesterday, everything should be fine. In other words, just do as you're told."

"I do get it Felixx, you know, and you don't have to keep rubbing it in."

"I know Davie, but I saw you smile when you got the medal and was a bit worried – capisce?"

"I fully understand so back off – let's go and get breakfast with the troops."

He mumphed and moaned a bit but organised another trip to the mess hall in short order. We did a slightly quicker walk through the crowds and once again, joined the queue for food about 30 minutes later. After a quick chow and a chat with some of the warriors, we got a lift back to the RV on what appeared to be a fully camouflaged Fairyland golf buggy.

As preparations started for the day – sound checks, technology checks, tactical updates, weather updates, makeup and the usual – Hoopik and I sat down in a quiet corner so that I could once again get my instructions.

"Essentially, it's the same as yesterday but it's not as controlled or structured. There could be more or less bouts and you'll see things moving a lot faster," she started.

I found the speed thing difficult to believe but she just explained that we were moving to a different level.

"So how does it end," I said.

"With these battles, we don't know. Sometimes we agree a finish with the other side, sometimes it's a sign that we hadn't thought of or there can also be the worst case scenario, someone else dies. I suppose like all wars, you can plan away until your heart's content but until you start the fighting, you don't really know the outcome. I'll warn you though; it could go on for days."

Great, I thought.

"If you could just behave like you did yesterday, with Snouques and Sandels back at base with the Noogmas, and me and you here, we should be a match for the Fs." she finished.

I was just starting to mull this over when the weirdest thing happened. I know that everything is already pretty weird so far but this was nuts: a half full coffee mug I had in my hand started to vibrate and one of the sharks stuck its head out of the top of it. I was struck dumb.

The best part, I have to say though, was the cat's reaction. It behaved like any other cat that is frightened or being chased and it took off round the room looking for an exit (there were none as they'd been closed off to allow us to bring up all the VR technology) and with its tail all bushed up, it finally hid under the seats I was sitting on. Not so cool now, eh Felixx?

With the cat shaking and the shark still bobbing in my coffee, no-one said anything so for want of anything better to do, I said,

"Yes?"

I said this as if it was the most normal thing in the world, mainly I have to say to show the cat that at least I wasn't scared.

The shark, speaking perfect English, said:

"King Dave, please accept my apologies for the interruption but something strange is going on in the Canooque-F camp. We don't know the whole story but appears that Ess has been relieved of her duties. Given she lost to you yesterday and the way Arverlang runs things, this isn't too much of a surprise but if it's one of his henchmen taking over, then be prepared for a dirty fight. Just thought you'd like to know."

And with that, the shark evaporated, taking the remains of my coffee with it.

This caused a bit of consternation. Hayley was called back from her flying duties and confirmed what the shark had said. She said to us that she'd been trying to find out more but hadn't been able to confirm anything. The message had also gotten out to the troops and there was a more sombre mood taking over out on the beach, albeit mixed with a bit of an edge as well. Even though we hadn't started, the odd arrow was already flying back and fore and there was a growing sense of anticipation. The cat had disappeared.

We got into the chair positions and linked up with Snouques and Sandels, checking everything was working. We had a quick confab and essentially just decided to take it as it came. We had no idea who would be in charge on their side so really couldn't second guess their tactics. We mustered the troops, I gave another quick rouse up speech which amazingly had the desired effect and we waited for their command crew to join us in virtual reality before hostilities began.

About 30 minutes later, we had a five second warning that the Fs were joining us. They appeared out of the ether and, like the day before, were positioned, like us, above the beach about

100 yards away on their side. However, in this type of battle and unlike yesterday, our positions apparently weren't fixed so if we wanted to, we could sail higher or lower and move around, retaining the full 360 degree view. The only thing neither they nor us could do was cross the front line.

As they materialised in front of us, I thought nothing of it. Ess had been replaced by some weird looking guy with yellow and black striped eyes, if my own eyesight was correct, and the other two who were there yesterday still flanked the main seat. I nodded by way of welcome and waited for the same from them and from our other three. This wasn't to be.

Firstly, old yellow eyes gave us the finger, followed by the other two. Then Snouques, Sandels and Hoopik all looked away while Snouques was furiously writing something on her command console keyboard. Joining in the fun I gave their leader a couple of not very complimentary hand signals (one of which inferred that he was used to playing with himself). I didn't realise at the time that many of the troops could see all of this and it was only later that I was also told that it had also had global TV coverage. There was great laughter from our amassed warriors and encouraged by this, my thoughts were: OK, the ante was clearly being upped but if they wanted to act like juveniles, we could too. So, just for fun, I also drew my finger across my neck as another gesture to their new leader.

Saying that this didn't go down too well either with them or their troops was a bit of an understatement. Everyone was horrified, including my team and yes, yet again demented David had unwittingly overstepped the mark. There was silence on the battlefield and you could almost hear the tumbleweed blow across the whole of Fairyland.

Of course, I wasn't aware of this, but apparently this gesture was the most insulting thing you can do to anyone in Fairyland and in many respects you didn't even do it to your worst enemy.

No-one could ever explain to me why it was so bad but right now, on the beach, it was clear even to me that I'd messed up badly. I could already hear the cat in my head saying, 'what did we tell you yesterday Davie, just do as you're told.' Then I realised he had reappeared at my feet, actually saying this and shaking his head at the same time. Realising that I'd was rapidly undoing all the 'good PR', as Hoopik put it, I said

"Sorry?"

This didn't cut it, in fact it didn't come near.

I was lucky, though, as old yellow eyes appeared to be one of those people who was very easy to wind up and he took the bait, fair and square. He stood up, got a dagger from somewhere and with his face going purple with rage, nearly cut himself as he repeated the gesture across his throat about ten times back to me as well as doing the Robert DeNiro 'I'm watching you' gesture with his other hand. So, I'd clearly got to him. Remember, this all took place over a few seconds in time, and as yet the message that Snouques was trying to send to my screen by text hadn't arrived.

His dagger performance had stirred everyone up on both sides now and the silence was rapidly disappearing. You could sense the anticipation starting to build. I mean, if the two Battlefield High Commanders were already at this level of insults, maybe this was going to be one special day. So at this point, just to complete matters, I pointed out my new medal ribbon, gave a 'freedom' fist in the air – this got a big cheer from our side – and once again gave him one of my special hand signals, while at the same time grinning and winking at him as if to say, the joke's on you pal.

This all led to complete bedlam and for the first time in history, there was nearly a battle start without all the music and other ceremony. However, things were brought under control by Sandels pretty quickly and with the normal dance music starting, the facing off or whatever they called it began. It was only now that I looked at my screen and saw the now famous message from Snouques:

"Oh my God, it's Arverlang in charge, don't do anything stupid 'til we work out what to do."

Oops.

I looked over at my team, kind of sheepishly and then the next message appeared.

"It's OK now, just carry on but with less hand signals if you can as it appears that he's even more stupid than you." You could definitely hear Sandels squeaking this breathlessly even in the written form.

I nodded at them, and then at Arverlang too. Unbelievably, he just nodded back as clearly he was getting the same sort of grief from his side. Maybe he had an annoying cat as well. Anyway, the opening ceremony was underway and order was almost restored. We waited for the last of the music to die down and for the signal to start. Again, no one was sure what it would be each time there was a battle of this magnitude but on this occasion, a flaming golden arrow came from the heavens, did a circuit of the beach and landed front and centre between the two front lines. Clearly accepting that this was a good enough hint to get started, once more, arrows and swords flying, everyone got ripped into everyone else. Game on.

19

Once again, it was quite good seeing the complete battle scene, as from my perspective I was really only an observer. Looking across at our adversaries, they were all wholly involved so this left me with some time to try to work out what was actually going on.

It was true that this time round the battle sequences were moving much faster than before. It was also difficult for the casual observer (like me) to keep up with what was going on and to compound matters we, as a group of four, moved around quite a bit. At times, we were even all facing in different directions. Update messages were coming thick and fast on to my screen and they helped me understand the moves that were taking place and I even recognised some of them from the evening with Sandels back at the Royal Mansion. It appeared that we were getting close to the first bout, which this time would be called by Arverlang or his buddies. True enough, the countdown appeared, he blasted some sort of hooter and made the necessary announcement. I accepted on behalf of the OutFax and the preparations started for a sword fight. This gave us time to get offline and take stock.

"It's looking good, eh?" I commented to the team.

"You think?" came back Hoopik, "we're getting cuffed and to be honest are lucky to have got to this stage and get some time to regroup."

"Yes," squeaked Sandels, "things are a bit more involved than I thought they would be and it appears that Arverlang showing up has galvanised them into action. We need to come up with something different."

"Give me a minute," added Snouques, "I'll log out just now and see what I can come up with."

I'll happily admit that I was now completely lost so did what I thought best in the circumstances – shut up and nodded. Felixx reappeared at this point and jumped onto my lap. He explained that in essence, we'd been caught napping and were falling foul of the fact that they had clearly prepared some new moves that we hadn't expected. He went on to say that we had actually gained some ground back just before the break for the bout but this was pretty much only down to one or two individual moves that Sandels had come up with along with a couple of the better warriors on the ground. He said he hoped that Snouques had something up her sleeve as maybe we'd bitten off more than we could chew by taking Del and The Sheep out of the equation. We were now ready for the bout.

We won this one, which clearly didn't sit well with the Fs, especially given that they thought that they'd had the upper hand up until now. Snouques had reappeared and had a quick discussion with Sandels and Hoopik and they all seemed a bit happier. I just sat there trying to look suitably regal after having congratulated our winning warrior, even though to me he looked like he'd be in a hospital for a good few weeks.

After a short ad break, some more music and some more facing off gestures, we started over again. Things were moving on to a more even keel and through the day, there were two more bouts, one of which was a sword fight that they won and the other a very rare boxing draw where both of the warriors managed to knock each other out at exactly the same time. We called a mutual halt to proceedings at about 8pm as the sun was going down, with us slightly behind due to having lost the sword fight but overall, the other three were happier than before. Arverlang couldn't resist another 'I'm watching you' gesture and I reciprocated with a wink and a grin. All of this pleased both sides and everyone retired for the night pretty happy with how things had gone.

Before getting some dinner, I headed down to the beach to

visit some of the injured. They were being tended to by the dust dispensers of the OutFax and seemed to appreciate my visit. Some had horrific injuries such as limbs cut off and really bad disfigurements for example, but I was reassured that over time, they'd recuperate and be back for more. I also tried my hand at dust dispensing for the first time when I sprinkled a little on a warrior's hand to help reaffix his thumb. Amazingly it worked and the moment was captured on a short video which immediately went viral on Fairytaks. I was told later that this had helped boost morale hugely. There you go then, King Dave, man of the people, although sensibly I didn't actually say this to anyone given my track record during the day so far.

Day two started pretty much like before, although this time without Arverlang and me having a go at each other, and after another golden arrow appearance, hostilities resumed. At times we were fighting on four flanks and by lunchtime, another bout had taken place; this time it was a swordfight won by us. We were marginally ahead at this point and it seemed that the momentum was starting to swing in our direction. Hoopik, Snouques and Sandels had gelled as a team and I was even starting to anticipate when I was to intervene and make announcements. We therefore started back in the afternoon of day two with reasonably high hopes that we might win this battle after all.

It was when we were orchestrating three separate on the ground flank battles that disaster struck – Sandels fell ill. We don't know to this day what happened but he just keeled over and stopped participating. Snouques, who was beside him back at the hill dumped what appeared to be a bag of dust on him but while it kept him alive, he was in no state to continue. This gave us a real problem though. Under the rules of engagement, we could officially ask for a time out. However, if we did this, we'd tip our hand to the other side – as it was, individual commanders dipped in and out all the time for mundane things like going to toilet or grabbing some food and it looked like the Fs hadn't twigged that Sandels's departure was anything more than this.

They would, however, work it out over time when he didn't reappear but we decided that we'd carry on without him while we worked out what to do. The obvious thing would be to bring Del back into the fray but the rules forbade this – we had one substitute and he wasn't it. Our sub was Raychell, one of Hoopik's Diven and a cousin of Naluke. Her day job was a labichen but she'd been brought in as a sub as, according to Hoopik, she was also a master tactician when it came to battles like this. She'd sat in for all of us at points in the battle so far so in order to keep up appearances, she just slipped into Sandel's space. She was physically with us on the beach so right now it was Hoopik, Raychell and me out in the islands and Snouques back at base.

To make matters worse, the Fs upped the ante, taking what I was told was a pretty unusual and risky move of adding some of their 'bout ready' warriors to the general battle. This was a gamble as it could be that if there were more bouts, they could end up with nobody to fight them as they'd committed their experts to the field already. This would lead to a default win for us but at the same time, it gave them much more expertise down on the front lines.

Houston, we have a problem, I was thinking.

I must have actually said it out loud as messages from the others immediately asked me what I was on about. I mumbled something about time and space and looked embarrassed as you would expect. Matters weren't great at all. It then got worse as we also started to lose ground a bit and towards the end of the day also lost two bouts in quick succession.

As we were regrouping after the second loss, we could see that both the Commanders and the troops of the Canooque-F were on a high. As far as they were concerned, they were winning hands down. There was further cause for concern when we realised that they were looking to launch a major offensive that would clear us off the beach. Although he couldn't take part, Del Fort had run an analysis of what was happening and with Jonnie The Sheep concurring, they advised us that a big, and possibly fatal push, was coming from the Fs. The others explained to me that if this was the case, we'd be forced to retreat and we'd lose the Western Isles. This would then give the Fs a foothold in Europe and a base from which to attack the Great Glen in pursuit of our dust. Overall, the prognosis was pretty poor and I was once again feeling that I was a failure. On reflection, we had probably bitten off more than we could chew and should have concentrated more on the battle as opposed to what had killed Naluke, but we couldn't change it now.

"I need a word King Dave," this was Snouques who had appeared beside me, offline from the others.

"I know", I said, "I'm not coming up to the mark and I've left us really exposed – if it's any help, I'm truly sorry but I don't know what else to say."

"But I might have a plan," she went on, "but it's pretty risky and while we've practiced it out in the Midwest where no-one's been around to see us, we've never actually used it in battle."

"I'm all ears," was all I could say, as at this point any suggestion would be very welcome.

"You'll have noticed that my Diven all have wings," she started with, "and we normally use them to flit about and cheer folk up as well as being more fleet of foot on the battlefield when dispensing dust to the troops. Well, what about if we used them to fight with – a sort of aerial attack solution?"

"But I thought that there was some sort of shield that meant aerial combat was ruled out?"

"Yes there is, but we worked out that as individuals, we can fly below it but still be above the battlefield. Although my lot have wings, they're not all as dainty as you might think and when some of them came to me with this idea a while ago, we thought we'd give it a try. On the pretence of dust dispenser training, we worked out a few formations and attack plans in the plains of Ohio. I have to say, it was less about keeping it a secret and more about hiding any embarrassment if it all went wrong."

"So why's no-one done this before?"

"We looked into it and it appears that it was tried in the past but they kept hitting the shield which immediately took them out of the equation. As such, it was just abandoned as an idea about 700 years ago. But we worked out that by using GPS and Geo Spatial software we can limit our height to just under the shield – it's a bit like a speed limiter on a car, if you get my meaning. It gives about 200 feet to play with over the field."

Thinking it through, I decided that I really had no option but to try her idea out on the others so we convened a quick battlefield conference. Hoopik was sceptical but along with Raychell, she too felt that we had no option. It also looked like the Fs were about to call it a day (this also worked for them as the sharks were telling us that they'd amassed more troops on Taransay which they they'd no doubt move on to the beach overnight) and this would give us the night to sort something out. As the current winners, the Fs did indeed call a halt before we could get started and everyone once again wound down for the day.

I nipped back to my bedroom for a quick break from everything. However Snouques, who was still back at the Hill, appeared in the mirror in my room and again asked me for a private word. I was so tired and worried, I just said yes.

"I want to give you something special King Dave," she started, said as always with that beguiling smile on her face.

"Look Snouques, I thought we'd sorted this nonsense outback at the bar –and even with that, your timing is not the best."

"No, King Dave, not that kind of thing – I meant this......"

And lo and behold, I grew a set of wings. I realise that this whole thing was mad but this was truly bizarre. I mean, even as I say it to you now, it's not right is it? – As in, yes, hello, my name is David Levante and I'm a lawyer's clerk. However, in my spare time I'm a great big Fairy King with wings to boot. See?

"Tug your earlobes." she was saying from the mirror, which I did. The wings disappeared into my back.

"This'll be our secret, King Dave. You see, you're equally accepted by each Diven and as you adjust to your role as king, you will be able to pick up and use the specialities in each of our areas. I saw you were ready to do this yesterday when you did the dust dispensing so these are my present to you. All you have to do is give another tug on your lugs and they'll come back. Also, flying is easy, so just imagine what you want to do, and it'll happen. If you want to try them out for size, I'd go outside though."

So I did, telling the rest that I needed some air. I went a bit of a distance away from the action and when I was by myself, I was met by a couple of Snouques's people that had done the dispensing bit with me yesterday.

"Come with us King Dave. Snouques has told us what's going on so we'll get you flying and we'll go and meet her at her Western Isles portal as she says that if we're going with the flying battalions, she wants to be here in person."

So we nipped off behind a low lying hill, I tugged my ears and with a bit of instructions I was flying out over the Atlantic. If I thought the battlefield command seat was great, this was awesome and I'll just leave it to your imagination to think what it's like; yes, just like that. Little things were also so right about it as well, for example my vision became almost 360 when in flight and I could sense other airborne creatures as if I had a form of radar. I was also kept warm by a bubble of air that covered me about half an inch from my skin. As I said, it was better than I could ever have thought.

After some playing around, my two guides and I hovered about 500 feet up and they explained that we'd be heading south, back towards Lochboisdale near where we'd picked up Hoopik. This time it would be a lot quicker and it would have the benefit of some great views as it wasn't quite dusk yet. So we set off and at some lick too. On the way, we had some fun and sat on the wings of the local Loganair plane that was making its way from Stornoway to Benbecula on the islands but as always, although we could see the passengers, they couldn't see us. After leaving the aircraft to land at the airport at Balivanich, ten minutes later we were circling Lochboisdale when one of the others said,

"So King Dave, where do you think her portal is then?"

Now, initially I thought, how would I know but then I saw the only place it could be. I pointed at the pink roofed Lochboisdale Cafe and said, "That's got to be it, hasn't it. I mean, pink and white fits with all of you lot and your fairy wings and stuff?"

"Yes indeed King Dave," came the beaming acknowledgement from them both. We hovered down into the car park and I tugged my earlobes once more nicely folding the wings away. Snouques appeared from behind the building with a big grin on her face.

"How's the flying King Dave? Didn't I say I could give you something special."

I had no real answer so when she came over, I just gave her a big hug and thanked her. Everyone appeared to be happy. I had one question though.

"Who in their right mind paints a metal roofed cafe bright pink?" I said.

"Well, we like it," said Snouques, "but I was in one day, coming up from under the kitchen sink the way we do and this guy in a suit and glasses who was buying a takeaway cup of tea was asking the girls in the cafe pretty much the same question. It appears that one of the owners' kids or something, a four year old by all accounts, was helping paint the outside walls white. She asked why they were doing it and the girls said it was to make the building easier to see from a distance by potential customers. Thinking a bit more about this, the little girl suggested that the roof would look good in pink to help with the cafe being seen. Mulling it over, they asked the local builders merchants if they could source a commercial amount of 'Barbie' pink paint and the rest, as they say, is history."

"Seems reasonable," was all I could think to say. After all, in the bigger scheme of things, this was pretty sane.

We then flew back up over the Western Isles – again, it was just magic. As we came in towards Luskentyre, Hayley swooped down and joined us.

"Hey KD," she shouted, "when did this happen?"

"Keep it quiet will you," said Snouques, "we want to keep this all up our sleeves right now."

This just led to a quick thumbs up from Hayley, after which she disappeared vertically at Mach One or something. Shortly afterwards, we were back in the RV, me with my wings packed away for the night and saying how I'd bumped into Snouques outside as I was doing the rounds. After dinner, we all sat down and planned the following day's tactics which roughly involved letting the Canooque-F get as many of their troops on to the beach. Then, via proper use of the flying battalions, we'd force them into the sea. It would either work, or it'd be us in the sea, heading to mainland Scotland in defeat. This time I went to my bedroom to sleep. Felixx came with me and, acting like the family pet he purported to be, fell asleep on my covers as I nodded off. At least some members of the Levante family were together.

20.

So onwards on to day number three. I see now what they mean about these battles going on and on. Most of it had been televised and it was getting audiences of millions across all five Fairyland territories. By now, it appeared that I was famous across the land and not just in the OutFax. The day started as usual with everyone setting up. The sharks had confirmed overnight that pretty much all of Arverlang's warriors had been brought across from Taransay so if nothing else, we were now probably outnumbered as well. We agreed that we'd try to take it to the first bout if we could and then, when that was over, we'd infiltrate each of the ranks with Snouques's people to get them as close to the frontline as possible. We thought about rigging the bout to lose it but in the end decided that it wasn't worth it as the Fs would all be pumped up either way.

So that's how it panned out. Arverlang and co appeared as usual although this time it started with him grinning and winking at me. I looked suitably chastised but hopefully not too defeatist and, one flaming arrow later, we were all back in business. We lost about 100 yards of our territory before the scoring called for a bout. We sent our best wrestler in and managed to win it, which gave our guys a bit of a lift. As everything was being set back up for the restart, we did as planned and put lots of winged warriors from the Diven of Hope into the ranks. They were dressed as dust dispensers and we hoped that if they were seen by the Fs, they'd just assume that we were expecting to take even more casualties in the next phase.

The battle duly recommenced and we waited a while, with Snouques, Hoopik and Raychell all analysing the best way to bring the flying battalion in. Then a Noogma alerted us to what appeared to be a breakdown in the Fs comms – this itself wasn't unusual as the IT power involved in all of this was pretty impressive and we too had had a couple of breakdowns in the last few days. But it gave us a window of opportunity which we took.

"Go, go, go," I said, "now's the time."

The other three nodded and agreed and the command was given to go ahead and launch the flying attack.

The winged warriors lifted themselves out of the massed troops, all armed with swords, daggers and bows and arrows. Some even carried stones for throwing at the Fs for good measure. They headed out over the front line and went to work. Honestly, the best way to describe it is like seeing vicious little cupids dressed in black coming at you from above. It worked a dream and was way more successful than we could have dreamed of. Their appearance caused chaos and of course, their comms were down so we had about five minutes of unchecked progress which was all we needed. The winged warrior attacks meant that each of the Canooque-F troops were now having to check above them as well as around them on the ground. This gave our ground troops just the opening they needed.

In two minutes we'd taken back the 100 yards and Snouques gave the word to just keep going. This was the fairy version of shock and awe – we'd even managed to get some fiery arrows to shoot at their mess tent (normally it would be too far away to hit, but if you can fly.....). It was almost an anti-climax as within minutes the Fs all turned and ran. We forced them into the sea (I did ask if they'd drown but apparently they wouldn't) and the sharks headed them off out past Taransay. We knew that they had a direct corridor back to Canada from St. Kilda and that's where we shepherded them to. Between the sharks in the water and the winged warriors overhead, they were off our land in less than hour.

When the comms came back on, Arverlang had gone, leaving his two lieutenants to take the rap. As was required with this kind of rout, they surrendered and at that point, we'd officially won the battle. To this day, we don't know exactly how Arverlang departed the scene so effectively but we did track him firstly back to Ontario and then within a week back to his cave up near the Arctic Circle.

There was mass jubilation on the beach, across the OutFax and beyond. In Fairyland terms, this was a pivotal battle that would be spoken about in revered terms for centuries to come. To celebrate, we had a huge party at Luskentyre with the music DJs turning the entire place into one massive open air rave. Snouques, Hoopik, Raychell and I went round the area on the golf buggy, both receiving and giving out all the thanks that we could muster. By the end of the night, a vast amount of dust had been used up for feasting and other partying uses but it was all good and everyone was delighted.

About midnight, we called in the battlefield commanders and delegated the clearing up and securing of our land to them. This included closing up the St. Kilda portal to stop the Fs coming back and getting all of our lot home, which was something that would take weeks rather than days. At about one in the morning, Jim fired up the RV and Felixx, the RPD and I headed off home. We left Snouques and Hoopik to make their own way back and I personally thanked Raychell for stepping in so well. We arrived back at the Ak-ram shop in darkness where we left Jim and his wife (they said they now really were going on holiday for a few days) and snuck back through Ded-i's Western Isles portal, on to a train and then home to the hill. By three in the morning, I was in bed sound asleep again, dreaming of flying through our lawyers office, laughing at my colleagues.

I was quite surprised when I woke up in the Royal Mansion as given the previous pattern, I thought I'd be back home either in bed or on the toilet, but no, here I was, being greeted by Felixx and P.S. with my usual big tray of breakfast. P.S. left the food on my lap and Felixx jumped up on the bed beside me.

"Well Davie, who'd have thought, you beat old Arverlang. I have to say that I'm impressed, although you'll agree that it was Snouques that saved the day."

"Yes, Felixx, I agree but it wasn't just Snouques, it was a truly great effort by everyone and don't worry, I'm not taking any credit. It would be nice though, if for once, you didn't damn me every time, OK."

"Only in private Davie, only in private – remember, I'm always going to be your grumpy little cat whether you like it or not. To be honest, this Fairyland thing is a real nuisance for me as well – I'm like you in that I don't know why I'm part of it and it drives me nuts that they're all like kids, as you've noted - and they get hung up on the most stupid things. I mean, this Yandermoo stuff is a prime example, to me it's just made up guff from millennia ago. But never mind, here we are, you're still the King of this nonsense and as part of my role in this madness, I've to let you know that you've got some duties to undertake today."

He went on to explain in his usual manner that I had to do a speech on the hill, meet with various heroes from the battle and hand out some honours, the way you'd expect a king to do. So I finished my breakfast and put on a clean version of the black jump suit. This time, overnight it had gained yet another medal ribbon but this one had a wing coming out of it to commemorate the inauguration of the flying battalion. In years to come, this would become the most sought after battlefield honour in the territory, and I had the first. All the cat said was:

"Bit of a fraud there Davie, eh? After all, it's not as if you can fly like the real warriors."

I just grinned and winked at him as I went up to the war room.

21

In the room, I had a quick chat with Sandels, who in amongst it all had just had a 'funny turn' as he said – I suppose at the end of the day, old folk are just the same in Fairyland as elsewhere. Other than that he was OK and was as happy as the rest about the outcome. I thanked him for his efforts and he squeaked his appreciation back. I also thanked Del and Jonnie as they were doing some serious advising in the background throughout but frustratingly, when I spoke with them, Struugs and Ded-i there had been no real progress on the killing of Naluke. I had a quick word with the Noogmas and the sharks, again thanking them all for their efforts and then I headed up to the hill for the speech.

It was like being back in the cemetery the day it had all started. I realised that this was actually less than a week ago in human terms but in many ways, it was more like a lifetime to me. Sandels and the four heads were there, all back in their normal togs, the Fairy subjects of each Diven were there in their thousands in each quadrant as before and we started with speeches from each of the heads. Sandels then asked me to the front and called out a roll of honour during which we handed out a significant number of battlefield honours. At the end of the procession, Hoopik, Raychell, Ded-i, Struugs, Del, Jonnie and Sandels were all presented with the winged medal and ribbon and Snouques was presented it in gold, the highest honour possible. She hugged me tightly, patted my back in a knowing sort of manner and whispered "come fly with me sometime, King Dave" as she hung on to me. I just laughed and so did she, so I think we were finally working out how to deal with each other.

I also presented a gold winged medal to Naluke's mother as a posthumous honour – this was very well received across the land and I thought it was truly deserved as, after all, there is no greater sacrifice than giving your life up for your country.

I then did a more serious sort of 'we did well, thank you to all but remember, it was a series of battles hard fought' type of speech that appeared to hit the mark. After some more roars and cheering as we once again rotated on the hill top, we went back under the hedge for some food. I nipped to the toilet before heading to the dining room, and as you'll probably have guessed, as I closed my eyes for a second, the next thing I heard was Bethany shouting:

"David, are you picking the kids up tonight or am I?"

I just reached for the headache pills on the shelf above the sink. However, the cat was still with me – after all, as far as the family were concerned, it had nipped into the toilet with me. It said:

"OK, Davie, remember, it's Monday morning and yes, you're picking the kids up from their granny's later. I'll also be reverting to normal when we open the door, so don't try to speak to me in any manner other than that of me being the family cat. What'll happen now is that, given Arverlang is back in his box, Ded-i and Struugs will continue to work on The Book and see what happens. If you wish, you can have a look too – you'll find it's still in your pocket – but don't try anything stupid. When the time's right, it'll be obvious and we'll all reconvene."

I was about to ask some questions when there was a bang on the door accompanied by "Come on Dad, we'll all be late!"

I finished up, washed my hands, let the cat out and just went to work, supposedly as normal for another week at the office. Before I left, though, I quickly nipped to the den and put the book back in its place in the bookcase because as far as I was concerned it could wait 'til later.

And that was it for a while. At work, remembering that Jim, Shona and Hayley had to all be present for me to bring up Fairyland, I tried a few times to make this happen. Every time, though, it wasn't to be as either one of them was missing (Jim being on holiday for the first fortnight, for example) or someone else was with them. More interestingly, when I looked for The Book later, it was gone.

I searched the den and as much of the house I could get through but it was to no avail. Notwithstanding what Felixx said, I tried to speak to him but I just got normal blank cat looks in return. I even tried to speak to Paws in Spanish but that didn't work either. I had a close one as I was reading the language to the dog from Google translate in the kitchen one day when TJ walked in and asked what I was doing. I mumbled something about Spanish clients to which she just shook her head and walked away. I even took on the job of forcing worming tablets down the cat's throat to see if I could get a reaction but other than making it sick, nothing happened. At work, I walked up to the hill a few times by myself but it was just the old graveyard it had always been.

Within a fortnight, I was starting to convince myself that the whole Fairyland episode had been a figment of my imagination. I'd read somewhere that sometimes people can have hallucinogenic reactions to certain types of food, for example, so maybe that was the reason. I didn't really know but over the next month, things just became normal again. I still tried to get my so called Halferlinc colleagues together every once in a while but it wasn't to be. So that was it then, I suppose. I'd had the best 'experience' I could imagine, but clearly couldn't tell anyone, and all I did was write it all down in secret so that I could maybe savour it in the future when I got bored. You'll see now why I was able to write this book.

About two months later I'd pretty much forgotten the whole thing. I mean, if I was hacked off at work, I had a quick smile to myself when I thought about the four heads and the battles we'd all been through and even Sandels' squeaking made me come over all warm and fuzzy in a kind of rose tinted glasses, looking back sort of way. But life went on and other matters took over. Milo was now a regular start in the football team and TJ was apparently taking the local music scene by storm so as a result, I was back to being a combination of proud dad and busy taxi driver. Bethany was promoted at work and overall, we were just a normal, busy family like many others across the world.

22

My illness or whatever it is returned about two and a half months later. I'd taken a day off work (made up of overtime that I'd built up – we counted the minutes) with the intention of doing some gardening and other outside 'tidy up' chores. But given the rest of the family had headed out at the usual time, I decided to relax and have a nice long lie. I'd got back off to sleep once the neighbourhood had all gone to work and was pleasantly dreaming of playing guitar in a country rock band when I heard it through the fug of sleep.

"Davie, Davie, wake up."

Yes, yes, the damned cat was growling at me again in that lovely accent. More than that, as I woke up, it was straddling my chest whilst shouting at me. I even felt it swipe my ear as I surfaced from dream land.

I threw it off me and the bed, turned over, covered my ears and closed my eyes.

"It won't work, you moron – I'd have thought that you'd get it by now."

"Please go away," I said pleadingly from below my pillow to no one in particular, "I'll definitely go see a doctor this time."

"I'll sit here as long as is needed, Davie, so you might as well just accept that it's back to Fairyland for you."

Now, at this juncture, I was really panicking. I'd come to terms with the previous 'episode' (as I now thought of it) and had effectively boxed it away in a corner of my mind, to be enjoyed in a personal capacity occasionally, but never spoken of. But here it was again, the cat was once more speaking to me in my bedroom. I even wondered at that time if it was the laundry powder that we used on the sheets that made me hallucinate. Needless to say, I also needed the toilet, so I quickly left the bed and headed for a pee. The cat just sat there and shook its head, saying "some problems never really go away, do they Davie?"

"Would you please stop calling me Davie," was all I could say from the bathroom.

"So, Davie, should it really be King Dave, spelled D-A-Y-V of course on a special badge with a golden winged medal ribbon below it for good measure, eh?" In my panic, I even decided that the cat must have read the notes I'd written down if it was saying this. The tumour must have grown.

"Look," it said as I looked round at it from behind the bathroom door, "let's do like we did the last time. You get yourself dressed and sorted out and I'll wait in the kitchen with Paws. When you get your act together, come on down and get some coffee or whatever you want for breakfast and we'll take from there."

However, being unable to go for any length of time without having a jab at me, it added "although it's a bit late to call it breakfast, ain't it lazy bones, heh, heh?" as it walked off through the door. "By the way, you and I need to have a serious chat about worming tablets," it added from the stairs.

I sat on the bed and cried. I checked myself out in the mirror for lumps in my head (there were none) and tried to think what I'd eaten the night before (nothing unusual) before reluctantly getting dressed. When I reached for my watch on the bedside cabinet, I realised that the nightmare was complete when I saw The Book of Groges had returned. Oh God, it's happening all over again.

I crept down the stairs and into the kitchen. Paws was sitting up in her bed and once again greeted me in Spanish. The cat was on the table, looking mean and furtive all at once so with no other idea as to what to do, I made a coffee and sat down in front of it, resolving to call my doctor as soon as our animals stopped talking to me.

"OK everyone," announced the cat after which the old team

arrived from under the kitchen sink. All four heads and Sandels came up to join the cat and me at the table but more ominously, the RPD appeared as well.

"No, no, no, no, no, no, NO." I also put my head in my hands as I said this.

"Aaw, come on KD," said Snouques as she fluttered over and sat on my shoulder, "aren't you even pleased to see me?"

"Help!" I shouted.

This caused the RPD to move round, flank me and point what looked like nasty swords at Snouques.

"Right, everyone, calm down." This was the cat, who hadn't moved an inch throughout. "Davie, once more, just accept it please. Snouques, we've been through this before so back off and you two, stand down, he's not in any danger other than to himself."

Snouques fluttered away and the RPD put their swords away. I nodded at them and they appeared a bit happier with this but still didn't move away. Sandels got all official and bid me a good day and once again, Struugs headed for the dog's bed. Ded-i looked at me expectantly and Hoopik just waited quietly. It was happening over again and I didn't know what to do.

The cat, however, was all business now.

"We've got a problem, Davie. Since the win over the Fs, the four Heads, Sandels and any labichens we could get hold off have been trying to sort out what happened to Naluke. At every turn, though, it's been made clear that the final interpretation will come from you. This is why everyone's come back to see you. I fully get that you were the most unprepared King in creation and I do still admit that you did a better job than I ever thought possible, but it looks like the good people of the OutFax need your assistance once more. Heaven help us all."

Other than the obvious sarcasm, I did think that his last comment was the most appropriate he'd said all day.

So, deciding that I'd managed to get through the last 'episode' by playing along with it all, I reluctantly said

"OK, good people of the OutFax, what's to be done?

They all started talking at once. I raised my hand and they all shut up. It appeared that I was still the king.

"Sandels – you first."

"Well, Sir, we were hoping that you would be able to make it back to the Royal Mansion to take over and lead the work. We've got some ideas of what may have happened and we've taken over the cinema in your absence with various reconstructions of the moves that took place when Naluke died. I have to say, though, Sir, that other than Hoopik, and especially Naluke's family, most of the OutFax now just see his death as a one off aberration and have moved on with their lives. It seems that the victory against the Canooque-F surpassed all expectations not just in the OutFax but also across the whole of Fairyland and has acted like a convenient catalyst for forgetting what happened in the run up."

"But I'm not happy," said Hoopik, "I'm not convinced that it was a one off, especially given that you turned up as predicted. I'd also like to put it to bed, so to speak, and if there is a solution, implement it so that we'll be on the safe side. The other problem I have is that Raychell has also gone missing and I don't know if the two issues are related."

So with that, and after a bit of outward sighing and a lot of inner conflict, I bid a quick 'adios' to Paws and led my people's representatives once more to the bathroom near our front door. I duly shrunk in size to join them and in no time, I was back in the mansion asking P.S. for a drink from the big island bar. He gave me a darker type of Fairie Broo ™ this time and he said that given it was morning, I would be best with the non-alcoholic variety. I wasn't so sure, I have to say.

Afterwards but before lunch, I went around the hill catching up with everyone. The War Room was being set up for an upcoming exhibition battle with the Sou-Pa territory. This was being led by Del and Jonnie who had moved back to their day jobs since I had left. I spoke with some of the Noogmas who were in top form and looking forward to the battle and I had a quick catch up with the sharks on the way past; apparently they now split their time between keeping an eye out in the Eastern Atlantic for any new F led activity near Taransay or St Kilda and also the Eastern Pacific near the dust mines of the Big Sur. The other rooms back in the mansion had been effectively mothballed in my absence but I asked Snouques to bring the food court back at least. This she did with a big wave of her wand and we all went for a mall style lunch. It was Vanda's and MexTexToo all over again.

Overall, this was both deeply worrying but at the same time very pleasant. OK, once again I had no idea what was going on but I also had a great time catching up on Fairyland matters with everyone. It seemed that a new school for trainee dust dispensers had been built in California and was working well, and some sort of college (as it was described to me) had been opened in the OutFax to formally train the Fairies of the world in new ways to wind up humans. Conveniently, it was located under a manmade island on the lake which was part of the new university campus in our town. Allegedly human students are great to practice on, especially when they've had a drink.

I know, you couldn't make this stuff up but apparently the new college lessons for the Fairies included inane ideas such as randomly changing the voice on vehicle GPS units and also grander things like making the White House appear Pink to some people. I was told that they did bigger ones like this to ensure that humans who were close to nervous breakdowns actually got the medical help they needed. I just decided to nod just after seeing Felixx shaking his head just as I was about to question the sanity of any of the above. All in all, though, I was actually enjoying myself and it was as if I'd never been away. Not good David, not good at all.

After lunch, I met with the labichens who had been working on The Book. At this point, it's probably worth saying a bit more about The Book of Groges and its contents. As I said before, it was 100 pages long and didn't look overly impressive as books go, although matters weren't helped by the tiny writing contained in it. Within it, the 12 chapters were:

Introduckshon
Wae bak at the begyn-ning
Wai Fairies eggsist
The Fairy koad of konduk
A lyffes jurnae
Wot mayksupp Fairyland
Polytiks an uther boaring stuph
Waw-ray-urs an Batelz
Uneckspektid Deths
Howe two deel wif chaynjes
Bee-yonde Fairyland
Yandermoo.

Maybe now you'll see how it really was a difficult book to read. The labichens had no problems as they were used to the spelling and grammar, but even they had issues with interpretation. I discovered that pretty much each of them had a different idea of what each section of the book was saying, which led to what were effectively big long philosophical debates.

Now, this might have been very nice but clearly wasn't getting us any closer to an answer and it transpired that since I'd been away, all they had done was argue over what tiny sections of the book meant. This, according to Sandels, was why they'd decided to call me back in. Great.

I had tried reading the book just after the last 'episode' and before it disappeared, but I found it impossible to make sense of. Now, however, I was going to have to sort something out. To do this, and given I really didn't want to read the book myself, I sorted all 20 labichens in the room into groups made up of individuals who had roughly the same interpretation of what the book said. Struugs and Ded-i agreed to stay with Sandels and me to help – Snouques and Hoopik went off to do their daily duties as usual, which apparently had Hoopik preparing the warriors for battle against the Sou-Pa and Snouques heading down the mines in the Great Glen to supervise a new method of dust extraction.

So, back to the book. We had five groups in all. One lot (which Felixx had of course also joined) thought that The Book was made up nonsense and was their equivalent of a Fairy Story. They actually said this to me with straight faces and it was only the narrowing of Felixx's eyes that made me say nothing and just nod once more.

The next two groups were pretty similar in their thoughts although they differed hugely on when the book had been written. One lot thought that Yandermoo had written, or at least dictated, The Book and the others thought that it was written by wise men who were predicting that Yandermoo would someday be amongst us, but hadn't yet arrived. I put them together because other than the timing issues, they both thought that the teachings, if you could call the contents that, were the same.

The next group took things literally. To me this was impossible given the style and form of writing but that was their take on it. By way of example, on the death by staring at daffodils thing, they took this to only happen with a group of daffodils that you came across but only after seeing someone having died from eating a mouse. They still got tied in knots though – how many is a group and what type of mouse; you'll get the picture. I put them in a back corner and let them get on with it as they were already giving me a headache.

The last group saw the book as having been written by early inhabitants of Fairyland as a general guide as to how to run your life. Their underlying philosophy was that given Fairies lived so long, they'd need some guidance at some point and this was why the book had been published. They didn't see it in nearly as much depth as groups two, three and four and at the end of the day, treated it more as a self-help guide. To them, if it was written by Yandermoo, great. If it wasn't, who cared - it was a useful reference book in times of personal or global struggle. I put them together with Felixx's nay-sayers as although they came at it from different angles, their philosophical interpretations were approximately the same.

I have to point out at this stage, though, that there were some labichens who had refused to even join the debate. As well as discounting The Book completely, they had their own codes to live by which they thought superior to any others. As King, I'd sent a message to them that this was OK with me, which seemed to go down well enough. My thoughts were that at the end of the day, unless they were causing any grief to others, they could think and live any way they wanted so good luck to them. Luckily, the Diven Heads and Sandels agreed.

Back at the room, I put Struugs in charge of leading the three debates and Ded-i in charge of looking for how the philosophical interpretations might actually lead to practical solutions. I asked Sandels to fulfil the role of 'wise old man' which he appeared delighted with. To get the best from the literal group, I told them just to concentrate on the paragraph that dealt with battlefield deaths. In earlier discussions, it appeared that so far they been unable to move past the first page of the first chapter due to differences within their own small grouping. Of course, they had ideological issues with what they saw as my short cut approach but eventually relented after Struugs had a half hour mini debate on the merits of only looking at a particular section of The Book. You'll see that this was already turning into a form of walking through treacle. I mean, as a lawyer's clerk I was very used to trying to make sense of unintelligible documents but this was a level beyond.

The others two groups saw the bigger picture and were happy to go to work on the problem. With my head pounding, I left them all to it and headed back to the bar where this time, a proper drink was waiting. I downed it in one. After a while, Felixx came to join me at the bar where I'd moved on to tea as a precautionary measure as the alcohol wasn't working very well with my headache. He jumped up beside me and took an EffBea Lite from P.S. We enjoyed a moment of silence as we looked over the town once more. I broke it by asking where Jim, Shona and Hayley were to which he said they were at work in a manner that suggested, where else would they be? We went back to sitting in silence.

I tried again.

"How long have you been at this Felixx?" I asked.

"About four years ahead of you," he said, slurping the EffBea Lite. "It was Paws who did to me what I did to you in the bedroom that day. I have to admit, but only to you, when the dog started speaking to me in a manner that I fully understood, I nearly wet myself as well. It took me about three months to get my head around it and, like you, I thought I was going mad. To be honest, the only way to survive this is to just accept it as real. Like that stupid Book, I've no idea whether we're really here or not but like I say, if you go with the flow, it all appears to work out in the end. It can also be great fun as you've already discovered, eh Davie?"

"So why us?" Here's me once again getting drawn further into possible insanity.

"God knows," he said, "although it does seem centre round you, Davie. I understand from Paws that ever since you had a family, all the pets you've had have been Haferlincs meaning that for some reason there would always be a link from you to Fairyland if it was needed. To make it work, though, you have to have some sort of contact with at least three human Haferlincs as well, hence Jim, Shona and Hayley. So, whether they were predicting stuff or, heaven forbid the Yandermoo guy actually exists and is pulling the strings, it looks like it was inevitable that you would enter the fray at some point. As you'll have worked out, I had my doubts but I have to say that your leadership so far has gone way past my expectations."

"Is it hereditary?"

"No, not normally," he said, "I think a few Haferlincs have offspring that are the same, but once again, the whole 'are you/ are you not' part appears to be pretty random."

At this point, I got him another drink and me a further top up of my tea. P.S. stood off to one side.

"P.S.," I asked, "has there been any others like me in the past?"

"Yes, there was," he said, leaning on the bar like a good barman does, "there was the Sou-Pa death thing where their guy just made them a bit bigger but I understand that about 900 years ago, the last King of the OutFax appeared. Apparently the crisis then was that the dust was drying up – at that time, it was just scraped off the ground but the new King brought mining to the territory and that fixed it."

"What happened to him?"

"Unlike you, he was single and decided to stay here. He married a Fairy Princess called Catked (this was pronounced Kai –yed, another spelling issue I think) and lived for another 300 years. Ask Sandels, he'll remember him but there was also some story about Catked going missing. She outlived him by about 200 years and was a hugely popular ruler but she just disappeared one day. However, in the usual Fairyland way, everyone just shrugged their shoulders, accepted it and moved on. Until Naluke's death, things just plodded on as usual and then you turned up."

"What was this other fella's name?"

"I think it was D'avud L'Vont, if I remember correctly," he said, without a single hint of irony.

Remarkably, neither P.S., Felixx, or the RPD who had by now materialised once more, had anything to say about this so I just tucked it away for looking into at a later time. Suitably refreshed, the cat, the RPD and I all headed back to the big debate. We listened in, made some suggestions and had a working dinner made by me as a dust dispenser and apparently welcomed by all. Later, I headed off to bed leaving them all to it. I slept soundly once more. At least Fairyland was a great place to get a good night's sleep.

The next day was much of the same. I couldn't see if any progress was being made but Struugs assured me that it was. He said that the structures I had put in made it easier to control although I found it hard to believe. My headache also came back with a vengeance every time I was in there for an hour or more, so more often than not, I found myself back in the war room chatting to the guys there. I even had a chance to address the troops again and it seemed to keep everyone happy. The one thing I did follow up on was the issue that Felixx supposedly had with the sharks. He'd headed off somewhere when I was up speaking to Del so I took my opportunity.

The story went that shortly after he'd found out he was a Haferlinc Cat, he was getting a bit too big for his boots. In those days, Paws came with him in much the same way as the cat now came with me to act as a minder, or as Felixx had put it, a guide. To put it mildly, Felixx was very quickly hacking pretty much everyone off, including Paws and the four Heads. As there was no pressing need for any help, he was just bored and to liven things up, he started to cause trouble (the Fairies just took boredom as normal and lived with it, so couldn't get why he was acting up). Even as a cat in our house, he was a bit like that anyway, so I could see what they were saying. However, the Fairies were getting annoyed with it and couldn't think how to calm him down. It transpired that their problem was that they had as much control over who could be a Haferlinc as us on the human side had – i.e. none.

Del said that it was Paws that sorted things out once and for all though. Equally as hacked off as the rest at his behaviour, she arranged to have a cinema night in the Fairy Lounge. Befitting the era that the lounge was decorated, they put on the Jaws films, partly as they'd noticed that Felixx didn't seem to like big aquatic creatures.

Now, I didn't say but I knew where this had come from. As a kitten and getting ahead of himself back home in real life, he'd got into our neighbour's garden and tried to catch fish that they had in an outside pond. We only know this is true because their CCTV filmed it, but one of the fish actually bit him when he had a swipe with his paw at it. At the time, after watching him take off at high speed back to our house on the film, we had a great laugh, and it also meant that he kept out of other gardens so didn't stray far from the house.

So with this knowledge, Paws had set him up. Del said that everyone enjoyed the films but it was clear that Felixx was not overly happy but given his recently acquired bravado act, had stayed throughout and tried to be nonchalant about it. Immediately after the films had finished, Del and the others had made up that things were hotting up in some battle or other so they'd all headed back to the war room with the cat front and centre, looking for some action.

It was at this point that they introduced him to the sharks, which he'd never had occasion to meet before and also didn't know existed. To make the lesson as effective as possible, Paws had apparently taken him down to the floor edge to supposedly ask him for his opinions on some tactical matter so he was right by the water when three sharks jumped out at him. He just screamed and took off.

Del said that it was a week before he showed up in the lounge again and to this day, he'd hardly been near the war room. When he did come back after his time out, Paws had a quiet word about his attitude and while everyone agreed he still had his moments, the general consensus was that it had finally put him in his place.

So that was the shark story, another one that I tucked away in case I needed it in the future. For the first time in my life, I was also considering getting some goldfish.

To be truthful, I was also getting bored. After the excitement of the last time I'd been in Fairyland, the labichen debates and no battles to fight were getting to me. That afternoon, I decided to practice my dust dispensing. I secretly wanted to fly again but for some reason I couldn't fathom, I'd decided to keep it quiet that I had acquired the skill. Also, Snouques wasn't around so I was pretty sure I'd crash and kill myself. So dust dispenser practice it was. I took over the sunken lounge in the Mansion and started to create things that I'd always wanted. I got a signed football shirt from my favourite player, a first edition of Alice in Wonderland (to see if it helped make any sense of what was happening to me) and best of all, a full £70k's worth of Linn Audio system. It came with a music streaming package and I was just getting into the groove of some of the DJ DarcRoola's latest Fairyland dance music when Snouques turned up.

Fluttering down beside me she started "What are you doing King Dave?"

"Having fun?" I continued to Dad Dance across the floor.

"But this isn't what the dust is for, King Dave. Unless you do good with it, there'll be an equal and opposite reaction somewhere else which given the value of that system, might have quite an impact. It's in the book."

This brought me up short. Here was Snouques being all serious and I'd failed again by not reading the book. Then the cat appeared. Just perfect.

"Can I just say that I was practising?" was all I could think of.

"I suppose just this once you might get away with it," she said.

The cat added, "You appear to have lived a charmed life so you probably will, Davie, but I'd stop while the going's good if I were you."

A bit like you with the sharks, I thought but didn't say. However, the cat was obviously in mind reading mode as its eyes just said 'coward'.

"Look, everyone, I'm a bit bored so I'm sorry if I've offended or anything. Is there anything else I could be doing – and don't say read The Book as I'm not at that stage yet."

"We could get you down the mines if you want" said Snouques "and I could get you there quite quickly," as she said this, she ran her hand across my back. Now, Felixx just took this as her flirting but when she winked as well, I got the gist and immediately agreed. Anyway, it would be good to see where the dust came from and maybe meet some more of the people of the OutFax.

So, with the cat heading off back to the big debate (saying something about dust mines and aquatic monsters that I didn't understand at all). I made my way to my room and got kitted up in the appropriate clothing for visiting a mine. Handily, it was in the wardrobe, labelled "fur duste myne visuts". I also gave the RPD the afternoon off, explaining that Snouques would be looking after me.

23

So Snouques and I duly went up from the Royal Mansion and out from under the hedge on to the top of the hill, where it was overcast but not raining.

"A perfect day for flying," was all she said.

To ensure that my secret would be kept for a while, we went down off the hill through the trees to the canal and hitched a ride on a boat for a couple of miles. We hopped off at the next set of locks and she took me to a nearby wood to get my wings out.

Now, let me tell you about my wings. No feathers or anything for King Dave – mine were pretty compact, spanning the equivalent of 4 feet in human terms and were a mixture of what looked like black leather with carbon fibre inserts, all in the shape of a stealth bomber. They were definitely part of me, however as they responded to my thought commands instantly. I asked would it be the Great Glen or the Big Sur. It was to be the Great Glen and following Snouques, I shot vertically out of the woods doing at least 200 miles per hour. After a quick orientation dive or two at 10,000 feet and practising some manoeuvres by buzzing a passing helicopter, we headed off at lightning speed towards the Great Glen in Scotland. Once again, the buzz was phenomenal and as we landed on the beach halfway down the south side of Loch Ness in the Great Glen, I was the happiest King on the planet.

With wings packed away, we went into the mines by the closest entrance, which transpired was through the turbine hall of a hydroelectric power station at Foyers, near where we'd come in to land.

"There are other mine entrances but when the electricity people built this and the associated tunnels running up through the hills, it was like a gift to us. We can get the dust straight out through the inspection tunnels and away in no time," explained Snouques as we passed through the control room, which appeared to have only one person in it running the entire place by himself.

"That's Starr," said Snouques as we passed behind the man, who was staring at a virtual power station on a big screen, "he's alright."

Not knowing what she meant or how to answer, I said nothing and just followed her. After going through a labyrinth of tunnels that went deeper and deeper into the ground, we came across a very un-power station-like old oak door with big iron bolts in it, which we duly went through.

This led us to a modern reception area, manned I assume like mine receptions everywhere. It was quite disconcerting, as I'd expected some sort of Dickensian hole in the ground with cobwebs and old wooden posts holding the roof up (you get the picture) but no, it was white, clinical and full of health and safety notices. It also had a very 'corporate' style waiting area with the history of the mine in an exhibition in the corner.

There was also a reception committee and the distinct smell of fresh paint. Yes, they were all set for the first Royal visit in hundreds of years. I nodded at a large, bluff man who was heading the line-up and Snouques made the necessary introductions. After doing the required and chatting to all of those present, Snouques said that she'd take me on the tour. After that, it was just a case of getting kitted up in overalls, a hard hat (with 'King Dayv' printed on it needless to say) and all the rest of the safety gear before jumping on a handily placed golf buggy, our transport for the afternoon.

Overall, it was a large well lit mine. The bright lights were attributed to having a power station as a neighbour ('they don't miss the little bit we take' said Snouques) and the overall layout was I was told a bit like modern salt mines - although cavernous was how I'd describe it. There was heavy lifting machinery and mechanised retrieval equipment and by and large, it was totally the opposite of what I expected. At the dust face (gettit?) I took control of the digging machine and did 15 minutes of mining, much to the amusement and then finally some respect from the miners. I then had dinner with them as the shifts changed, did another speech in the dining room in which I said that to me, the miners (who were of all ages and both sexes) were every bit as important as the warriors out in the battles. This went down well and as a bell rang and they all filed out, it looked like it was time for home.

"We're not finished yet," said Snouques, "follow me."

I did as I was told and we went off on the buggy once more. This time, we went off the main drag and quite quickly we were in older parts of the workings that, while they were still lit and maintained, hadn't been used in anger in centuries. I was half expecting to meet King Solomon himself in this part of the mine. Nipping through the tunnels at ever more worryingly higher speeds, Snouques shouted at me:

"This is the original mine workings that the last King set us up with. It was before my time, but when he did it, it was a huge breakthrough. The special thing he did was put venti-birds in. These were mentally big canaries who did two jobs – they hung off the ceiling flapping their wings in unison thus bringing fresh air to the miners and at the same time, being canaries, tested for poisonous gasses. Nowadays, we don't need them but there is still an open nature reserve for them out on the surface and all miners revere them to this day."

I'd noticed that the mine 'insignia', for want of a better word, was what I thought was a big scary bird and now I knew why.

"But that's not why we're here, King Dave," she carried on shouting as we flew along the mine workings, doing little jumps as the buggy lifted off the ground, "I want to you meet the guardian of the dust".

Now, you might remember that way back, I'd made a flippant remark about the Loch Ness Monster which no-one else had thought anything of. Well, was I about to be brought right back to Fairyland proper as we turned the corner.

"Here we are," said Snouques, hand brake turning into an opening by the tunnel. Through a window in the far off wall, I could see a big red eye having a look in our direction which didn't look very promising to me.

Following Snouques's led, I went through a door near to the window and we were in a large cave, complete with a beach that headed down to some water.

"Hi Kelpy, how's it going?" shouted Snouques.

The nicest, singing voice came back, "Hang on Snouques, I'll just be out."

And with that, I was introduced to the Loch Ness Monster. She came from behind a big boulder and was much smaller than you'd imagine. Think of a horse sized dragon and you'd be about there. She had flippers come paws, a big tail and yes, red eyes. I looked back at the window and saw that the red eye there was some sort of decoy. The monster must have seen me looking and said:

"Hi King Dave, it's great to meet you. And yes, that's just there to put off anyone who finds themselves this far down the trail. I'm a pretty old lady and like the peace and quiet, although it's a pleasure catching up with Snouques every once in a while."

I went over and did some sort of high five with hands and flippers and we settled down on the indoor beach. Snouques and Nessie had a bit of a gossip and I answered any questions that came my way. She had some servants who brought out tea and cakes which went down a treat and I heard more about her story. The Loch Ness Monster was indeed the guardian of the dust in the Great Glen and she also said something about a distant relative called Tahoe Tessie doing the same job on the Pacific coast of North America which meant nothing to me. She made it clear that the name Loch Ness Monster was not to her liking as apparently she wanted to be known as Kelpy, which I was fine with. Allegedly, the 'monster' title had only come about in the last 80 odd years but for the 1400 years before that, she'd just been 'Kelpy' and had been the Guardian of the Dust, which I discovered was actually pretty much an honorary title.

This rounded off a really interesting day. At least it was a break from the work on The Book and I got to fly again. Speaking of flying, we made it home to the hill in the dark but like before with the x-ray type of vision that I acquired when flying down the Western Isles, in the dark I was blessed with night vision, making the whole thing a bit of a breeze. When I finally went back in under the hedge, I didn't see anyone else in the Mansion so I said my goodnights to Snouques and made my way to bed, wondering what the next day would bring, or would I once more wake up back at home on my day off.

24

Well, I wasn't destined to be back home. The day started with Hoopik banging wildly on my bedroom door, waking me up with a start and creating a bit of panic.

"King Dave, King Dave, wake up," she was shouting, somewhat hysterically.

"Hold up," I shouted back, getting myself out of bed and into the royal dressing gown. I opened the door to see what all the racket was about.

It wasn't just Hoopik; behind her all four Heads were lined up and the cat was there as well. I led them all through to the lounge where the RPD had thoughtfully arranged for some coffee to be delivered. Meanwhile, everyone was shouting at once and had been since I opened the door which actually meant that the four Fairies where shouting at me and Felixx in turn was screaming at them. I put my hand up as I sat down and again thankfully, they all shut up. I looked around and decided that the cat was the best place to start as the rest were back to behaving like hysterical children.

"Felixx, what's the matter?"

"It's Raychell," he started "she…"

"Arverlang's got her and we can't get her back," shouted Hoopik.

"Enough, everyone, enough," I said, trying to look Kingly. "Felixx?"

"As I was saying," he said, jumping on to the coffee table in front of me, "and as our Hooligan friend has just jumped in with, it appears that the reason Raychell disappeared is because she was kidnapped by the Canooque-F. The story is that she's now been taken back to Arverlang's cave."

"And we know this how?"

"It's all over the TV." This time it was Ded-i joining the fray.

"He's paraded her as what he calls a prisoner of war."

"Once more, would everyone just shut up until I tell you to speak. Felixx?"

"It's true, Davie, but other than the obvious concerns about her safety and wellbeing, the problem is that she's a labichen so he'll be able to make her read. He's also got some sort of copy of the book as well that he's been waving in front of the cameras, so you can imagine the kind of threats he's making."

"Right, everyone, first up I'll be getting dressed and then having some breakfast. Then we'll convene in the dining area as before. By then, I want you all to have calmed down but more importantly, I want the following. One, a report on how she is. Two, how did it happen. Three, how can we get her back and four, how are our lot getting on with the analysis of the book. Be back here at the table in one hour. Now go – Felixx, you stay. RPD guys, go find Sandels and Del, will you and get them here in half an hour but first can you get my usual breakfast to the dining room in ten minutes."

Yup, King Dave was back in charge and I have to be honest, it felt quite good that some action was required.

This had the desired effect and apart from the cat, they all disappeared. The RPD did as I said and half an hour later, the remains of breakfast were being taken away as Del and Sandels appeared at the big table. While I was eating, the cat had run through a summary video clip of the news stories and by the time I'd finished my grub, I was as up to speed as the rest.

I got a bit more sense from Del and Sandels who were already working on a plan to get Raychell back. What it meant, though, was that we really had to get ahead on why Naluke died as the latest from the Fs was that they were intending to force Raychell to tell them what the book said, work out what had happened and then take us all back on in a 'once and for all' battle.

Shortly afterwards, the four Heads reappeared, this time

in a slightly more organised manner. I then discovered that as far as we could understand, Raychell was taken by the Fs when she was travelling between readings in the Midwest of the USA. She was apparently travelling overland from St Louis, Missouri to Topeka in Kansas when she accidently crossed into newly held Canooque-F territory near Kansas City. It was an opportunistic capture by all accounts. The heads went on to say that such things happen all the time and normally the prisoners are released after a daft ransom is paid (pay us three chickens and a 1960's tape player was one example they gave). However, in this case, someone recognised Raychell from the Luskentyre battle, gave Arverlang the nod and she was taken to his cave way further north.

On her wellbeing, there was no real danger of her dying and actually, the Fs were treating her with an element of respect. The only concern Ded-i had (he'd taken on the task of finding this out) was that they had access to hallucinogenic drugs that they might use to force her to read the book. I said we'd address this if it came to pass. On getting her back, there was no consensus at all as this was something that no-one had ever had to deal with before. I asked about negotiating and sending intermediaries but they all just looked at me blankly. They had no idea what to do next and unfortunately, neither did I.

We then had a discussion on whether we should cancel the battle with the Sou-Pa but it was decided that if we did, this would be handing an advantage to Arverlang. Furthermore, it transpired that The Sheep got on pretty well with his opposite number in the Sou-pa and they had agreed to do some manoeuvres that looked like they would kill Fairies to make Arverlang think we were further on than he thought. I agreed to let this happen. I also wouldn't be in any way in charge of this battle as it would be back to the normal set up with Del, Jonnie, the Noogmas and the sharks running our side.

We were back at square one it seemed and with a bit of urgency now, we really had to get going on the book. The latest was that all the groups (including the 'extremists' as I now though of the literal thinkers) all agreed that it was some million to one confluence between the flight of the arrow and something to do with Naluke's physiology. I know that this might sound fairly obvious but the mumbo jumbo they'd all gone through to get to this point was astounding and wouldn't make any sense to anyone outside Fairyland. I told them to carry on, especially now that each of the groups appeared to at least recognise the others' points of view, if not fully agree with them.

So they all filed out, except Felixx and Sandels who stayed at the table. Before I could say anything, the glass panels came down, went opaque and the VR projector came out of the ceiling.

Sandels squeaked breathlessly. "This is really serious, Sir, and we're about to have the first multi territory summit in at least 400 years. I know that it's a bit quick, but overnight we worked on it with our contacts elsewhere as everyone is really sick of Arverlang and his nonsense and would like to put it to bed. They're all now worried that with having Raychell, he'll work out what happened and basically, the rest don't want to be next in the firing line."

I didn't know what to say at all, so Felixx said, "If in doubt, Davie, stick to nodding, Sandels and the other representatives of the territory heads will be doing most of the talking anyway so all you need to do is look like you know what's going on. I'll nudge you when you have to say 'yes' to anything."

I duly nodded.

Now, at this point I should probably tell you a bit about the other territories. The Sou-Pa (which was just short for 'South Pacific') was really just South America as we know it. Like the OutFax before I came along, it was led by a counsel of Diven Heads – they had five – and today they were represented by their elected head Mydaxxa.

The reason I've never mentioned the other territories up to this point is that I hadn't really asked anyone about them. You'll understand that so far, I was having enough difficulty with things like my bathroom having a train station behind it and my cat talking to me, without worrying about global issues in Fairyland. But never mind, the other two that were coming today were the DgfhlM territory (we'll call them the Ds) which was, as far as I could see, the Middle East on a human map and the final group made up the Mallbaste territory which was essentially just Africa to you and me.

This, as you'll have noted, left a lot of the human globe out of the equation. I had asked previously what about China, India, Australia etc and all I got was very blank looks. As far as the people of Fairyland were concerned, they just didn't exist although they did admit that you couldn't go east via the DgfhlM to us or to the Sou-pa, for example. There was some mention of fog and wolves that were in the way, but at the time I didn't enquire any further about it, so that was that. The Ds, who had a system like Divens but was sufficiently different to confuse me completely, were represented today by some sort of queen called Azyullch, and the Mallbaste, who had the equivalent of 4500 Divens (don't ask), sent along a Fairy appropriately called President Mallbaste.

So back to the present and over the next ten minutes, they all appeared by virtual reality around my dining room table, each with their speaking representatives in tow. Sandels said a few words of welcome, I did some nodding (as did the others) and it was the Ds representative that led off.

"Thank you Sandels for arranging this."

More nodding, suitably grave this time.

"We're all genuinely concerned," the D went on, "and we think that it might be in our best interests to collaborate. As such, we thought that a quick meeting like this to agree such an action at leader level was appropriate."

We all nodded again. The Mallbaste guy took over.

"We would like to add our labichens and interpreters to your efforts King Dave. We all have different versions of the Book of Groges, but having had a brief look in the past, we think that the overall philosophy is the same so we should be able to help." The rest all nodded in agreement.

The Sou-pa representative then added, "Is this acceptable?"

Felixx, sitting under the table, gave me a nudge and I said "Yes, thank you all very much". I went to say more but he nudged me again, so I shut up. Sandels looked at the other leaders and they all said "Yes" in turn. Everyone nodded gravely again and Sandels thanked them all for coming before they faded out. And that was it – nothing more, nothing less, with me wishing that our lawyers' meetings could be so quick.

Once we were again by ourselves, I asked what would happen next and Sandels just said that he would arrange what had been agreed. It didn't seem to me that much has happened but given the risk of again making a fool of myself, I just said 'thank you' to him and left it at that.

I was about to get up and get a coffee or something, when Felixx came back up on to the table and Sandels indicated that I should stay put. Given the walls were still in place, I really had no option so I did.

"Sir, we also think you should seek an audience with Aitchnee."

Felixx nodded this time, gravely I might add. There was silence, during which I was clearly supposed to say something but as usual, was floundering badly.

"Sorry guys, but what's Aitchnee?"

This was followed by suitably disgusted looks.

"You didn't read the book at all, did you Davie." This was

Felixx making me feel even smaller, if it was at all possible. I just shrugged and as King, thought 'so what'. He clearly saw what I was thinking though and while not too happy, went on.

"Look, in Chapter ten, the one about dealing with changes, it says that in extreme situations, you can ask for an audience with the territory seer. It gives details of each of them, including Aitchnee, who is ours, and also how to approach them, address them and also the likely cost. The cost is the bit Sandels and I were weighing up but we think it's worth it. For a King to get an audience with Aitchnee, it'll cost about three months of dust supplies, but we have that and more in stock so we think, on balance, we should go ahead and arrange it. We've put it past the Heads and they agreed, but given the state they were in about Raychell, they'd probably have said yes to anything."

"Why does it cost so much?"

"Well," this was Sandels, "it's very rare that anyone needs her help and she's also immortal so when someone does go, she has to come out of a deep hibernation type sleep that takes a lot of energy. Afterwards, there's the same amount expended going back to sleep safely for the next time. It's also graded on how important the visitor is and I'm afraid a King is top of the list and is therefore the most expensive."

Felixx carried on. "We checked if it was going to be cost effective with your new pal Kelpy and she gave us the nod – she's had a word with the dust diggers and says that with the new methods that Snouques was working on recently, we should be fine. She was also getting like everyone else is – do whatever it takes to sort the Fs out once and for all."

"But what'll this Aitchnee add," I asked.

"According to her website, she should be able to shortcut the work of the labichens quite considerably," said Sandels, without even a hint of irony or anything else. "We should also be aware that if Raychell doesn't come up with the goods, Arverlang will probably try his seer as well, although he'll almost certainly bankrupt the Canooque-F's dust supplies in doing so."

"Ok, let's do it," I said, in as regal a manner as possible, but really having no other option that I could think of or, to be honest, not having any idea what I was agreeing to.

And so it was to be. The plan was to visit Aitchnee when the battle with the Sou-pa was taking place. Hopefully this would give us the cover needed to ensure that Arverlang didn't get wind of what was going on. I asked where I'd meet the seer and was told 'Fyrish' as if I knew where this was.

Again, the cat took great delight in informing me of my poor judgement in not reading the whole of The Book but in the end gave me the details. Apparently, it was close to the north of the Great Glen near the Loch Ness mines, had some sort of big stone pillars on it and was one of the most sacred places in all of the OutFax. I asked if it would be appropriate for Snouques to escort me there as she had managed to get me to the mines and back and Sandels thought that it would be OK. As you might have worked out, I really just wanted another crack at flying, which apparently even Felixx still didn't know that I could now do.

The battle was set to start the next day and the required 24 hours notice was given to Aitchnee's people to get her awake, and that was about us for the day. By now it was lunchtime and after I'd had a quick bite, I decided to try to work with the labichens to see if we could make any headway. Over the next few hours, we sat down and went through the relevant lines one by one as I was hoping that it might also help me with the audience with the seer the next day.

So, back to the paragraph in question:

This may occur when the pentagonal balance of the territories of Fairyland is disturbed and one or more territories gain a power advantage over the others. OK, this must be the fact that

Arverlang was a dictator nutcase and it had somehow affected a balance or other – this made sense when it made the other territories upset as well.

This power shift can lead to circumstances in which what would be normal exercisional behaviour can actually kill, without the possibility of a dust resurrection. We knew this to be the case.

It is recognised that the cause of this is the creation of a triple vortex impact of force. We'd repeatedly looked for three arrows, or a combination of arrows and daggers or even a random stone or stick but everything pointed to there only being two hits when Naluke died. The post mortem backed this up – one on his ribs and one directly to his heart.

with a subset of balanced projectile trajectories combined with concurrent impact orchestrations, Again, yes there had been two hits which we took to be the 'balanced projectiles' but we knew all about them and this added nothing.

into the lateral subjugation of the victim's postural and energy receptor acceptance. Even the best of the labichens had no idea what this was about and needless to say, neither did I. I mean, was he standing up and facing the sun – no. Was he sitting down in front of a fire or eating food – no. Was he going in the opposite direction to everyone else – no. Was he overcome, yes in a sense but how was it related to the rest. The other issue was that plenty other warriors had seemingly been in exactly the same way as Naluke had been and they survived.

So where we were at was that we were missing a hit (there were two that we could see and not the predicted three) and lateral subjugations/energy receptors were proving difficult, putting it mildly. I guess I just had to ask Aitchnee what it all meant - at the cost of a lot of dust. To properly prepare, I went off for an early night and once again just before I nodded off, I enjoyed watching Hayley set Fairyland up for the battle the next day in the night sky.

I hung around in the war room the following morning to say a few words of encouragement to those that were about to battle the Sou-pa. Again, it was a TV spectacular, taking place on Miami Beach and the audiences were in the millions. There had even been a new soundtrack written which was a more melodic form of dance music, but still with an underlying bass beat to get the warriors going. The battle was quickly in its full flow first phase and a good couple of hours away from the initial bout so when Snouques poked her head into the war room and winked at me, I was good to go. Aitchnee, here we come.

Sandel's squeaked, "Good Luck, Sir," and quietly tapped his staff. The cat was nowhere to be seen.

I asked Snouques about how to deliver the dust payment. I mean, knew I could fly but I didn't fancy hauling bags of dust through the air as well. It transpired, though, that there was a ready built tunnel from the Loch Ness mines through to Fyrish that had been used when the previous King had paid to see Aitchnee. Kelpy had informed us that in the past, Aitchnee's people had just called off the supplies as she needed them, hence this was why the tunnel was still in existence. So, other than a pretty significant down payment that had been transported north overnight, the rest would be delivered as and when she required it.

So, once more Snouques and I went out to the top of the hill, this time to a bright sunny day. We snuck away on the canal boats again and then took the same flight path to the Great Glen. We ducked in over the power station and by way of support, Kelpy came up for one of her rare surface breaking appearances on Loch Ness, which would no doubt be on lochnesssightings.com by tonight. I'm pretty sure I saw Starr with a pair of binoculars nodding as well, but I'm not sure.

We then made pretty good time heading north east, landing

at a small car parking area in the trees near the bottom of Fyrish hill. Snouques explained to me that we couldn't land directly on the hill, due to its revered status and also because, by way of ritual, we had to make our way through the Fairy Gate to be able to see Aitchnee. The trek to the top, which was actually part of a network of forest walks in the area, involved a mile long walk and a 1000 foot climb, which to an unfit me was bad enough, but when you're on 18" tall, takes at least twice as long. Already, I wasn't looking forward to it at all.

"Is there no other way up?" I asked as we set off into the trees that surrounded the hill.

"No, King Dave, this is it. It's part ritual like paying homage and also, there's all sorts of protections in the air around Fyrish to stop people like you and me flying in unannounced."

"But surely as King, there'd be an exception made?"

"Unfortunately not, we'll just have to walk it."

So we carried on into the woods, crossing a river on an old wooden bridge and then started on the seriously steep bit that took us to the gate we had to go through.

The 'Fairy Gate', which made me think of gold and diamonds and big fancy columns etc, was in fact a gap that had formed under a tree that had fallen down over the path a bit of the way up the hill. True enough, we could pass underneath and Humans wouldn't be small enough, but I have to say that it was pretty underwhelming.

As we climbed, the trees thinned out and the pathway started to plateau out on to a more level footing. Taking a break at my insistence, we stopped off at a small lake that was further up on the left near where the hill flattened out on top. The views were fantastic and went nearly as far as the mines at Loch Ness and as we sat catching our breath, I lay back against a tree and looked to the skies.

"So how come you can fly and the others can't?" I asked Snouques

"It comes at birth King Dave. When a Fairy is born, it's checked to see if there are shoulder blades and if there are, then it's automatically allocated to our Diven. The others who can't fly don't have shoulder blades and therefore will never have wings. While they are kids, those with the blades can stay with their family even if they are in another Diven but when they come of age, it's over to us."

"And is there any pattern to this?"

"No, there isn't and likewise, some of our flying Fairies have kids that can't fly. It's just the way it's always been and everyone accepts it."

"And what about yourself – how did you become the Head of the Diven." I was asking these questions mainly in a bid to sit a while longer so that I could recover from the climb.

"It's a long process but effectively you're born into it. At first, future heads don't know what's in store for them but when an existing head dies or retires then the next one is just magically installed, whether they like it or not. It's a process known as the new Head 'bekumingaparunt' and it's all explained in the Book of Groges."

"So you didn't have any inkling beforehand?"

"Not really. I think there are a few sort of heirs apparent who are tested out in secret during their lives up to that point so like in any society or government structure, there are people who rise above others in the pecking order and it's generally one of them that becomes the new Head. I suppose it's Yandermoo that makes the final decision and the process is the same in each Diven."

I thought that the mention of Yandermoo was a good place to stop and anyway, I could see that she was getting set to move on again. So, with Snouques keeping the pressure on, we left the last of the tress behind and carried on across the heather covered flat top of the hill. There were also human people there as well passing us on both directions, but they seemed to be in some sort of parallel universe and were, as usual, unable to see us.

I still couldn't get my head around the fact that when I went back, I'd only have been away for microseconds when here and now, the world was obviously still carrying on as normal, but like trying to work out why the universe exists, I'd long ago decided that it wasn't worth the hassle and inevitable headache.

As we approached the top, a light mist descended on the hill, so when we arrived at the big stone pillars (which I was told were called the 'Gates of India' in the human world for some mad reason, given they were thousands of miles away from anywhere in India), there was a suitably ethereal quality to the whole experience. Snouques said that by tradition, she had to stay away from the actual audience so went and hid behind the pillars. Before she disappeared, though, I was directed to some guardian Fairies who had come out of the mist and took me away towards the actual summit. We stopped at a big, flat stone and waited. One of the guardians said:

"Welcome to Catked's stone. Your audience will commence shortly."

I was a bit confused, after all I thought it was Aitchnee I was meeting, not some lost Queen but having learned some protocol in this world, I kept my mouth shut.

And then she appeared, apparently from no-where, just sitting on the stone. With long blonde hair and dressed entirely in white, she had under her arm a picnic basket, the contents of which were now spread out on a tablecloth in front of the stone. In a very pleasant Scottish Highland lilt, she said in a fairly normal tone, "Welcome, King Dave, would you join me for some lunch?"

Given this was costing buckets of Fairy dust, I just said yes and sat where she indicated. We then had the sort of conversation, aided nicely by a glass of Fairy Wyne I might add, that you have with an old friend that you're catching up with after a long break. She asked how things were going, I gave her the history of why I was here, Naluke's death and Arverlang's capture of Raychell and she just asked some fairly innocuous questions along the way. We were on to some tea and shortbread when she brought matters to a head.

"OK, King Dave, I know this is costing a bit but a seer's got to live and I have to be able to guide those who come by my place as best I can. What do you need help with?"

I pulled out a copy of the notes that I'd made from the last meeting with the labichens which were pretty much as I'd written above.

"I need to know what this all means, Aitchnee. As you'll see, we haven't made any headway at all as there are definite contradictions and not putting too fine a point on it, I'm led to understand that the whole future of Fairyland depends on me working out why Naluke was killed."

She didn't reply. At the same time, I reflected on what I'd just said, and seeing some lost humans wandering about in the mist, once more questioned my sanity.

Aitchnee brought me back, though, as a guardian appeared with a notebook and pen beside me:

"You may want to write this down, King Dave," she said "You will have to look to the heart and when coopid's arrow doubles up and causes the inevitable pain as it hits both its targets at once, you'll again find the path to long and fulfilling lives."

And with that, she faded away - along with the full lunch ensemble and all her guardians. I was left in the mist, all alone with a message that meant nothing to me and Snouques shouting from behind:

"Can we go now, please, it's freezing?"

So, with no other better plan, we made our way back down to

the car park. At least the mist lifted and the sun came out, but I was truly none the wiser. On the way down, I asked Snouques why it was called Catked's stone and not Aitchnee's to which she said it was because Catked had placed it there so that she and her King D'avud could enjoy the view when Aitchnee was asleep. Maybe I shouldn't have asked after all.

We made it back to the war room by late afternoon by which time the battle was in its latter stages. It was less a battle than a celebration but both sides had emulated what appeared on the video feeds to be the cause of Naluke's demise. As promised, this had been done to make it look like we were trying out various theories and also, with the Sou-pa doing the same, make it look like all of Fairyland was joining in. I didn't know if it would work at all but I hoped that it would buy us more time as I didn't trust Arverlang at all. The battle then wound down, having comprised three bouts but with the usual unfathomable Fairyland way of scoring, it was a draw. I did a brief 'thank you' to both sets of warriors and Mydaxxa did the same for the other side and after some chill out music from the DJ, that was it. I was really tired from the day's exertions and went off to lie down to mull over Aitchnee's message. As I nodded off, wondering if it was 'coopid' or 'cupid?' I still had no idea.

Back in Canada, Arverlang had moved south again to his Ontario base. He'd taken Raychell with him and was deeply unhappy when she tried over and over again to say that she had no idea what the book said. She also explained that the best labichens in the OutFax had looked at it and they had no idea either.

He didn't buy this at all. After all, he'd seen the moves in OutFax/Sou-pa battle and was convinced they were both on to something. He'd also heard rumours that there had been an all-Fairyland meeting which just added to his paranoia. He decided to feed some drugs to Raychell in a bid to find out more.

As she went under the influence, inside her head she said over and over again to herself 'Naluke's ghost', 'Naluke's ghost', 'Naluke's ghost', 'Naluke's ghost'. She finally floated away. Having been told by his minc-lings that she'd been given a truth serum (they were now at the stage of basically telling him what he wanted to hear) when under the influence, she read the passage from the book and with her plan working, ended every sentence with an involuntary 'Naluke's ghost'. Arverlang just became even more paranoid.

Not knowing what else to do, and giving up on the book, he got his henchmen together and planned another attack, this time near the Big Sur. If he couldn't outwit them through reading the book, he'd surely get the OutFax and their dust this time, given most of their warriors were in Europe and not the West Coast USA.

25.

I was again surprised to wake up in Fairyland the next day. As each day passed, I was becoming more accepting of the whole situation but at the same time, I couldn't work out whether this was a good thing or not. Today's job, however, was to add Aitchnee's advice to that in The Book and see if the labichens and others could make any more sense of it. After breakfast and a sports review type of chat with P.S. about yesterday's battle, I trotted off to the conference room to join the debate.

The seer's comments had just added another layer of confusion. There was a heated discussion going on about cupid v coopid in one corner and the main believers had moved on to a more philosophical discussion about long and fulfilling lives. Some labichens from the other territories had also arrived as promised and if anything, appeared to have confused matters even more. Nothing appeared to be getting anywhere, which was confirmed by Struugs.

"I really don't know, King Dave," he said, "in the past, the seer's always been very accurate but this time, we're not so sure. Are you absolutely convinced that this is what she said."

"Yes," I answered, "I even asked her to clarify the spelling, which she did, so what's written down is what she said. If it's any help, I have about as much idea as you have and I was the one who met with her."

He shook his head and went back to the groups where it was like a political debate gone mad. I left and went back through to the bar for a cup of tea. Felixx and Sandels came to join me.

"If you would be so good as to come and join us at the dining table, Sir," was how the next glorious phase of my illness/dream/nightmare began.

Back at the table, it was down to business right away.

"We've got a problem, Davie, the sharks are telling us that a massive force of Fs are heading south from around Vancouver. They've hitched a lift on an oil tanker that was coming south from Alaska, clearly in the hope that we'd miss them. As you know, the sharks and I have never really got on, but in this case, one of them was sniffing around Vancouver Island looking for some dinner and happened across the boarding sequence, so I suppose it's fair play to them for once."

He really didn't like giving ground at all, did he?

"Yes, Sir, we'll have to mobilise quickly – we're assuming that he's going for the mines at the Big Sur."

This truly was turning into a nightmare. I mean, here I was apparently again leading a whole people into another war when all along, my life was set up to be an office clerk and a Dad. So I wearily said:

"OK, let's get the team back together."

An hour later, Del, Jonnie, Hoopik and Snouques joined the cat, Sandels and me at the table. The walls came down, went opaque and once more, the dining area became the situation room. This was all too familiar and I said as much.

"Look folks, to be honest, I'm getting sick of all of this. We're getting nowhere fast with The Book, Raychell's still with the Fs and now they're at it again. Why?"

"We can only assume, Sir, that they're running really low on dust," came the squeaky explanation, "We know that Arverlang hasn't gone to his seer, which he would have done if he could, so it's likely to be that this is one big push at trying to get to our dust mines. Unfortunately, we've got to fight for real again."

We decided to call in all the help that we could and as a result, Jim, Shona and Hayley also joined the fray. The rest of the day was spent planning what to do. We also informed the other territories of what we thought was happening in the hope they might join us, but as I suspected, global politics in Fairyland were the same as elsewhere so they all elected to sit on the fence at present.

So it was the OutFax Territory v Canooque-F Territory, Major Offensives of the 21st Century, Round two, the Battle for the Pacific. (This was actually the title of the bestselling book that was later written about the tactics and methods we eventually use. You'll understand that it was clearly written by an academic author).

Even before the end of the day, the winged warrior battalions had made it to the Big Sur and were camped out around the mines. Jim had left early to get the RV to the California coast where there were at least plenty RV parks and surfing camp sites to park it up in. We estimated that it would be two days before the Fs would be fully in position, which would allow us to all make it out west and be ready for whatever came next.

This time round, Jonnie and I would take up seats in the Mobicom-C command room and Del and Sandels would do likewise in the war room back at the hill. Snouques and Hoopik would meet us in the RV but would be on the ground with the warriors, wherever the battle would eventually take place. Felixx? He'd no doubt be somewhere around, telling me what to do, although he'd already left with Jim. Much as we could also have done with Ded-i and Struugs on the ground, I reluctantly agreed that they could stay and keep the big debate going and finally, with Hayley out doing a galactic reconnaissance job and Shona acting as the Chief Operating Officer at the Hill, we were as set as we'd ever be.

Sandels then turned the situation room back into a dining area and those of us who were left had a working dinner which I just hoped it wasn't the Fairyland equivalent of the Last Supper. Afterwards, Hoopik said:

"I'll see you at my Pismo beach restaurant portal."

And Snouques added, "I'll see you at the tree."

Not having a clue what this meant I just nodded, this time to no-one in particular, as they headed off.

Soon after, it was just Sandels and me left.

"Thank you, Sandels, for all your help," I said, looking down the table to him sitting at the other end.

"It's been a pleasure, Sir. I have to say, a bit like Felixx , although I'm not always happy agreeing with your cat, when you arrived and the first thing you did was wet your trousers, I wondered if you were up to the job. However, it's been a real pleasure watching you grow into the role. I remember the last King – he was a bit like you when he arrived but over time, he became a truly brilliant leader. I think Catked might have had a lot to do with it, though, so I'd say that given your wife can't join you here and you're doing this alone, it's job well done so far."

"Well, we'll see what everyone thinks after this next battle, won't we," I replied, "a bit like a football manager, I think I'm only as good as our next battle."

This time, it was he who just nodded.

The RPD then arrived, saying that my transport to the RV was sorted and would I like to come with them. I did a quick once around in the War Room, chatting briefly to the Noogmas, sharks and Del before sorting out Shona in the Fairy Lounge which had been turned into an ops room, with all sorts of comms kit linking everyone up. Bidding farewell to P.S. and his staff, I grabbed my bags (I still wasn't entirely comfortable with the whole servants thing) and followed the RPD to the Tomna Hill station.

26.

Within two hours, I was unpacking in my room in the RV, which Jim had parked up for the night just to the north of the Golden Gate Bridge in Northern California. As I went to bed, I asked why we were so far north but he just said it was because we were picking up Snouques and offered no other explanation. Jonnie and Felixx nodded in agreement so I just went to sleep.

We were pretty sure that we still had 24 hours' grace but even then, it called for an early start the next day. Jim (with his wife in tow again) drove the RV to the nearby Muir Woods National Monument and given we were early, managed to park close to the Visitor Centre - we were also lucky as our RV was just under the 35 feet limit that the National Parks Service had set for the surrounding roads.

Felixx and I jumped out of the RV and once again following his instructions, headed off up the main trail to Pinchot Grove, breathing in the clear sweet air as the sun rose on the massive trees in the valley. He did a quick check of a map he had, and we took a right up some steps onto the Ocean View Trail path. A little further on we came to the second large tree on the left and lo and behold, it had what could only be described as a proper Fairy door in it. As we looked around, Snouques magically appeared from the tree, gave me a hug and the cat a high five. I now understood why she'd said she's see us at the tree.

"Thanks for coming to get me King Dave," she said bending over to pick something up from the forest floor, "here you go, this'll bring you good luck."

She handed me a four leafed clover.

"You see King Dave, if you come here as a human and find a four leafed clover, it shows that you're probably a Haferlinc."

With that, she winked at Felixx and me, and skipped off down the path towards the car park. We were soon all back in the RV and shortly afterwards with Jim in charge, we were driving back over the Golden Gate, heading for the Big Sur. It still was only 9.30am.

About an hour later as we were heading steadily south, and had by now made our way on to Highway One which took us along the Big Sur, I popped up to the cab and asked Jim where exactly we were going.

"We'll be heading south to the San Luis Obispo County line," he said. "We'll be there by the mid-afternoon"

"And what happens then?"

"There's a little parking area right on the county line, just before a property that's numbered 20001. We'll pull in there and Snouques will take you up into the hills for a quick look at the Big Sur mines. At the same time, it'll give Jonnie and Felixx a chance to check on the progress of the Fs. After that, we're heading on south to Pismo Beach."

None of this made any sense to me so, given Jim's wife had headed back with the others to make some lunch, I just stayed up front in the passenger seat and enjoyed the view. I now see why people try to do this route at least once in their lives – bright sunshine, spectacular scenery and at times a challenging drive, all makes for great fun. If you're a surfer and like the idea of life on the beach in an old VW camper, then this is also seems to be the place for you.

I also lost count of the number of open top Ford Mustang rentals and Harley Davidson bikes that we passed as it seemed that these were the default transport on this particular highway. It was also quite interesting from a Fairyland point of view as, given most of the drive was along the side of big cliffs, I could see that it would be quite difficult to mount a seaborne attack on the mines here.

When we arrived at the county line, we pulled over as discussed and Snouques took me outside into the sun.

"OK, King Dave, let's walk away from the RV down towards 20001- that way, we can nip off the road and you can get your wings out."

This was what we did and about ten minutes later, I was looking up the length of the Big Sur from 5000 feet up. Wow, what a view. I then followed her about a half mile inland to an innocuous looking hill where we landed, walked over to an equally unassuming rock and found ourselves morphed through the hillside and into another reception area, almost identical to the one at Loch Ness.

It was the same as the last time: Fresh paint, a big line up of staff and this time, a truly great Californian buffet lunch. I also dug some dust out with the guys and having practiced over in Scotland, made a much better job at it. Then, like the Loch Ness Monster, I had a brief introduction to Tahoe Tessie, Kelpy's cousin and guardian of the West Coast dust. I discovered her name came from the fact that when things got a bit hot in the California summers, she went off to Lake Tahoe for a cooling dip, causing Loch Ness type sightings there. After all the necessary goodbyes and thank yous, we found ourselves back in the RV in the late afternoon, heading for Pismo Beach. This, apparently, was where we would find Hoopik.

On the journey south, Jim and his wife reclaimed the front seats and Jonnie, Felixx and I fired up the command room for an update. First up from the hill was Shona with a five minute briefing .

"Hi David, here's where we are. The guys took a guess that any battle would be at Oceano Dunes just south of Pismo beach because it's been used before. There's about five miles of beach to play with and the bonus is that Jim can drive the RV right on to the sand. The sharks have just an hour ago confirmed that this is indeed the case with Arverlang's warrior divisions streaming off the tanker as it passed by the beach. They've made it onto land and are setting themselves up near the refinery end.

She carried on, "We've held back, letting them think that it'll all be a surprise but right now, Snouques's Winged Warriors have moved from the mines and are hidden in some RV storage yards behind the beach. The rest of our primary force are making their way to the station portal at Pismo as we speak. When you get to Pismo and pick up Hoopik, she'll arrange the move on to the Dunes. I'll pass you to Del."

"King Dave, while you were at the mines, we went through some likely manoeuvres with Sandels and Jonnie. The beach is a bit longer and narrower than Luskentyre and has dunes as well so it presents some opportunities, as well as other issues. We've got another force mobilised and by tomorrow, we'll be up to full strength so hopefully, it all go to plan."

"And the plan is?" I thought this was a reasonable question to ask.

"The plan is to once again put him back into the sea. We won't have the element of surprise this time with Snouques's flying warriors but we know that they've been unable to replicate the flying performance. You'd never believe it but the reason for this is that as they have no labichens, they've not been able to read the instructions for GPS units and therefore keep bumping off the shield if they try the moves. We also heard that Raychell has used the fact that he gave her drugs to pretend that she's now totally out of it and permanently brain damaged so cannot read anything – as an aside, she apparently also keeps mentioning something about a ghost which causes Arverlang to keep out of her way. We'll keep you up to date on the battle plans."

Then it was Hayley's turn to jump in as she appeared on the big screen.

"Hi all," she started, waving her torch around, "I've been out and about, and liaising with the sharks we reckon that we'll be about man for man in number terms with the army Arverlang has sent south. He's not full strength – there's talk of deserters and he's pretty much out of dust so is depleted anyway – so I'm hopeful that we'll be fine. Tonight, you'll see the night sky light up with all sorts of signals – although the other three territories won't send troops, they've allowed their equivalents to me to join up with us and spread the message of support for what we're doing. This should also add to the disillusionment that the ordinary people of the Canooque-F are feeling right now as they'll know something's up, but won't be able to read it as none of it will be in their galactic code. I'm off to charge my torch up, so to speak, so I'll catch you all later."

That was it and they faded into the ether once more. Snouques and Jonnie went off for a rest and apart from the RPD, Felixx and I were once more by ourselves.

"Felixx, I need to ask you a question."

He looked at me enquiringly.

"Well, I could ask lots but right now, but where does all our intel come from? I mean, throughout all of this, I keep hearing that we know what's going on with the other side – like we 'understand' that things will happen and then it all appears to be true – where's it coming from?

"Spies."

"Would you like to elaborate?"

"No."

"Why not?"

He said nothing. I didn't like this; after all if they'd made me King, surely I could ask this type of question and get an answer. With that and as was his want, he disappeared, and I was left pretty much by myself. The RPD guys were on their tablets doing only knows what, so not knowing what to do next, I lay back in one of the big leather command room chairs and shut my eyes. I was soon dreaming of sharks in my coffee mug, wands and flying Fairies.

"Pismo Beach guys," came the shout from Jim that woke me up. Snouques and Jonnie were back too and Felixx reappeared as I woke up. I headed back up to the cab.

I discovered that Pismo was a holiday resort like lots of others the world over. Motels, hotels, apartments, restaurants, hire companies and gift shops all fought each other for a good place to do business as close as possible to the big sandy beach that gave the town its name. After coming off the Highway, we headed along Cypress Street where Jim slowed up close to the Pismo Fish and Chips restaurant. As we did, I heard the little gas door open on the side of the RV and a couple of seconds later, Hoopik was with us in the Mobicom-C.

"Hi everyone. Jim, could you keep going along to Addie Street and then park up somewhere – I'll get the troops out when we get there. How were the mines, King Dave?"

We then duly had a chat about the mines and Tahoe Tessie while Jim found Addie Street and a parking place for the RV.

"Right King Dave, let's get you out on to a Californian beach – you haven't lived until you've had the warm sand under your feet."

So we went through the adjacent parking lot, over a wooden boardwalk and on to the sand. I ran about a bit, and like kids on a day out played Frisbee with Hoopik, and yes, the sand was warm, the sun still up and there was a very pleasant breeze coming off the Pacific. Right at that moment, I could see why lots of Americans had wanted to move out west through the years.

"OK, King Dave, enough fun."

Dammit, just when I was getting to enjoy myself too.

"Come on, let's meet the troops," and with that, she disappeared under the boardwalk with me following quickly behind.

In this portal, there was a massive holding area attached to the obligatory train station. To give you an idea, in relative terms it was probably bigger than Grand Central Station in New York and there were thousands of Fairy warriors lining up, with still more coming off trains. Hoopik led me to a little raised dais at one end where, when we got up on it, a hush fell over the crowd.

This time round, Hoopik did the warm up speech and I just nodded behind her. I'd waved at the crowd as we arrived and spoken to a few individuals but given I was still in a Frisbee frame of mind, I decided just to leave it to her. After she spoke, one of her field commanders took over and explained that as darkness fell, the move out to Oceano Dunes would start. We then bade our farewells at that point and I was delighted that there was a general mood of anticipation in the air. As we came back up under the boardwalk and out on to the beach, she said

"I think we're just about there, King Dave – it'll probably all kick off early afternoon tomorrow."

With that, we headed back to the Mobicom-C and Jim drove us out on the Dunes, where we parked up amongst a whole lot of other RVs. As before, they couldn't see us (although a few Californian dogs definitely could – Felixx stayed well indoors, I can tell you) and after getting more updates from the war room and some dinner, I headed out on to the beach to see if Hayley was right. She certainly was and the sky was ablaze with what up until then I thought was shooting stars, twinkling planets and the northern lights. It just shows how little us humans really know.

27

The following morning started with the sun rising and a briefing from Ded-i and Struugs. They also said that they'd managed to get Aitchnee's message to Raychell to see if it meant anything to her as Naluke's cousin. I was going to ask something about spies but thought better of it when my ever present (unless it suited it), mind reading pet cat narrowed its eyes and ever so slightly shook its head. So I just said 'well done'. It then licked its lips. I didn't know what this meant, so I hurriedly went on to other subjects. The upshot was, though, that we were still no further forward with the analysis of The Book. No surprise there then.

So it was back to the battle in hand, or 'round two' as it was now being called across Fairyland . Overnight, the big mess tent, field dust dispensing units (hospitals to you and me) and all the other paraphernalia of war had magically appeared on the beach by the dunes. It was the same on the Canooque-F side, with a clear 100 yard no man's land having been formed in between. It looked like we were ready to go and after some off line briefings, we all took our seats for round two.

"Are we really ready for this," I asked Jonnie when we were still offline.

"Yes, King Dave, I think we are. With Hoopik and Snouques actually out on the ground, we've got extra flexibility as they both know what they're doing, and they've been through the last battle in these seats, so will also be able to see the bigger picture. We're pretty sure that the Fs don't have the same capability."

We were then joined in our virtual world by Del and Sandels.

"Are you up for this, Sandels?" I asked. Not only was I worried in battle terms but I was also quite concerned for my squeaking confidante as after all, we'd effectively taken him out of retirement and put him in the front line again - and he's had his 'turn' the last time.

"Absolutely, Sir, I've had a blast of dust each day which has rejuvenated me and Del and I have been through a proper plan regarding where I can fit in with what they do."

"Excellent," I replied, "and one more thing - if it's OK with all of you, I'll just do what you tell me to on my screen."

Three nods of approval came back.

We then tested all our equipment. I was determined that we wouldn't fall foul of the same issues that created Arverlang's downfall the last time. After that, we just chatted and waited for our adversaries to appear.

Which they did about 15 minutes later. This time, there was no sign of Arverlang (no surprise there as far as we knew, he was hiding out under the playground). This time up, they had four in the seats, all of whom were battle hardened veterans and looked like it.

The gravity of the situation didn't stop the ceremony, though. We had the normal speeches, including one from me and then the music based dance off as well. Like the last time, there was an edge to proceedings with various random projectiles making it over the 100 yard buffer as the anticipation grew. We waited for the signal to start.

It came when three commercial refrigeration units fell in unison from the sky into no man's land.

I said, "Really?" to no-one in particular and off we went.

I have to say, the rest of the day was a bit of an anti-climax. There was a lot of nervous probing and attempts to gain tactical advantages and eventually, hours later, the first bout (a dagger only fight, but this time with two from each side in the ring) took place. The Fs won it by a whisker and promptly called it a day. One nil to them, then, but we all knew that this battle would be fought to the bitter end and the scoring on the way through was to all intents and purposes irrelevant. We all duly listened to a quick chill out set, had a brief chat with Del and Sandels back at the hill, wound the VR down and sat back in the command room to catch breath. Hoopik and Snouques came to join Jonnie and me. The cat appeared as well.

"It's not going anywhere," started Hoopik, "we're all just testing each other out."

"Yes," said Jonnie, "but whoever makes the first major move better know what they're doing as any weakness could be catastrophic. You and Snouques will have to keep the lid on some of our more volatile characters as any breaking ranks could also leave us weakened."

"It's OK Jonnie, I'm already on it." this was Snouques. "I'm flying around keeping the morale up but at the same time co-ordinating the various battalions. Hoopik is keeping our maniacs warmed up but under control."

"It seems different this time," I interjected.

"Yes," this was Jonnie again, "they honestly thought they could win the last time and were probably at the end of the day overconfident. It's clear that they're getting desperate – you can see this in their commanders' eyes at times – and desperate armies are unpredictable. They're also likely to be more fearless and they will no doubt take any chance they can to break with convention. In other words, the little trust there was has now well and truly disappeared out the window and we've got to be alert to any signals we get that they're on the move."

"We've got lots of night patrols, King Dave," added Snouques, "at the moment, I'm using the winged warriors only for surveillance and then, only at night. The hope is that this'll discourage them from any silly moves through the hours of darkness."

And with that, we headed to the mess tent for some grub with the troops. It was a funny atmosphere that was both boring and tense at the same time and I didn't really enjoy it at all. I left the rest to it and headed off to my bedroom.

I was missing my family again. I'd been away for days and although I was fully engaged in the whole king and wars thing, at times I wished that I was back doing the gardening on my day off, just waiting for the kids to come home from school. I dreamt of them all that night.

Day two dawned with the news that the Fs had tried an overnight move against us on the water side flank. It was nipped in the bud by the winged warriors and when the Fs realised that they had lost the element of surprise, their warriors all backed off. While expected, this was a complete no-no in the rule book and was being widely reported in news bulletins across all of Fairyland. I went on global TV just after breakfast to make a comment.

"We kind of expected this but it was always going to be unacceptable," I told their field reporter, "we will raise it in the normal way with their command team but unfortunately, I just see this as an example of the desperation that Canooque-F army must be facing right now. I actually feel for the ordinary people of the Canooque-F who by now are running out of dust and are having their daily lives ruined by a lunatic dictator. Understand, though, that no matter how many crazy moves they try, the OutFax will win in the end. I also want to make it make it clear, however, to the citizens of the Canooque-F territory, this is less about winning and more about freeing them from the oppression that they currently face."

I felt I was getting into the swing of being King and was walking away from the interview with the RPD in tow, quite happy with myself when Felixx appeared and said:

"We've a problem, Davie, let's go over here – quick."

He headed off to one of the many field latrine banks that, by necessity, followed the army around wherever it went. He must be caught short was what I was thinking.

When we reached the toilets the queue disappeared (I suppose being King does that) and to my surprise and I have to say mild annoyance, I was ushered into one of the stalls. With no other option I sat down as the cat jammed in as well, blinked, and then I was back home again. It seemed that my personal portal was of the bathroom variety, just great eh?

"What now," I said as the cat and I were once more in our hallway bathroom, "what's going on with you and what's the problem?"

"It's TJ. She's hurt her ankle and in about two minutes, Beth's going to call you to go and get her from school as it's your day off. Let's get to the kitchen."

We duly did and found Paws sitting up and wagging her tail. She said something in Spanish which Felixx said was her confirming the situation. It appeared that she did indeed keep an eye on things when I was gone.

Still confused and thinking of overnight manoeuvres, I didn't understand what was happening at all but I also couldn't get my head around the timing issues.

"Why does this matter, Felixx, when even if I was away for a month, it would be less than a second in the bathroom according to what you all told me before."

"It's not working right this time, Davie, and the best that Hayley can get is a minute per day. It's something to do with the number of interactions you're having with Humans this time round but other than that, like I said, it's best to just accept the situation. Given you were on a day off, ordinarily it wouldn't have mattered if you lost even an hour, but this TJ thing has mucked things up."

With that, the phone rang and I did my best to sound surprised, and then had to defend myself when Beth accused me of probably still lying in bed. If only she knew.

So I went and got TJ. She'd gone over her ankle in gym

lessons but it was just sprained and not broken. I took her to her grandparents as they had more experience in such matters than I did. They were delighted to help and she also saw the chance to be spoiled for the afternoon. I then headed back to the house where my cat and dog reception committee was waiting.

"Come on Davie, we have to get back. That was an hour and a half and the battle's about to restart. We managed to delay it because they'd acted up through the night but if you're not there in your seat when we start, it'll send all the wrong signals."

So with that, it was back to the bathroom where Felixx threw some dust over both of us and I was in seconds magically back in my en-suite in the Mobicom- C.

"How do you explain me making it here from the latrines," I asked the cat as I washed my hands out of habit.

"Easy, Davie, we told everyone that it was diversionary tactic to get you away quickly as we said we'd heard there was an assassination attempt coming. This also helped with delaying the start as the Fs were adamant that it wasn't them – I think they were trying to get some credibility back after last night. Anyway, let's go, the others are waiting."

I made it back on to my big seat with about 30 seconds to spare and as the F's commanders appeared, we were all once again hovering over the battlefield. I was still impressed by how this all came together and I briefly thought about TJ who would no doubt be setting down to an old X box console that her granddad had – I wondered what she'd think of her dad doing this.

28

The Fs guy started with

"We would like to apologise for last night's incursion. This was one of our field commanders taking matters into his own hands – it will not happen again."

I duly accepted his apology. I had no idea if this was the truth or not, but either way, they were obviously having to show some sort of contrition in the face of international condemnation.

Then the fridges dropped again and we were underway. We moved our command group view over towards the dunes and orchestrated a concentrated attack on one of their brigades that we knew had been up all night wandering the sands as sentries. At the same time, on the ground Hoopik and Snouques took up positions towards the water, looking for possible ways to attack on that side. Our tactics worked as within an hour, we'd defeated their dune brigade and were on to the first bout of the day. It was a wrestling style fight which gave us, still up on the virtual command platform, time to plan.

"I think we'll try to win a few bouts and go in ahead tonight." This was Del speaking from the Hill War Room. "You see, we're getting intel that the failed night time attack, combined with the outcry that the TV news has managed to create will by tomorrow cause them to try something really stupid out of desperation."

"We agree," This was Hoopik, "I actually tend to believe what their guy said about them having mavericks on the sea board flank. As you know, every so often they (and us) change up the next battalions to the front line as the previous one gets depleted or worn out. They're working on a rotation of five at the moment and the second lot are nutcases. They're trying all sorts of stupid things which so far we've been able to hold off but if they double up, which we've seen the do in the past, we could have a real fight on our hands"

Jonnie this time, "So, we go for two more bouts and try to win them. If we're there by late afternoon we'll be in the lead and I'll call it a day – everyone agreed."

We did and by putting our best wrestler on early (you wouldn't normally do this apparently and the Fs weren't expecting it) we won bout number one of the day in short order.

We were settling down to get going again when Felixx popped up in my virtual world.

"Hey Davie, we might be getting somewhere with The Book. The Mallbaste labichens said they had a similar issue a few centuries ago and they reckon the triple hit is the key. We also discovered that the F warrior who killed Naluke was nick-named 'Stoopid Coopid' due to his behaviour with women so that clears the spelling bit up. Struugs has taken the decision to now concentrate on the triple hit aspect – just thought I'd let you know....."

And with that, he faded away. The rest had heard this as well and again, although to you and me this decision wouldn't be exactly rocket science, in Fairyland such agreement was a major step forward and gave everyone a boost.

The Canooque-F command team reappeared and within minutes, were we all going full tilt again, this time hovering all around our side of the battlefield. I had very little to do except make the one off comments that came up on my screen, accept the bouts when offered and generally look like I was in charge. This allowed me to watch the others in action.

Del and Jonnie were very obviously a really experienced team. They split the battlefield into sections and had separate Noogmas deal with each. They could also almost second guess what the other was thinking so had a real grip on what the state of play was at any given time. As I've already said though, the scoring was beyond me and the battle was fought at lightning speed, so these guys definitely knew their stuff.

Added to that, Sandels's centuries of experience came into play exceptionally well this time. Now that he was up to speed on the technology and given that Jonnie and Del were back in charge, he could take a step back as it were, and just be an extra pair of super perceptive eyes. Twice, his interventions on how things were progressing got us big scores and it was this that got us to the next bout, just around lunchtime. This time it was swords and we gambled our best swordsman this time as well. I'm glad we did as they had done the same, so anything less from us would have been dicing with a loss. We won again, but this time by a tiny margin. We were in front, though, and Jonnie's plan was intact.

It was much the same throughout the afternoon and we came to bout three, pretty much as planned by Jonnie and Del. It was a dagger fight and we had a dilemma. We went offline as required.

"What do we do here?" said Del.

"Dunno," replied Jonnie, "We should really put our best guy in but we know their fella is better – he's possibly the best in all of Fairyland."

"I've an idea," interjected Snouques, "my winged guys have been practicing and one of them is pretty good. It's never been done before, I know, but we could have a flying dagger warrior in the ring. Hoopik and I worked on it last night with Sandels in case this came up and looking at past bouts, we're at more than 50:50 by our estimate."

Hoopik nodded in agreement.

"What do you think, Sir?"

What I thought was 'cheers, Sandels for putting this on to me' but in my head I could also see the cat making comments about being unable to step up to the plate, so I said:

"OK, if we're likely to be beaten anyway, let's do it."

And we did.

Let me explain in more detail how the bouts go. Although there was all the ceremony and music and whoever was winning called the bouts, the actual type was randomly picked by big blue eagles that appeared in the midst of it all. What this meant was that we didn't know what each bout was beforehand. The TV audiences loved it and furthermore, the only gambling that was allowed in Fairyland was on what type of bout each one would be and then who would win it. This was why there was always a delay in getting them going as the bookies needed time to accommodate all the betting and the TV people ramped the excitement up at the same time. By way of example on how hyped up this all was, the commercials aired just before the bouts, and then at the time outs, cost the equivalent of 'half time' air time at the Superbowl or World Cup in the human world.

There was also the warrior selection issue. As you'll have probably worked out, each side makes their own choice before finding out who the other side have selected, so there is a bit of guessing and gamesmanship there as well. Both participants have to be chosen and formally lodged with the eagles before any announcements can be made.

During the bouts, the time outs were for a maximum of five minutes at a time and only very limited amounts of dust were allowed to be used. In essence, this was to ensure while each of the warriors weren't able to benefit from a full treatment during time outs, there would be just enough dust to enable the bout to continue, giving the good people of Fairyland their money's worth.

You'll see from all of this that there were many arcane rules that had been developed over the centuries, but at the same time they had moved with the times, allowing technology to be used where possible. So at this juncture, we lodged the winged warrior's name with the eagles and waited. To be fair to the big blue birds, they did send a message back double checking our choice but we gave them the OK. The Fs then did the same and no surprise, it was their top guy. I had the pleasure of ringing the bell and calling the bout.

After they'd accepted and all the music and ceremonial stuff had started, we went back offline. Snouques and Hoopik had headed off to be part of the ringside support team and Del and Sandels were on a comfort break or something so it was just Jonnie and me.

"What do you think?" I asked.

"Might work", he said, "for all her nonsense, Snouques is a pretty experienced battle hand and Hoopik has worked really hard with all of our warriors on different tactics since Luskentyre. Remember, Hoopik has a point to prove as other than the winged brigade, most of the warriors are from the 'other' Diven."

"What'll the Fs do if we win this?"

"Dunno, but we'll immediately call it a day if we win, which we can do as we'll be ahead, so unless they do anything stupid or illegal, we'll get some breathing space until tomorrow. I don't think they'll try it on, though, as last night's illegal attack has made them look like idiots to the whole of Fairyland – Arverlang won't like that at all."

"And tomorrow?"

"We'll see King Dave, we'll see. I'll be on to it with Del and Sandels tonight so we should have a reasonable plan. Let's just see how this bout goes though."

The bout started and was actually quite funny for a bit. Our guy was physically much slighter than theirs (remember, Fairies are uniformly 18" tall, but they can be, and most definitely are, many shapes and sizes within that). This meant that his tactic was to run away from the other guy's dagger as much as possible, which caused much hilarity. In fact, what was really happening was that Snouques was trying to tire the other man out as normally in dagger fights, it was close up and personal and involved sort of wrestling hold stand offs that lasted for ages as they each tried to inch towards stabbing the other.

Our man did get nicked a couple of times by the opposing dagger which also allowed Snouques to call a couple of time outs, although medically they weren't necessary. As a result, she started back really quickly thus catching the others on the hop. After two legs of their guy running around after ours and all the attendant laughter, they then called a longer time out. This was going almost exactly as our side had predicted so it was with baited breath that I awaited the restart. We were gambling entirely on the fact that we thought the Fs didn't know that our guy could fly. We'd find out soon enough.

And it worked. Like the flying attack at Luskentyre, it was one of these rare moments when a plan falls into place beautifully. As they came back from the third time out, our man did four laps of the ring which caused the beginning of dizziness in their fighter. He then popped his wings out, went up in the air and flew straight down sticking the dagger in their man's head. By the rule book, a hilt deep stab to the head was a winning move and given he flew directly on to the F's head from about 100 feet up, this was achieved and we won the bout. Jonnie, as promised, called it a day and that was that for now. After the chill out ceremony, we once more convened in the Mobicom-C.

"Congratulations to all," I said, "As King, I am genuinely impressed at the foresight, work and tactical moves that were used. Tomorrow, I will bestow a battlefield honour on our new dagger man."

This was well received as you can imagine and we had a premature celebration. The cat though, back to its usual morose self, did say something about never counting chickens but I was just so happy I ignored it. It went away in the huff, proving to all that it really was just a normal pet cat at heart.

Day three started as before. The Heavenly Fridges descended and very heavy fighting ensued. Once more, Jonnie was proved right. The next bout, a wrestling one, was won by them but the intensity carried on afterwards. Hoopik came on the intercom, sounding like she was speaking to us from the set of Braveheart or something.

"King Dave, this is crazy."

"Why?" It all looked just like the usual carnage to me.

"You probably can't see it, but at hand to hand level, they're using every dirty and illegal tactic going. They're also using others as a shield so that the Noogmas and TV cameras aren't picking it up. This means that they're managing to hurt our side in a manner that they're off the field for at least two days. We're in danger of running out of our best trained warriors."

The problem we had was that, as I've already said, we had to ship our army into California at short notice. Not only were we behind the curve on numbers, although more were coming by the day, we also had a shortage of really good dust dispensers, hence injured warriors were taking longer to recover. Also, the sheer desperation or fear or whatever was by now driving the Fs gave them that little edge on the ground.

"OK, Hoopik, let's go to Flying Plus," instructed Del, confirmed by Jonnie.

"Moving to the formation now, confirming that it will be their second battalion that we'll hit," she replied.

This new tactic I'd heard about but not seen. After the winged warriors had their success at Luskentyre, Hoopik and Snouques had worked on the next big move, called Flying Plus. Essentially, it was part flying attack, part diversionary tactic. It worked like this:

Four winged battalions surrounded one of Hoopik's top archer battalions at the front line. The winged warriors then took to the air in a big circle, the hole in the middle being where the archers had been. The circle moved forward as one and attacked the other side's warriors who were below them. This meant, of course, that there was a similar sized group of opposition warriors to the archers on the other side who weren't being attacked by flying enemies (in this case, it would be the aforementioned 'nutcases'). Distracted by who to attack, bearing in mind that they were surrounded but their colleagues were engaging the flying warriors above them, they were then hit by multiple waves of arrows from the OutFax's archers, fired in over the circle of winged warriors. The intention was that as those surrounding the 'hole' saw all their comrades decimated by arrows, they too would be distracted, allowing the winged warriors to take them out as well. Everyone would then retreat to allow follow on attacks elsewhere on the front line.

We watched the formation taking place and then Hoopik said:

"Go, WW, GO!"

With Snouques taking the lead in the air this time, Hoopik waited to give the signal to her archers. The timing would be critical and would be called by Jonnie with his virtual view, working with Snouques in the air. This was deemed of such importance, I was told via my screen to count it in and give the command 'FP FIRE' when we reached zero.

The count started at 20 and erratically made its way down to five over a period of about two minutes as the winged warriors engaged the opposition under them. Jonnie then raised his hand, Snouques did the same and the numbers went red. The count went smoothly to zero.

"FP FIRE!" I shouted.

I don't think I've ever seen so many arrows fired at once and the Fs were to a man taken out. They also couldn't escape as they were unable to pass through the close quarter fighting that was taking place with the winged warriors around them so it was a little bit like shooting fish in a barrel.

But then we were all taken completely by surprise.

Klaxons went off everywhere and the whole battle scene went purple. I had no idea what was going on so mindful of possible feline rebukes, I did and said nothing. Everyone stopped. I mean stopped still, completely and absolutely.

I discovered that this was the equivalent of a 'kill' or 'total reset' button on a Smartphone or tablet. It could only be used in one circumstance and could only be done by whoever was in charge of each side in a battle. Incorrect usage meant immediate defeat and a ban from fighting for some undetermined period of time. It wasn't me who had done it so it must have been the Fs. Their leader broke the silence as everyone, and I mean everyone, bowed their heads – although I was clueless, they all knew what had happened.

"King Dave of the OutFax, I am deeply saddened to announce the irrevocable death of one of our warriors at the hand of your archer brigade. We will, as is now required, suspend all hostilities."

They faded away as we all went offline.

A bit lost, I was very happy when Felixx took me aside as we 'descended' once more into the command room.

"Let's go to your bedroom, Davie, and by the way, make it look like someone close to you has died."

Once in the room, he said:

"This is unprecedented, Davie. Two deaths in Fairyland in such a short time will send everyone nuts. You've got to completely step up to the mark this time and be a true king now and calm the people – you've seen what they're like at the best of times, they're like hysterical kids, so it's up to you to keep the peace I'm afraid. We'll also have to put a rocket up Struugs and Ded-i to see what's causing this. I'd never normally say this, Davie, but this is really serious."

I nearly wet myself again. I'd been getting totally into the battles and meeting Tessie and the like and was really enjoying all the glory that comes with winning. Now someone else had died and although they weren't from the OutFax, it was my direct command that had started the move that caused it. I genuinely felt sick to the core.

I went out to join the rest. To say the mood was sombre was an understatement.

"Get me the TV people, will you," I said to the RPD. They took off at high speed.

I followed them out of the RV with Jonnie and Felixx and we were joined en-route down on to the Oceano beach by a morose and defeated looking Snouques and Hoopik. There was an eerie silence across the whole area.

We made our way through ranks of silent warriors to the TV reporters' stand that I'd been interviewed at earlier. Everyone seemed stunned. For want of anything better to do, I shook hands with the reporter I'd spoken with in the past. The cat had nipped off somewhere as we went up to the TV people but he now reappeared and jumped up on a little platform in front of us.

"Ok, everyone, this is what we're going to do." This was Felixx at his best.

"I've sorted out that this channel will share a live broadcast with the other three main TV companies that work across the whole of Fairyland. Lots of people were already watching the battle so everyone will know what has happened, but a cross channel broadcast will reach anyone else who wasn't watching and get a consistent message across the land."

There was continued silence as he went on.

"If Arverlang was here, it would be a joint broadcast between him and King Dave, but we've been unable to contact him. Sandels has confirmed to me that protocol dictates that King

Dave should then broadcast by himself."

Never mind wetting myself, he was now setting me up to crap myself as well.

"What he's agreed to say," he went on, looking directly at me now, "is that he is deeply sorry etc. etc. and that while the battle is suspended, he'll call an all Fairyland summit in Arizona...."

This led to some gasps from some who could hear him but he went on:

".... to which Arverlang will be invited along with the heads of the other three territories will be invited. He will then, Blah de Blah, talk sensibly about really making an effort to find the reasons for the killing etc. And then sign off. It will be brief, conciliatory and to the point. Let's do it people."

And they did – everyone listened to the cat, would you believe. I took him aside as all the necessary setting up was done.

"OK, first, thank you for telling me what to say"

He actually purred.

"But what's with the gasps about Arizona – I mean, I understand that it can be hot and dry but I didn't get the shock they showed at all?"

"It's an effort to show how serious this all is, Davie. You'll be meeting in the Betatakin cliff dwellings at the Navajo National Monument near Kayenta in Arizona. I'll fill you in later, but if you thought that Fyrish was sacred, the Betatakin place is heaven on earth to this shower. The choice of venue will reinforce how important you think this is and will hopefully allow you to keep an elevated standing in Fairyland until this mess is over."

This seemed reasonable enough, so after dusting myself down and practising a few lines in my head, I went over to do the live broadcast. I was counted in, which just reminded of my own fatality inducing count, and then we were on air. I started:

"Good people of Fairyland, I am speaking to you today less as the King of the OutFax, but more as one of you. Many of you will know of the tragedy that occurred at Oceano Dunes earlier today, which has, I can assure you, truly saddened all of us gathered here at the beach. Firstly, I want to pass on my deepest condolences to the bereaved family of the stricken Canooque-F warrior. We, the OutFax nation, know more than most the personal and territory-wide effect such an event can cause and we extend our sympathy to the people of the Canooque-F at this difficult time. Moving forward, I am extending an invitation to each of the other four territory heads, including Arverlang, to meet at a summit at the cliff dwellings in the Navajo National Monument in Arizona."

I stopped momentarily for a pause and I could see from the gathered warriors around us that it had had the desired effect.

"I hope that we can all put any differences behind us to enable us to work together on behalf of the whole of Fairyland to finally decipher what has caused the death of two fine warriors in such a short period of time. You will be kept abreast of developments through the usual channels. May I bid you goodbye at this time, but also say that as a united global people, we will find the answer and move forward as one."

The crowd's reaction started with a few claps around the TV platform but then it grew in volume and spread across the battlefield and beyond. I just hoped that the applause meant that somehow, I'd given them a little bit of optimism at a difficult time.

I decided to stay in the RV rather than go back to the hill. I could undertake all the necessary functions of state just as well from California and it would be quicker getting to the cliff dwellings from here anyway. Back at the hill, Shona was in full charge and was sorting out the diplomacy issues and travel arrangements with her opposite numbers across the other four territories.

Sandels joined us in a virtual capacity and while Jonnie,

Hoopik and Snouques went out to speak to the field commanders, Felixx, Sandels and I got together.

"Will they all turn up to this meeting," I started with,

"Oh Yes, Sir, there is no way that they can miss this. If nothing else, their people would lose all respect for their leaders and here in Fairyland, that's career death in a manner of speaking."

"Arverlang too?"

"I'm pretty sure he'll come to his senses on this one," said Felixx, " after all, one of his own has now been killed, which I'm sure you'll understand is about as serious as it can get around here. If he doesn't come, I don't know what the outcome would be as for one to deliberately miss such a summit is unheard of."

"There's also the possible interaction with the Gods, Sir, which I'm led to believe you'll experience at the Navajo dwellings. I'm told that those who meet there can at times be introduced to Yandermoo. And it's only leaders that are allowed into the houses so I doubt Arverlang will miss a chance for such an opportunity."

This was turning into some experience indeed. First the Fairies, then I'm a King and now I might meet God. You can understand why I don't really speak about this too much when I'm back at home.

29

The meeting was set for two days hence. Each of the other leaders did similar broadcasts to me but there was an ominous silence from the Canooque-F. At Oceano, they'd just remained and did as we were doing, regrouping, but other than that, nothing. There was a wild rumour that Arverlang was dead but then pictures were released proving he wasn't. It was simply that he didn't seem to be playing ball but the assumption was that he would turn up at betatakin no matter what.

Needless to say, the TV cameras were ever present and there was a huge build up across the networks as the preparations were made to meet at the cliff houses. The dwellings in question were sometimes out of bounds to humans as well, given their archaeological importance and even then, it was only a few very fit hikers who took the ranger guided tours to see them when they were open. In other words, they were pretty much undisturbed. The buildings were actually adobe structures located under a massive rock overhang in a valley in the middle of land owned by the Navajo tribe. Maintained as a national monument, they were also pretty special to the native people as centuries ago they'd been abandoned as dwellings. The legend was that the people of the day had left about 700 years ago but were coming back, but no-one knew when. Visitors to the site could learn more at the obligatory visitor centre and then take a path to view the betatakin dwellings from across the canyon. This was as close as the general public got which made them perfect for a big Fairyland summit.

So it was like a pilgrimage as each of the leaders was televised making their way to the viewing area. As you can imagine, there was much pomp and ceremony with stops along the way for each of us. There was a little used station at the visitors' centre which led to a portal in the reconstructed adobe houses in the grounds.

I travelled there with Sandels as an elder of the community, the RPD as always now in tow and the cat to keep me right. Given the dwellings were located in the OutFax, I arrived first to greet the rest. Needless to say, the place again smelled of fresh paint and the staff all looked like they had just been given brand new uniforms. I disembarked from the train, did the line-up thing and then waited for whatever was to happen next.

"How do I welcome them?" I asked Sandels.

"We'll now stay on the station platform with the cave staff and the TV people. When each leader's train arrives, they will exit and come up to you. You should shake their left hand, give a small nod and accept any gift that they bring. They will then move off up to the visitors' centre where, when everyone has arrived, we'll have a press conference."

It seemed simple enough.

President Mallbaste was first to arrive. He was a jolly sort and brought me two camels. I received them graciously. Azyullch came next, with an entourage that you would expect from a queen. She gave me a transistor radio. Oh well. Then Mydaxxa came in on a gold train. He was pretty straightforward as well and presented me with a speedboat. Somehow, the RPD managed to take the camels, boat and radio away in a reasonably civilised manner. I never saw any of them again.

I then waited for Arverlang. To be honest, I wasn't looking forward to meeting him at all. His eyes gave me the heebies and his reputation went before him – he was a nasty piece of work. Then the word came that due to his rampant paranoia, he would make his way directly to the canyon. There was no mention on how this would be done so I didn't ask – at least if he acted up when he joined us, maybe this Yandermoo could sort him out if he was there.

With that, we all made our way to the press conference. Broadcast once more across the land, we all said the normal politically acceptable stuff that you would expect. We then made our way out on to the trail. Imagine the crowds that turn up for the Pope wherever he goes added to the annual Hajj at Mecca, and the triple them. There were thousands of Fairies lining the route as far as the eye could see, sitting on and in between all the scrub like trees that grow in that part of the high desert. You'll see that as a result, it was a long slow walk that we took in the desert heat. Finally, we arrived at the viewing platform, which thankfully had been kept clear of people. We got out first sight of the betatakin houses through binoculars that the Navajo folk had thoughtfully provided for tourists. They were at least half a mile away and 500 feet down on the other side of a valley with very steep sides. I turned to Felixx.

"Do we have to do some mountaineering now or, heaven forbid, join a ranger led tour?"

"No, you idiot, the transport will be here imminently."

"What is it, exactly."

"You'll see."

And with that, he walked off. Sandels was in deep conversation with one of President Mallbaste's people so I just sat down in the sun and waited.

Back in Ontario, under the playground, Arverlang was having a huge fight with his senior minc-ling advisors.

"I'm not going to meet with these halfwits," he said, "they're beneath me."

"But Sir, it's protocol."

"Stuff protocol, you moron – we'll attack the OutFax tonight when that clown Dayv is meeting with these other idiots in Arizona."

"But you can't do that, Sir."

"I think you'll find that, when you're locked up you fool, that I can do whatever I want."

With his eyes blazing yellow, he turned and went off to have a meeting with his henchmen.

Next door, Raychell was still locked up but unknown to Arverlang, she had been well looked after by the staff. They were gradually turning against him and were delighted to revolt a little bit where they could. They'd smuggled in the latest debates from Struugs and Ded-i and she's been working away on the problem. Luckily Arverlang now left her alone – it was all the chat about the ghost that had worked wonders as by chance, she'd stumbled across his Achilles heel which was that he was terrified by spirits.

The day before, the staff had managed to get Aitchnee's message to her as well. She now thought she had the answer and had asked for a postcard to write on. With this, she drew the following:

One arrow, like cupid's, but going through two hearts with a big rock following it.

And she addressed it to 'King Dave at 'Tomna Hill'. The staff, thinking it was some sort of hero worship thing she had going on, agreed to post it for her and that afternoon, as Arverlang *was plotting an ambush and the other leaders were awaiting his presence in Arizona, the postcard was dropped into the postal system and started on its journey to The Hill.*

#

30.

I was actually nodding off in the sun when it seemed to go a bit dark, like when a cloud passes by. When I opened my eyes thinking it how was this possible when it was a cloudless sky a minute ago, I discovered that it was in fact four huge phoenix birds carrying a vintage Rolls Royce on ropes underneath them – and they were heading straight for the viewing platform. Seriously?

"Here you go," said Felixx who had reappeared, "first class travel all the way to the buildings in the cliff."

"You've got to be kidding," was all I could muster, but as everyone else appeared to be in awe of the spectacle unravelling in front of them, I just decided to once more 'go with the flow'. All four of us leaders got into the car and we started our 'flight' over to the big cliff overhang. If this was how we got there, how on earth was Arverlang going to turn up, I thought.

We landed with a gentle bump and we all got out. The birds and car promptly took off again and we were right outside a 700 year old Indian house. None of us had ever been there before so we all looked around, and conscious that the eyes of Fairyland were no doubt on us, waved over to the other side – it was a long way away – and went into the house.

Inside, it was like a 21st Century doctor's surgery waiting room, all white and functional, brightly lit and with full air con. I almost laughed when I saw it but managed to contain myself, although I could see that the other three were equally bemused. There was a very pleasant lady, who looked to be of Navajo descent, behind a reception desk and I could see other Betatakin staff behind a glass partition working away doing office things.

"Welcome to the Navajo National Monument, Fairyland Division," she said.

We all nodded.

"There is a conference room to the right," she pointed to an open door through which we could see a modern table and chairs set up, "and a couple of breakout rooms to the left. Toilets are over there" more pointing "and we serve food through the back behind me. There's no overnight accommodation as no-one in 2000 years has ever needed it but if you need a facilitator, please let me know and I'll ask our office manager to help."

We all nodded silently again. She went on,

"Now, I understand we're waiting for Arverlang to join us. While we wait, coffee and Danishes are now being served in the dining room. Please follow me."

We did, and like a million meetings across the world, we sat with our coffees and traded gossip about how best to run territories and the like. The rest were very keen to hear first-hand what it was like to be a Haferlinc so I regaled them with the stories about appearing and disappearing via my bathroom, for example, and in general, the overall mood was fairly congenial. After about an hour, Mydaxxa said:

"Look guys, notwithstanding when Arverlang appears, let's get to it?"

"Ok," we all said in unison and we trotted off to the conference room. The lady who had welcomed us led everyone to their seats.

"Will you need a facilitator?"

No was the consensus, but we asked about comms links and TV feeds.

"Sorry guys, there's none of that here. We could do it of course, but it's not in keeping with the gravitas of the site and also, when you leave, you mustn't tell a soul what it's like in here – we've got to keep the mystique up as I'm sure you'll understand. I mean, we could have left it with bare floors and walls, like it was 700 years ago, but we wanted to make it as comfortable as possible so I hope you like it."

We all murmured assent and then she left us to get on with

it. About an hour in, she came back in with the first bombshell. With a knock at the door, she entered and said,

"Excuse me leaders, apologies for the interruption but our sources say that Arverlang has decided not to come. I've no more information and no other comments to pass on so I'll leave you to it."

"Does anyone else know?" asked President Mallbaste.

"Not yet, but it won't be long – you know what Fairyland's like," she said before leaving us to it.

This was a blow. We'd all hoped to sit and thrash it out in a manner that would mean that Arverlang would basically back off until we found the reasons for the killing and that also he hopefully agree to some sort of diplomatic solution to his ambitions. We'd naively thought that because he was running out of dust he'd come along and we'd be able to get his OK for all of this. How wrong we were.

So, given we now knew that he'd effectively got one over all of us, we quickly decided to add more effort to the Book analysis and the others agreed that, if he kicked off again at Oceano or anywhere else, they'd all send in troops if I asked. In other words, it wasn't just the OutFax he was facing now, it was the whole of Fairyland.

We had a light lunch, chatted to the staff and then the receptionist called up the phoenixes for the return journey. All four of us thanked our host and the staff very much and as we heard landing noises outside, we made our way back into the desert heat. As the car took us back across to the viewing platform, I had a real look around and saw the attraction of the place. It was isolated but easy to defend, although it was in the desert (and therefore had pretty good weather) the valley floor was lush with vegetation and had a good water supply. As we landed, I wondered why the locals had abandoned it all those years ago.

We had all agreed to remain silent until we made it back to the visitors' centre so we duly made another slow, hand waving journey back through the crowds, all the while ignoring questions about Arverlang. The second bombshell was awaiting us back at the press conference area.

"Psst, Davie..Davie.....DAVIE."

"Not now Felixx," I said from the side of my mouth as I walked along the last of the path to the centre, doing the royal wave and smile thing that I was getting so good at.

"But it's about Arverlang," he carried on in a loud whisper, "the word is that he's going to attack us again tonight."

"Give me a minute," I whispered back, as we all went to reconvene in the visitor centre, before facing the press.

The other territory heads had heard the news as well and it was very apparent that the press had too. I asked for five minutes to myself and got Jonnie up on the my tablet.

"What's the story?"

"Not good King Dave," he came back with, "it was Hayley that got an inkling then the sharks saw a couple of their flyers coming down the coast well out to sea. About 30 minutes later, their troops were all abuzz – well, some of them, as others are not happy about this at all."

"So what do we do – and what do I tell the press?"

"We'll have to prepare for the worst, King Dave, and get our guys ready to fight. The problem is that they're not too keen either as no-one else wants to die."

"Can we hold them off for a couple of days?"

"We can try, but like I said, it's not looking good. I was speaking to Del and the only hope is that given what we now know, he might hold off on trying anything stupid. Also, we took the chance in the break to get some more warriors here as well, so numbers wise we're OK. It's just the morale issue that's a worry."

"OK Jonnie, thank you for this – I'll speak to the other leaders and we'll see what we can do."

He then faded away into the ether.

"Felixx, what's the quickest way back to Pismo and Oceano Dunes?"

"The train, Davie – if we step on it, it'll only be a couple of hours."

"Right, get our train up to the platform – we're off as soon as this TV stuff is over with."

And with that, I headed off to again join my fellow leaders while Felixx found Sandels to get the train ready for departure.

We were pretty brief in the end. The whole Arverlang episode – first not turning up and then this attack plan – had put everyone on edge. I did get the others to (reluctantly it has to be said) agree in public to send us some warriors if we needed them. As there was now a true danger of death, they said they would call for volunteers only though. So that was the gist of the TV message – you've done it this time, Arverlang ,and we're going to join forces to push you back right to the top of Canada if we need to. They did also then ask for volunteers and then, after thanking them all offline, I headed off at speed for our train and then back to California.

31

The return journey went by in a flash as we talked through various scenarios with Shona, Del, Sandels and Jonnie on the way. I had a quick chat with Struugs who mentioned something about me getting fan mail from Raychell, which I just put down to Fairyland rambling - after all, amazingly to me it has to be said, my royal mailbag had grown almost exponentially with this sort of nonsense since the Luskentyre win. The cards all had drawings on them (they couldn't read so definitely couldn't write anything) and were quite frankly somewhat juvenile on the whole. I did think that maybe Arverlang's drugs had done something permanent to Raychell if she was sending me cards from captivity, but I gave it no more thought.

On the way, both Sandels and Felixx asked me about the cliff dwellings but I wouldn't discuss it at all. Sandels was particularly keen to see if I'd had a 'Yandermoo experience' to which I confirmed that I had not and he looked deeply disappointed. However, we were soon back at Pismo beach and shortly afterwards I was on a golf buggy heading to the RV. To say that matters were tense was an understatement. We gathered in the command room as the sun set over the Pacific. Hoopik and Snouques joined us as well.

"We've got major morale issues, King Dave," started Hoopik, "The warriors are really not happy about the chances of dying."

"And it's the same with my flying battalions," came Snouques, "as they can get much closer to the action, they're seeing the same issues."

"But the other side must be the same," I said.

"They are," said Jonnie, "but they've also got the whole fear factor – we're hearing that anyone who doesn't fight will be sent to the Arctic to scrape what little dust there is off the tundra for the rest of their lives, so they'll fight I think."

"How do you think we should play it, Del?"

"To be honest, until any other warriors get here from the other territories, we should just try to hold our ground and defend. I don't think many of our guys have the heart to attack full on right now. I'd hope that their field commanders go to exhibition mode – if they do, this would suit everyone but I also think that Arverlang would rumble it pretty quickly. For me, I'd defend for as long as possible but if any real maniacs start on their side, we should ask for volunteers to do a Flying Plus on them again."

We agreed that this would be the case and all went our separate ways to prepare for what could be a long night.

In the end it was a bit of a damp squib. Never mind the threats about tundra, it seemed that the Fs didn't have the heart to go full on again, and the chat was that they were saying that if he wanted them to fight, Arverlang could come and lead them himself. Overnight, a few loose arrows and rocks were traded but nothing of any substance happened and most of us even got some sleep.

The stand-off continued throughout the day next day which allowed me to properly speak to Ded-i and Struugs for most of the morning.

"Come on guys, you've got the best on the land with you now, surely there's something?"

Not the most regal of appeals but I was tiring of all of this and to be honest, just wanted to go home. The whole killing episode and then Arverlang not playing ball had made us all weary, and I was no exception. Being Fairies, they were of course a bit offended by my comment so Felixx jumped in.

"Ok, everyone, let's not let things get out of hand. Struugs, you've got to understand, your King here has gone through a lot and until a couple of months ago didn't know that any of this existed. And KING DAYV, please be a bit more sensitive, alright?"

We all calmed down and got to business. Sandels joined us while the rest were all keeping a wary eye on the Fs.

We were just going round and round in circles as usual and it was when we were having a break, I mentioned to Felixx and Sandels that in amongst all of this, it was also quite sad that Raychell was clearly not well as she was sending me love letters. They both looked at each other and said in unison.

"What?"

Struugs told them about the postcard.

"Get it now," said Sandels, who if it was possible managed to squeak and shout at the same time.

"NOW!" shouted Felixx and Struugs disappeared from the VR link. I asked what the panic was.

"For God's sake Davie, she wouldn't be sending you love letters, she's a labichen and they are specifically banned from sending anything frivolous, and posting love letters to you is definitely frivolous in my book."

"I didn't know," I said lamely, acutely aware that David the lawyers' clerk was clearly back in the fray.

"Never mind, he's back, Sir. Struugs, did you not think?"

"I'm really sorry King Dave," he said. "It never crossed my mind – when we were discussing her drug taking, I thought she'd just gone mad. I also didn't tell anyone else as I didn't want them to think badly of Raychell."

"It's OK, I didn't know either," I looked directly at the cat willing him to take me on. King Dave was returning.

"Right, take a copy of it and get send it here," ordered Sandels, and within minutes it was with us.

I took a look and said, "Why two hearts, the arrow didn't hit two people."

They all looked at me as if I was stupid.

"Well?"

"All Fairies have two hearts," said Sandels, "in fact, while you're here, you have two as well. Everyone knows this."

Apart from me that is. I felt my chest with both hands and sure enough, there were two distinct sources of heartbeat but as they worked in sync, ordinarily, you wouldn't know there were two separate beats.

"So, let me get this straight," I said, "what Raychell is saying is that she thinks the arrow hit both his hearts but if that's the case, why didn't the post mortem pick it up?"

"We looked and it definitely didn't hit both his hearts – it was stuck in one." This was Struugs, "The funny thing though is that in Raychell and Naluke's family, their hearts are both on one side, one in front of the other. This isn't uncommon, though – lots of the 'Other' Diven are like that."

"Ah ha," I said, "so the arrow must have gone through the first and nicked the second". There you go guys; King Dave solves the mystery of the third hit. Simple.

"No, it didn't, we checked," said Struugs, looking at me the way the cat normally did, "we thought that that was a bit obvious and it was the first thing we looked for. Anyway, the back and sides of a Fairy heart is like bone and an arrow won't go through it."

Back to square one then.

"But in the drawing she's also got the rock that hit him following on after the arrow," I said, "does that mean anything."

"Well, we're pretty sure that the sequence was arrow to the heart and at the same time the rock to the chest, breaking some ribs and puncturing his lung," replied Struugs, "but although this would kill a human, as we've established over and over, this is not nearly enough to kill a Fairy."

"Have you got pictures of the arrow?" I asked.

They did and there was what appeared to be the answer. You'll see that Raychell had put a few black spots on Naluke's second heart in her drawing. This turned out to be heart disease.

Now, the two heart thing is one of the reasons that the Fairies live so long; if one goes out of action for a while (you know, arrow blow, disease or even broken in a love tryst I was also told), the other takes over until the first repairs itself. In normal circumstances, Naluke's heart disease would not be relevant but from what I could see of the arrow, it looked like the rock had hit the arrow shaft square on at the feather end, before bouncing off and breaking his ribs. This jolted the already embedded arrow against the bone which thumped the diseased heart behind it. This was the extra hit and with the good heart already out of action, the thump was enough to stop his other, already weakened heart. This was my explanation and they couldn't see that it wasn't plausible. The only way was to check it against Aitchnee's proclamation.

"Does this mean another ton of dust and a trek back to Scotland?" I asked.

"No, Sir," said Sandels, again with that look that well and truly put me in my place, "you can hold the note you made – this is why they made you write it down – and as you do this, speak your explanation and any solution you've come up with out loud. If it's correct, the writing will turn green. It's part of what we paid for and saves the seer from being woken up so soon again."

"How many goes do we get at asking?"

"Two," came the answer in unison from all of them.

"After that, we have pay some more dust to get more chances." said Felixx.

After working out a solution, which Ded-i worked out mathematically was to put an arrow proof nameplate across the part of the chest where the hearts were, thus stopping arrows hitting the front of the organs, we were ready. So we got the original note, I held it and spoke through the explanation and solution and the colour didn't change. One chance was gone.

"And it seemed so good, Sir." He actually sounded genuinely disappointed.

There was something missing and it was annoying me like an itch that wouldn't go away. I went off for a walk round the troops to see if I could clear my head and also if it would come to me. I took a tablet in case they needed to get hold of me and headed off out with the RPD for company.

I had a coffee with some of our warriors in the big mess tent, caught up with Hoopik and checked on the dust dispensers. It was pretty clear that the word had got out that I'd blown one of my chances at settling the issue and everyone was feeling down. I ended up sitting on top of one of the dunes with only Hoopik for company. As she was there, I gave the RPD the OK to have some time off as I needed time to think.

"Don't worry King Dave, it'll come. I mean look at what you've done so far – beaten Arverlang off and also held the rest of Fairyland together against him. You should be proud." Hoopik was trying to cheer me up.

I appreciated her thoughts but I couldn't accept them fully – after all, the reason I was here was simply to find the cause of death, come up with a solution and then hopefully, if this was indeed some form of reality, go home.

"Let's look at the videos of Naluke's demise again," she said, "maybe something will show up."

I doubted it as we'd looked at them from every angle so many times already but with no better idea, I fired the tablet up and we had another look. As we were watching, the itch was scratched so as to speak. What was niggling me was the 'concurrent impact' bit. After all, if the arrow hit, then the rock hit it and then hit Naluke's ribs, this wasn't concurrent – it was three hits one after another. Even if the arrow was hit by the rock concurrently with going into the front heart, then the rock hitting the chest afterwards, no matter if it was micro seconds, it was two concurrent blows followed by a single hit thus not all three together.

I said this to Hoopik and with this in mind, looked again. And then we saw it. It was so fast and the camera angles were so random and shaky (remember, this footage came from Naluke's and others' helmet and body cams) we'd missed the cause. There were actually two rocks and unless you were looking, with one being ever so slightly smaller than the other, it was masked by the larger rock in most of the footage. We finally worked out that the second rock had hit the end of the arrow at exactly the same time as the other one hit his ribs. This was also exactly the same time as the arrow punctured his good heart. It looked like we had it.

As I still had the note in my pocket, I said to Hoopik, "Well?"

"Please let us be right, King Dave," was all she said, very quietly.

So, sitting all alone on a sand dune with my Hooligan friend whose issues had started all of this, I held the note in both hands, gave the explanation, then added Ded-i's nameplate solution and waited.

By some miracle, the writing turned green. I almost collapsed with relief. Hoopik was hugging me and crying all at the same time. Against all the odds, we'd done it, and most appropriately, it was Hoopik who was there with me when the result was achieved.

"Right," I said after a minute of lying back and looking to the skies, "no one must know the explanation, at least until we sort Arverlang out – OK?"

"Definitely," she said, with a grin a mile wide and also, for the first time in weeks, these little stars coming back into her eyes, along with a few spectacularly blue tears of joy.

"We'll get Ded-i on to making the nameplates for all those

with back to back hearts, and we'll show the green message to the world, but the explanation will be our secret. This means that it's us that has the advantage over the Fs now and, because I could really do with seeing my family again, I'm going to use it to try to sort them out once and for all."

"Agreed." she said.

And with that, we headed back to the RV with a spring in our step. I called the whole team together and when they were all there virtually or in person, I did a 'Tah, Rah' moment with the note. To say there was jubilation was an understatement – even Felixx was happy but then I remembered, maybe he wanted to go home too.

32

Afterwards, they all of course wanted to know the explanation, which I refused to reveal. Hoopik joined in by saying that she didn't know because after all, The Book had said that it would be the King that came up with it. She did wink at me when saying this though and I'm sure I saw the cat once again narrow its eyes when she did this, but I didn't care.

We formally disbanded the labichen room, Ded-i went off to design the nameplates and Snouques went away to get the right amount of dust to make them in short order. Struugs said that while the labichens were delighted to have been released, some were actually staying behind to debate what 'A Lyffes Jurnae' meant. I wished them well. He seemed delighted.

So, for the first time in ages, things were looking up in Fairyland. Once the nameplates were made and distributed (much dust was used to get a super quick result), I took to the TV to tell the world that we'd come up with a solution, it had been verified by our seer and that with this new knowledge, anyone who took us on should remember that as well as having the solution, we also knew the cause so they should maybe be a bit cautious when thinking about fighting us. This, as you will understand, was a direct attempt to get Arverlang to back down and hopefully surrender.

Unfortunately, I'd find out that it didn't work quite as well as I thought it would.

However, back at the beach the rest of the day was spent celebrating with our warriors and doing some more TV interviews. I was rapidly becoming the celebrity King and if I'm honest, I was enjoying the attention. I went to bed that night fully expecting to finally wake up the next day at home and excused from this whole 'experience' and then just head back to work, after doing the garden chores of course. As I nodded off,

I was just thinking that if the hallucinations ever came back, I'd just go to the doctor straight away the next time.

Unfortunately, I woke up the next day in the RV.

Dammit.

The cat was on my bed looking at me, shaking its head. I wanted to cry again.

"Up you get, Davie, there's work to do."

"But I thought that doing as the book said would be the end of it."

"No, you clown, Arverlang's still around, Raychell's not home yet, their warriors are still out there and if you were any decent sort of King, you'd see it through to the end. They love you Davie, God help us, and it would be bad form to bale on them so soon."

"Ok, let me get up," I said, with that weary feeling descending on me once more. When would this ever end?

So once more we all gathered in a virtual meeting. It was a bit like the morning after a really good party or celebration – everyone was feeling a bit deflated. Worse still, it appeared that the Fs hadn't got the message.

"So," I started, "Where do we go from here?"

"I think, Sir, that the only alternative is to take the fight to them."

Everyone else nodded.

"All our warriors now have Ded-i's name plates so we're ready to go." This was Snouques, who had worked through the night with her people and Ded-i to make this happen.

"OK, folks, once again, let's do it," I said, somewhat wearily.

And we did, although I sat this one out and let Del and Jonnie do their thing alone. We took another crack at the 'shock and awe' tactics that had worked so well at Luskentyre and after about an hour of them trying to hold out, we got the better of the Fs and, for want of a better word, they ran for it. I later found out that they had intended going anyway (well, most of the saner ones) but they'd been waiting for a suitable oil tanker ship to be heading north so that they could get a lift back home. As we drove them into the sea, our sharks made sure that they all got to a tanker when it appeared and by the end of the day, we'd won and Oceano Dunes was ours and ours alone. The dust mines of the Big Sur had joined those in the Great Glen in that they were once more safe from attack. We didn't celebrate that night because to be honest, it was more like relief.

33

The next day was the beginning of the clear up operation and, along with Jim and his wife, we bade farewell to Hoopik and Jonnie who were staying on to supervise the withdrawal. This left Snouques, Felixx, Sandels and me in the RV with Jim and his wife up front. We drove out of Pismo and on to the Pacific Coast Highway again, this time heading north. Sandels took to his bed as his age was catching up with him and it had been a hectic few days.

"Let him sleep it off, King Dave," said Snouques, "he'll sleep until we wake him up. I've asked Jim to get us up to Muir Woods again so that I can get back through the portal and when we get there, I'll rouse him and take him home to the hill."

"I might join him," said the cat, as it headed off to some corner or other to have a nap as well.

"Do you think that's it?" I asked Snouques as we were left alone. Even the RPD had agreed to a few days off so it was just Snouques and me.

"I don't know, King Dave, I mean, we've beaten Arverlang, found the cure and he's got the whole of the rest of Fairyland on his back but with nutters like him, you never know. I'm concerned about the land we lost in the Midwest so I suppose that if we were to finish things off, we'd take that back while we're ahead and try to depose him at the same time."

I said I'd give it some thought and we left it at that. Snouques also decided to have a rest, so I popped up front again and chewed the fat with Jim and his wife as we made our way north. As we'd left quite late, Jim pulled over for the night at one of the RV parks on the way up the Big Sur. Felixx and Sandels were still asleep so Snouques and I left the RV as darkness fell and went for a bit of flying. She showed me some more advanced manoeuvres and after a couple of hours, I felt I was getting the hang of the intricacies of having a pair of wings. We made it back just as Jim and his wife were heading to bed. We followed suit.

We made it in jig time back to Muir Woods the next morning. This time round, we decided that we'd all go back the Hill through the tree portal, convene at the Royal Mansion and then take it from there. So after packing my gear up again, waking Sandels and Felixx up and bidding Jim and his wife goodbye, we all went back into the woods and along to Snouques's tree. After heading through the doors and climbing under the tree, we went down about 50 steps on a narrow staircase and finally descended into a mini bullet train station.

Let me explain. The bigger subway trains went all across Fairyland at very high speed, through a network of tunnels that had been developed through millennia. The bullet network was separate and went way faster than even the speed of sound. The tunnels were very narrow and immediately outside each station became a vacuum, hence the speed availability.

The carriages, if you could call them that, were actually single people pods and each 'train' had a maximum of four. This was a network that had been developed by and for Diven heads and, it appears, Kings and their cats. Snouques called up a train, we each got in what to me was a combination of a bobsleigh and a coffin. There was muted blue light and some background music in my pod which I lay down in as the lid/door shut. This was not a good place to be if you were at all claustrophobic. I felt a little push as we set of and within minutes were slowing down to come out of the vacuum and arriving at a separate bullet train platform at the Tomna Hill station. Impressive stuff indeed. I was also, I felt, back within touching distance of home and as I took a welcome drink of EffBea Lite from P.S. at the bar, I looked wistfully out at the town in front of us. Struugs wandered in.

"Hey, King Dave, congrats and all that." He sat down and got himself a drink as well.

"Thank you, but it was really a team effort once more, Struugs."

"But The Book was right, King Dave, you came, saw what had happened and came up with an answer."

"Yes, I suppose you could look at it that way, but I prefer to look at the huge combined work that took place on the battlefields and in your room that led to the eventual answer."

He seemed quite happy with this and over the next hour, we were joined by Sandels, Felixx, Ded-i and Snouques. We just sat and chatted until Sandels got all serious again.

"We should convene another meeting, Sir," he said, looking over to the dining room table.

"What, another summit with the other leaders?" I asked.

"No, just our people – we really need to round this all off."

I was quite pleased that everyone seemed to be on the same page so we agreed to meet in an hour. He also said he'd get Jonnie and Hoopik in by VR so that everyone was there. I asked about Jim, Shona and Hayley but was told that Jim was off on holiday again and the other two were back at work.

An hour later we were round the table, walls down and opaque, Sandels at one end and me at the other and Hoopik and Jonnie in the ether. Feeling a definite sense of déjà vu, I nodded at Sandels.

"Sir, I asked for this meeting as I have considered what the next move should be."

I was thinking that mine was to go back to my family if at all possible but you can guess who gave me one of his special looks.

"Please carry on Sandels."

"It is apparent, Sir, that we have an opportunity to get rid of Arverlang once and for all. We've had a message from Raychell that she can lead a coup if we can somehow distract Arverlang once more. The citizens of the Canooque-F have had enough, just as we expected. The plans that Ess had put in place before Naluke's killing have been resurrected and they're good to go if we agree."

"So, what kind of diversion are thinking of?" This was Del.

"We should go to the Midwest and take back our land. After the Oceano debacle, there are virtually no warriors left in the area he took so I think that if we divert the troops up to Kansas, we might just be able to walk in and take it back. Snouques has agreed that the winged warriors can be used to nail any pockets of resistance. Remember, Sir, they know that we now have the knowledge of how to kill and they don't, so I don't think we'll meet much opposition."

This met with general agreement, and given Jonnie and Hoopik were just starting to get our army off Oceano Dunes, it could work out well. We agreed to transfer them all to Kansas and just start moving quickly up to the Canadian Border. We'd be ready in two days and we adjourned to get everything organised.

I asked Felixx if I could please go home for a bit and after discussing it with Sandels, they agreed. I ran as fast as I could to the nearest toilet, and with Felixx in pursuit, went in, sat down and closed my eyes. Thankfully, when I opened them I was back home and only four minutes had passed since I'd left after coming back from dropping TJ off.

"You've got just over a day, Davie. Enjoy." And with that, he disappeared into the house when I opened the door.

To try to get my mind back in order, I went to work in the garden. Over the rest of the day, I managed to get a pile of work done that I'd been promising to do since whenever. In the late afternoon, I retrieved TJ from her grandparents, came home and started dinner. When Bethany and Milo made it home, it was a scene of domestic tranquillity. This led to a very pleasant evening as TJ was feeling much better, Bethany was both delighted and surprised at my gardening and cooking endeavours and Milo was just happy that everyone else was happy. I'd had a fruitful day off work and, unknown to them of course, had saved a nation as well. All in a day's work, David, I thought to myself as I smiled and went off to sleep that night.

The next day was just normal. TJ went back to school and I went back to work. With Jim being on holiday again, there was no chance of a Fairyland catch up, but I didn't mind as I was actually enjoying the normality of it all. I got home sharp, had dinner as usual and then we heard the cat meow loudly from the hallway.

"David, could you see what's wrong with it." This was Bethany up to her elbows in dishwashing.

"Yes, Dad, it seems to get itself locked in the hall bathroom a lot. I don't know how but it's probably done it again." said Milo from behind a football magazine.

So off I trotted to see what was up with the cat and as you will by now have expected, about 10 minutes later I was back in the War Room at the Hill.

Here we go again – and I hadn't even managed to get a cup of coffee after dinner. Then I remembered about the shark/coffee episode and decided it wasn't such a big deal after all.

"Evening all", I said to the assembled group, including the Noogmas and all the rest of the team.

"Good evening, King Dave," came back the uniform reply.

"We're good to go in the morning, King Dave," said Del, "but we thought it best you were back here tonight so that we could all get up to speed."

"Yes, Sir," said Sandels, "the plan hasn't changed since yesterday –we're amassing everyone as we speak and we're just going to move at speed to the border. If we're lucky, it'll all be over in a day."

And that was really it for the day. I got my long awaited coffee in the Fairy Lounge and had a fun evening watching Fairyland football with the guys, but believe me, it's so unbelievably complicated I'll leave any explanations to another day.

#

In Perth, Ontario, Arverlang knew something was up, but didn't know what. It appeared that his five most trusted henchmen had gone missing, one after the other. He didn't like this but with them gone, he felt it wasn't safe to move to his cave, which was his preferred choice. He'd also made the mistake of seeing Raychell again but all she'd done was chant about Naluke's ghost with such an intensity that he was sure he'd started to feel the presence. All in all, he was in paranoia overdrive, and for the first time in a long time, not overly sure what to do.

What he didn't know was that the revolution was underway and his henchmen were in prison. Ess was leading the revolt and to make it public, all they had to do was wait until the OutFax went on the offensive the next day. They knew this would draw Arverlang from his hideout and it would allow them to capture him publicly. Everyone waited.

#

The next day dawned on The Hill with great anticipation. The word from the Canooque-F ("Spies, Davie, remember the spies") was that as we started our 'invasion' Arverlang would be captured and that should be that. It was expected that there would be some areas that would be loyal to him, but overall, the impression was that the support for Ess and her group was overwhelming.

I was on the viewing gallery and nodded to Del who gave the order to advance through the north of Kansas and up to Canada. By lunchtime we were halfway there, having met minimal resistance and by dinner, our field commanders were at the border taking selfies with the perpetrators of the Canooque-F revolution. Even the capture of Arverlang was a bit of a let-down. As we went started to move north, he went out for a rare breath of fresh air. Thinking he'd got wind of what was up (it transpired he hadn't) he was captured as he sat unawares in the kids' play area.

At the end of the day, Ess was in charge of the Canooque-F territory, all the other leaders (and us) had sent in peacekeeping forces to help quell any backlash from his supporters and over time, it would become known as 'The Quiet Revolution'. I gave the obligatory address to Fairyland but was very careful not to gloat in any way and the bravery of Ess, and especially Raychell, was mentioned in despatches by the other leaders of Fairyland in similar speeches. Arverlang was being held pending an appearance at an international Fairyland court (a bit like the Human war crimes court in The Hague) and it looked like peace was being restored to Fairyland at last.

I found myself sitting with Felixx in the sunken lounge of the Royal Mansion.

"So that'll be that then, my feline friend. We'll be back to being cat and the clerk in the normal sense, eh?"

I was in part a bit deflated, given the excitement of the battles and then finding the cause of the killing, followed by the almost uneventful overthrow of Arverlang. I also liked the adoration part that came with being King and I loved the travel but at the same time, I was looking forward to regaining my normal life, or sanity, or health, or whatever it was again.

"You've a bit to do yet, Davie."

"How do you figure that?"

"You have to sit in arbitration at Arverlang's trial."

Oh, No, all I could think of was how long would this take. I mean, working for a firm of lawyers meant that I knew that it could be months or even years before he stood trial. I said this to the cat.

"You'll never learn, will you Davie, this is Fairyland where things are definitely different. The trial's tomorrow and after that, you can go home. Remember, the last King, the D'avud fella, only stayed on because he was single, had no real ties in the human world and he fell for Catked at the same time. Don't worry, The Book's pretty clear that once you've discharged your duties, that'll be it."

"But might it happen again?"

"Honestly, I don't know. As you'll have gathered, we all thought you were an unusual choice for King, especially as most Haferlincs have an inkling that something's up and you most definitely didn't. This is the reason why we deliberately didn't teach you how to go back and fore by yourself – if you're just here to sort out what The Book required, then why potentially ruin the rest of your life with unnecessary worries about these guys."

"So this might be the end of our little chats," I said with a grin.

"Maybe so, Davie, maybe so – and I've got so much to still

discuss with you at a personal level. But remember how it all started to fade into your memory after the Luskentyre part; well that'll be what happens to all of us – you, me, Paws – when we're done here. We'll be dog, cat and servant to the cat again."

He never gives up. If you've never seen a cat grin, then this was the moment. I realised then that he'd actually done a fantastic job keeping me on the straight and narrow so I just smiled back and shook his paw as Hoopik came in. He purred in a sort of feline acknowledgement.

"Hi King Dave, Felixx, just wanted to come over and thank you both in person. It was my problem that kicked all of this off and it's now been solved – and Arverlang is going to be a thing of the past."

"You're very welcome," I said, while getting that feeling that I might burst into tears again.

Then the rest came by and it was clear even to me that it was a goodbye party for King Dave. I could see the dust covers that had appeared in the Royal Mansion, obviously to close the place up after I went home. To celebrate, we partied into the night in a suitable regal manner and I barely remember getting to bed.

The day of the trial dawned. No hangover either – this dust has many uses, I can tell you. The hearing was taking place up on the top of Tomna Hill because we had assisted in the capture of Arverlang. Overnight, President Mallbaste, Mydaxxa and Azyullch had arrived and had been billeted in the Mansion. We all enjoyed a breakfast together, for once using the dining table for what it was designed for. They too expressed their gratitude for what I'd done and a large part of me wanted to stay to find out much more about them and their territories but in the end, I was accepting that this wasn't to be. At the appointed hour, we all went off to change into our judging robes. Shortly after, we were called to the Hill.

With Felixx guiding as usual, and Sandels the master of

ceremonies, it reminded me a bit of the first day that I came here on that fateful walk. We sat on the four chairs that the Diven Heads had used when meeting me and Arverlang was brought from one of the doors that appear in such circumstances. He was in chains and was led to the open area in front of us. This was the closest that I'd ever been to him and I could see how deeply unpleasant he really was.

"Order, Order," squeaked Sandels. There weren't many Fairies on the hill but the whole thing was, as normal, being broadcast live across the whole of Fairyland. As it was on our turf, though, Jim had been recalled as the guardian of the hill, Shona acted as the organiser of all the personnel that were there and Hayley gave the whole event a bit of bling by bouncing off the atmosphere and causing daylight shooting stars. The four Diven heads sat to one side and Sandels stood to the other.

"Today, the Supreme Court of all of Fairyland sits to decide the fate of Arverlang, who is charged with the most grievous of crimes in all of Fairyland – wasting dust at a territory wide level."

There was a collective gasp and I tried my best not to giggle. However, never to be outdone, Felixx had made it under my robes and actually bit me as he knew what my reaction would be. I continued to look very serious. I discovered afterwards that this is the worst crime you can commit in all of Fairyland, believe it or not – even worse than the dagger across the throat stuff Arverlang and I had done to each other in the past. Sandels then read out a massive long list of dust wasting activities that Arverlang was accused of. No mention about him being a homicidal, dictatorial lunatic though.

Unfortunately, Arverlang didn't look fazed at all. Sandels carried on.

"The other leaders of the four remaining Fairyland territories will sit in judgement. The punishment shall be either locked in a mine of our choosing forever, under house arrest but having to eat three fir trees each day or being made into a football for use each day around Fairyland".

The others nodded gravely and I did too, not wanting another bite from the cat. Each punishment had been met with gasps of incredulity as they were read out. Please take me home.

So we deliberated and after an hour, during which I said pretty much nothing but nodded an awful lot, a decision was reached. Sandels reconvened the court.

"Sirs, madam, have you reached a decision?"

"Yes," replied President Mallbaste, our elected spokesman.

"And that decision is?"

"Arverlang will be under house arrest at an address of our choosing and will have to eat three fir trees each day."

You could actually hear the cheering across Fairyland as this was said. Apparently, this would cause most ridicule and I had to agree with them that given his demeanour, it was probably the most fitting punishment.

"Would the convicted now like to address the court."

"Yes, I would," boomed Arverlang, yellow eyes glowing.

Calming down he said, "I would like to apologise to all of Fairyland and especially the people of the Canooque-F territory."

This was a turn up for the books.

"But most of all, I'd like to apologise to the Head of the Other Diven of the OutFax territory, Hooligan Pict, for causing the death of her brave warrior Naluke and thus creating all of this furore."

There were certainly plenty gasps this time round, I can tell you.

"Please, Miss Pict, come forward and accept my hand as an apology."

Hoopik, doing very much the correct thing in the circumstances, went forward to take his hand as a proper

248

gesture of reconciliation. Maybe things would indeed be OK in Fairyland when I left after all. Even Felixx stuck his head out to watch.

And then it all went badly wrong. In hindsight, we should have seen it coming but I guess everyone just wanted the whole thing over with so that they could go back to 'exercisional' battles and winding up us humans. As a result, we all took our eyes off the ball a bit.

As Hoopik innocently stood in front of Arverlang, he put both his hands out. Although still manacled, he had enough movement to slide a dagger out of each sleeve into his hands. He quickly stepped forward and stabbed her in both hearts while at the same time smacking his head against her skull – a concurrent triple blow and as it wasn't a battle, she hadn't worn one of Ded-i's nameplates. She collapsed, unconscious and bleeding heavily. He shouted,

"And you thought you were the only ones who could work this out."

Ded-i was first to react, taking Arverlang's daggers (he was still chained and Jim and Struugs had got hold of him) and did the same back to him. Clearly he was more accurate as Arverlang was killed instantly. As I ran to Hoopik, I was fighting back tears and was joined by Ded-i who was in the same state as me.

"She's dying King Dave, please help her, please," he pleaded.

Behind me, Snouques appeared saying,

"The only hope is for you as King to take her to the Affwurld, King Dave. Lift her now and I'll help you get there."

Once again not having a clue what was happening but deciding to do as I was told, I bent over to lift Hoopik and then slipped on some of her blood. I promptly fell over, hit my head on the ground and everything went black. I then found myself spinning through space and time and shouting 'Help me, please help me, help me please'.

I came to, bathed in sweat and in the dark, thrashing about under the covers of my bed at home with Bethany sitting up beside me saying, 'David, David, it's OK, it's just a nightmare.'

Then I heard some frantic scratching at the door and a very Spanish sounding 'woof' from elsewhere in the house.

'And you've woken the animals'.

'It's OK,' I said wearily. 'I'll see what the problem is – I think I might have to go to the bathroom anyway'.

End